Right Place, Wrong Time
Judith Arnold

HARLEQUIN®

TORONTO • NEW YORK • LONDON
AMSTERDAM • PARIS • SYDNEY • HAMBURG
STOCKHOLM • ATHENS • TOKYO • MILAN • MADRID
PRAGUE • WARSAW • BUDAPEST • AUCKLAND

ISBN 0-373-71141-7

RIGHT PLACE, WRONG TIME

To Ted and the boys

CHAPTER ONE

"DO YOU HAVE any idea what you're doing?" Kim's father asked.

Good question, Ethan muttered. No, he didn't have any idea what he was doing. But he was doing it anyway. When in doubt, he usually just plowed ahead and hoped for the best.

"You're driving on the wrong side of the road," Kim's father pointed out.

Ethan glanced at the man who might someday be his father-in-law. Ross Hamilton sat rigidly in the front passenger seat of the rented Oldsmobile, his jowls just beginning to go soft, his silver hair thick and precisely styled, his skin preternaturally tan and his eyes framed with the sort of creases that implied he squinted a lot, presumably at people he didn't approve of. Ethan suspected he fell into that category.

"People drive on the left side of the road in St. Thomas," Ethan explained.

"St. Thomas is part of the United States," Ross argued. "Why don't they drive on the right?"

"I don't know."

"This is an American car. The steering wheel is on the left."

"Yes." Ethan was having a hard enough time getting used to left-sided driving. He didn't need Ross undermining his concentration by badgering him with questions.

"Perhaps you should have arranged for someone to pick us up at the airport," Ross chided.

"My friend Paul told me the cabs on the island are overpriced. By renting the car for the week, we'll save a lot of money." Surely his thrift would win him a few points in his potential father-in-law's view.

"In the meantime, we might wind up in a head-on collision."

"I'm on the right side of the road. The left side," Ethan corrected himself. Even with cool air blasting from the vents, he felt dampness gathering at his nape. Ross exuded not a single drop of perspiration, despite wearing a linen blazer over his polo shirt. July in St. Thomas—it was *hot* on the other side of the windshield. Ross Hamilton didn't sweat, though. He was obviously a chilly man.

Ethan wished Kim hadn't insisted on including her parents in this outing. He'd gotten access to Paul's timeshare because, as Paul put it, no one in his right mind would want to go to St. Thomas in July. Paul's regularly scheduled week at the resort on Smith Bay was in January, but last January he'd had the chance to go skiing in Aspen with friends, and he'd chosen that over the tropics. So he'd traded his week with a woman who owned a week in July in the same unit, and then offered the July week to Ethan if he wanted it.

Ethan had thought a week in St. Thomas, even in the middle of the summer, would offer Kim and him a fun getaway. Kim had been elated. "I hear jewelry is dirt cheap and duty-free down there," she'd said. "Maybe we could do a little shopping." *Hint, hint.*

Okay, she wanted an engagement ring. Ethan was

willing to concede that the time for an engagement ring might be drawing near—and if that time arrived, why not buy one that was dirt cheap and duty-free? In March, when Paul had first offered him the week at the condo, this had all seemed like a good idea.

Then Kim had heard that the unit had two bedrooms, and she'd come up with the clever idea of bringing her parents along. "It will give them a chance to get to know you better," she'd argued. "I want them to love you as much as I do. We could have great fun, Ethan."

Kim had been naked when she'd mentioned this, sliding her hand in provocative ways over his chest while simultaneously stroking his shin with her toes. She and Ethan had been having great fun at that moment, and he hadn't been thinking clearly. So he'd said, "Sure."

The van behind him was tailgating so closely Ethan could practically see the pores on the driver's nose in his rearview mirror. Steep hills rose to one side of the road and a turquoise sea spread along the other side. He was in alien territory, surrounded by palm trees and brilliant crimson flowers, squat stucco houses and sprawling, cliff-hugging mansions. Cars, jitneys and small buses kept coming at him on the narrow, winding road—and they were on his right. The entire experience was disorienting.

Adding to his tension was a goat ambling along the asphalt no more than a hundred feet ahead.

"Oh, my God!" Kim shrieked from the back, where she and her mother had spent the entire time since they'd buckled their seat belts thumbing through guidebooks and plotting shopping expeditions. "It's a goat!"

Ethan tapped on the brakes to slow down and prayed that the driver behind him wouldn't rear-end them. A

fender bender would not be an auspicious way to start
this vacation.

"I've got to have a picture of the goat," Kim declared. "Can you pull over, Ethan?"

"No."

"Where's the camera? Do you have it in front? I don't
have it back here."

"It's in the trunk," he told her, slowing even more
as he drew within a few yards of the animal.

"My first St. Thomas goat, and I don't have a camera," Kim wailed.

*My first St. Thomas headache, and I don't have an
aspirin,* Ethan thought. During a brief lull in the opposite
lane's traffic, he swerved around the goat, which glanced
up from its grazing. Thin and brown, its jaw pumping
and its black eyes piercing, it gave Ethan a contemptuous look, as if to say, *This is paradise, pal. Mellow out.*

Ethan wished he could. If only Ross Hamilton weren't
occupying the seat next to him and Delia Hamilton
weren't occupying the seat directly behind him, her un-
naturally blond hair as flawlessly arranged as her husband's, her skin as free of perspiration and her face lacking incipient jowls because Santa Claus had left some
plastic surgery under the tree for her last winter. If only
Kim Hamilton, the woman Ethan was contemplating
marrying, weren't squawking about her camera in the
trunk.... Ethan would love to mellow out, but at the
moment, the thought of leaping out of the car, slamming
the door on the entire Hamilton family and joining the
goat in a nice little snack of roadside grass held an odd
appeal.

He promised himself he would mellow out as soon as
they arrived at Palm Point, the beachfront complex
where Paul's time-share was located. Until they reached

their destination, he was going to have to fight his natural inclination to steer onto the other side of the road, and he was going to grit his teeth at being cooped up inside a fat American sedan with Kim's parents.

Vacations were for relaxing. He'd damn well better get to relax—and if everyone would just shut up, he might survive the half hour it took to drive to the place where relaxation would be possible.

If only he hadn't agreed to let Kim's parents come.... He and she could have escaped here by themselves for a week of exclusive togetherness. A week alone with her, when neither of them was distracted by the demands of their hectic lives, their careers and other obligations, would have given them the chance to make sure a lifetime commitment was right for them. He supposed having the chance to sample the Hamiltons as future in-laws would help him make up his mind, too. But he wouldn't be marrying Ross and Delia Hamilton. If he and Kim got married, he wouldn't have to see her parents more often than a few times a year, since the Hamiltons lived in Chevy Chase, Maryland, a good three hundred miles from Arlington, Connecticut.

He glanced at the screen of his PDA, into which he'd entered directions to the condo. Paul had provided a route that would allow Ethan to avoid Charlotte Amalie. He'd neglected to mention that avoiding the bustling capital city of St. Thomas required them to drive straight up the side of a mountain. If Ethan had thought the road leading away from the airport had been narrow, he'd been mistaken. The road up the mountain, a barely paved trail of twists and switchbacks and thirty-degree inclines, lacking shoulders, lacking railings but not lacking the occasional goat, would have been alarming if Ethan had been behind the wheel of his beloved Volvo—and driving on the right. In this alien environment, with lush, unfamiliar foliage—palms and ferns, shrubs with vivid puffball-shaped pink flowers and erotically red blossoms scattered across their branches, viny ground cover and ghostly moss dripping from branches—he felt totally out of his depth.

Ross Hamilton sat rigidly next to him, his scowl eloquently communicating that he, too, believed Ethan was out of his depth.

"Paul said there's a golf course just up the road from Palm Point," Ethan said, hoping this news might improve Ross's opinion of him.

"I didn't bring my clubs."

"I'm sure they rent clubs."

"Kimberly tells me you don't golf."

"I've never tried it," Ethan said, "but there's always a first time." In truth, he thought golf sounded excruciating. Hit a ball, walk a little bit, hit a ball, walk a little bit more.

"Perhaps we'll golf a round together," Ross suggested, a dry smile whispering across his lips. "I could teach you a few pointers. Although God only knows what kind of equipment this golf course will be renting."

Delia piped up. "Ross, it'll be too hot to golf. You'll have a heatstroke."

"I will not," he retorted, as if he and he alone determined whether he'd be afflicted.

"Where is Charlotte Emily?" Delia asked, peering out the window as the car strained up another precipitous incline.

"Charlotte Amalie," Ethan gently corrected her.

"I just love that they named their city after a woman. Or is it two women?" Her smile reached Ethan via the rearview mirror. "Did we pass the city?"

"We're circumventing it," Ethan told her.

Her smile morphed into a delicate pout. "Well, if you boys want to golf and get sunstroke, that's your business. Kim and I will be strolling the streets of Charlotte Emily. The guidebooks list all these wonderful shops...."

Ross shared a knowing grin with Ethan, who forced himself to grin back. "Something tells me your friend's generous donation of his time-share is going to wind up being the most expensive gift you've ever received. Angels tremble when those two are set loose in a shopping center."

"It's not just shopping," Delia informed her husband. "It's duty-free shopping. Bottles of Absolut at prices you wouldn't believe."

Ross Hamilton glanced over his shoulder. "Really?" he asked, eagerness underlining his tone. "Absolut?"

"Absolut, Stolichnaya, all the big names, darling. You can restock the bar while we're down here."

"I can restock the bar at home."

"Not at these prices."

Ross gave Ethan another conspiratorial grin. "Women," he muttered. "They think we can save a lot of money by spending a fortune on airfare to fly to some island with duty-free shops. We could have bought vodka at the duty-free shop at the airport and skipped the trip."

Too bad you didn't come up with that idea sooner, Ethan thought. A weary dog, part Lab and part a dozen other breeds, slouched across the road. Either Kim didn't think dogs were as photogenic as goats, or she was too busy planning shopping excursions with her mother to have noticed the poor mongrel. Its tongue lolled to one side and its eyes looked sad. If Ethan weren't in an air-conditioned car, his tongue might be hanging out of his mouth, too.

Around another hairpin turn, and they started down a decline. "Oh, my God!" Mrs. Hamilton shrieked. "There's no railing! Slow down, Ethan!"

"I'm doing ten miles per hour," he assured her. Yes, the road was steep, and no, there wasn't a railing, but he wasn't going to steer them over the edge. He'd had his driver's license for thirteen years and had never been in an accident. Of course, he'd never driven on the left side of the road, either.

They'd get to Palm Point soon. According to Paul's directions, it was only a couple of miles down Smith Bay Road, a scenic route skirting mountains that dropped sharply to the most tranquil, turquoise water Ethan had ever seen. Let Ross and Delia visit the duty-free shops in Charlotte Amalie by themselves, he thought. Let them stock up on enough liquor to keep them swilling martinis until they left this world for the next. While they were oohing and ahhing over the discounts on Stolichnaya and Absolut, Ethan and Kim would be lying on one of the pale, inviting beaches that fringed the sea. They'd be racing on the sand, and plunging into the water, and then sprinting back up to the condo for a quickie before her parents returned from their tour of duty-free liquor stores.

He would turn this vacation into something good, he resolved. He would not let Kim's parents rattle him. He would not knock himself out to win their favor. He would not play golf against his wishes. He worked damn hard in Connecticut, but he was out of town for a week, out of the office, out of touch, and he wasn't going to waste the opportunity.

He cruised past the gated entry to a hotel, then another…and then he spotted the sign for Palm Point. He turned onto the drive, which was appropriately lined with towering royal palms, and maneuvered over the speed bumps. He passed a parking lot and a series of tennis courts surrounded by green chain-link fences, then followed the drive as it zigzagged down the hill toward the ocean. Beige stucco buildings dotted the road, their ocean-facing facades marked by vaguely Spanish-looking wrought-iron balconies. Ethan imagined sitting on a balcony with Kim, both of them flushed and sated after making love. They could be sipping drinks—beer for him, nothing with Absolut or Stolichnaya in it—and watching as the sun slid down toward that breathtakingly blue sea, and not sparing Kim's parents a single thought. This was Ethan's vacation. It was his fantasy.

"Here we go," he announced, pulling into a parking lot beside a building identified by a small sign as number six. Paul's unit was 614, on the second floor. Ethan's mood brightened. He'd found the place without incident or accident. In ten minutes he'd be unpacked and in a swimsuit, ready to take a walk on the beach.

"It doesn't look like much," Mrs. Hamilton said with a sniff.

"Oh, Mom," Kim scolded. "It looks lovely."

It looked fine to Ethan. The stucco was freshly painted, the gardens surrounding the building well tended. When he opened the car door, the air that hit him was heavy with heat and thick with the scent of those red flowers.

"Hibiscus," Kim answered his unasked question. She threw open her door, climbed out and circled the car to him. "I just love the smell of hibiscus. Isn't this *beautiful?*" she gushed, as if to nullify her mother's disparagement of the place.

"As soon as we unpack, let's go to the beach," said Ethan.

Kim gazed up at him, her hair golden and her eyes a blue paler than the sea but darker than the cloudless sky. *She* was beautiful. From the moment Ethan had seen her stepping out of the elevator into the lobby of the building where he'd worked, he'd been almost uncomfortably aware of her beauty. It was as overpowering as the fragrance of those red flowers.

"We'll have to help Mom and Dad get settled in first," she said.

"They're adults. They can get settled in without our help."

"I really appreciate your taking the convertible couch in the living room," she added. "I know that wasn't what you wanted."

A ripple of resentment passed through him, impeding his evolution to mellowness. Sleeping on the living-room couch was definitely not what he wanted. Paul had told him one bedroom had a queen-size bed and the other had two twins. Ethan had thought he'd been demonstrating admirable selflessness by ceding the queen-size bed to Kim's parents. He and Kim could snuggle together in one of the twins—and they could rumple the other bed's blanket each morning so it would appear that they were sleeping separately.

But Kim had maintained that such an arrangement wouldn't work. They couldn't sleep in the same room, not with Mom and Dad right across the hall. If they were married—or even, perhaps, if they were just formally engaged—she might consider it. But without anything official declared between them, she just wouldn't feel comfortable sharing a room with him when her parents were present.

Ethan had contemplated calling off the whole trip at that point. But that would have made him seem like a sex maniac. After all, he and Kim slept together often enough in Connecticut. It wasn't as if he had to travel all the way to St. Thomas to get his rocks off. For Kim's sake—for her parents' sake—he could be a gentleman.

He didn't have to like it, though.

Unlocking the trunk, he gazed at the array of luggage Kim and her parents had brought. A folding garment bag, a large pullman, a midsize pullman, a tennis tote containing racquets and fresh cans of balls, and two carry-ons—all in a matching tapestry pattern—belonged to Ross and Delia Hamilton. Given the option, Ross probably would have brought his golf clubs, too—and he probably kept them in a golf bag with the same quaint tapestry pattern. Kim had packed an enormous wheeled, leather-trimmed suitcase for herself, as well as an ergonomically designed shoulder tote she'd ordered from a catalog company specially for this trip.

Ethan had fit everything he needed into one modest duffel.

Nonetheless, he knew that as the young man of the party, he'd be the one hauling all the luggage inside.

He hoisted his duffel out of the trunk and slid the strap onto his shoulder. Then he pulled out Kim's wheeled suitcase and the Hamiltons' garment bag. "I'll get the rest in the next round," he promised the Hamiltons, who had finally emerged from the air-conditioned car into the broiling Caribbean afternoon.

"The condo is air-conditioned, isn't it?" Delia Hamilton asked her daughter anxiously.

"Of course it is." Kim grabbed her ergonomic shoulder bag, handed her mother one of the carry-ons and her father the other, then stepped aside so Ethan could close the trunk. Why she didn't close it herself—she had two free hands, after all—he couldn't guess, unless it was to prove to her parents that the man she intended to marry was properly chivalrous.

Feeling like a packhorse, he lugged the bags along the walk to the stairway and up to the second floor, the wheeled bag thumping as it hit each riser. Kim and her parents trailed him like baby ducklings following a mother duck. Sweat slicked his face and dampened his collar as he trudged along the open-air corridor to the door marked 614. He balanced the luggage on the concrete floor, then dug into the pockets of his khakis and pulled out the key Paul had given him. It slid easily into the lock. Smiling, he twisted the knob and pushed the door open.

He was greeted by a blast of cold air and an skull-splitting scream.

IN THE HOUR since they'd arrived at Carole's unit at Palm Point, Alicia had changed into a swimsuit and run circles around Gina, investigating their vacation digs and announcing her discoveries: "They got a microwave, Aunt Gina! Can we make microwave popcorn?" and "This TV doesn't get the Disney Channel!" and "There's a balcony!"

That announcement had torn Gina from the dresser drawer into which she'd been dumping her underwear and sent her flying down the hallway, past the bathroom and through the living room to stop Alicia before she ventured onto the balcony. Alicia was seven, and in general she was smart enough not to fling herself over the balcony railing, but "in general" had nothing to do with this week. Alicia was wired. She'd just taken her very first airplane trip, and now she was in an ocean-view condo on a Caribbean island. Remembering to be careful on a balcony would not be high on Alicia's to-do list.

But when Gina had joined Alicia on the terrace, gazing down the gentle slope toward the palm-studded beach and the vivid blue water beyond, she'd felt almost as wired as her niece. The air smelled tangy and sweet, so different from the usual sour scents of Manhattan in July that Gina could almost believe she was on a different planet, with its own separate atmosphere.

This was exactly what Alicia needed, she'd thought— a safe, happy planet for a week of carefree fun.

"Don't lean over the railing," Gina had warned, even though Alicia was too short to fall over accidentally.

Alicia had rolled her eyes and issued a long-suffering sigh. "I *know*. Look at the beach, Aunt Gina. Isn't it great? I want to go down there."

"You'll have to wait until I finish unpacking."

"You're taking too long," Gina had complained.

"I unpacked all your stuff first so you could put on a swimsuit. Now I've got to unpack my stuff. You'll just have to be patient."

"I hate being patient." Alicia had folded her arms across her chest and pouted. Her skin was already golden from swimming at the day-camp pool. Her swimsuit was a garish orange, the color of those vests road construction crews wore to make themselves more visible to passing motorists. Ugly as it was, Gina appreciated the color. It would make Alicia easier to spot on the beach.

"I'll go finish unpacking, and you will win the Most Patient Girl of the Year award, and then we'll go to the beach. I promise."

"Can I have a cookie while I'm being patient?" Alicia had asked.

Gina had asked the cabdriver to stop for ten minutes

at a grocery store on the way from the airport to Palm Point so she could stock up on food. She would never complain about New York City cab fares again. Compared with the rates in St. Thomas, New York's were a bargain. "One cookie," she'd told Alicia. "If you eat too much, you won't be able to go in the water."

"I won't eat too much," Alicia had promised her before scampering through the sliding-glass doors and heading for the kitchen.

Gina had returned to the master bedroom, but had bypassed her open suitcase for the window, which offered the same view as the living room and terrace. God, what a beach. What an ocean. What heaven. She and Alicia were going to have the time of their lives—

And then she'd heard the scream.

"Alicia!" she roared, charging out of the bedroom, nailing her shin on the corner of the queen-size bed but not stopping to rub the bruise. "Ali! What?" She stumbled to a halt at the sight of four luggage-bearing strangers hovering in the condo's open doorway. Actually, only three hovered—an older couple and a young blond woman. Their leader—a man who looked to be about thirty—was standing inside the room, his face glistening with sweat as he let assorted bags and suitcases drop to the carpeted floor at his feet.

Alicia darted from the kitchen to Gina's side and pressed into her. Gina wrapped an arm protectively around her niece and gaped at the four invaders. They didn't seem dangerous. Actually, they looked as if they could have stepped out of the pages of a Ralph Lauren fashion spread. The older couple had the refined appearance of people who belonged to elite clubs and indulged in his-and-hers facials. The man wore a blazer with a crest on the pocket and the woman had on the sort of pearl earrings favored by politicians' wives. The younger woman was almost painfully beautiful. She could be a refugee from one of those teenage cheerleader movies.

If the man in the lead looked a little less polished and a little less sure of himself, it was only because he was sweating and because he'd been loaded down with all the heavy luggage. His reddish-brown hair was mussed, his brows skewed upward and his mouth twisted into a quizzical shape that was half a smile and half a frown. His face intrigued her, all sharp lines and planes, his eyes the color of jade.

"Who the hell are you?" he asked.

"He said a bad word," Alicia announced in a stage whisper.

"*Hell* isn't always a bad word," Gina assured her. Alicia didn't have to know how often her aunt uttered words a lot worse than *hell*. "It's just the name of a place."

"A bad place."

"We can turn that bad word right back on him, okay?" Gina stared boldly at the man and said, "Who the hell are *you?*"

"I'm sorry," he said. Gina wasn't sure if he was apologizing for the invasion or only for his language. "There's obviously been a mistake."

"Obviously." If he could be diplomatic, so could she. "I don't know how you got in here, but you're in the wrong unit."

"Six-fourteen," he said, glancing behind him at the open door, on which that number appeared. He turned back to Gina and lifted his hand so she could see his key. "This is how we got in here."

There's obviously been a mistake, she thought, her

brain scrambling to figure out just how serious a mistake it was and how she was going to get these strangers out of the unit. "Okay—this is a time-share. We've got a key. You've got a key. My guess is, someone's here the wrong week." *You*, she wanted to say. *You're* here the wrong week.

"We're here the week of July 19," the man said calmly.

"Um, no." Gina smiled. "That's our week."

"That's *our* week," the cheerleader said, stepping into the room. "Come in," she ordered the older couple, "and shut the door. All the air-conditioning is escaping." She sashayed past the man to confront Gina, who sensed not a hint of diplomacy in her attitude. "This is our week. We planned this trip back in March. This week belongs to Ethan's friend Paul, and he gave it to us."

Gina shook her head firmly and felt her smile petrifying into something stiff and lifeless. She didn't like the cheerleader. The man had opted for courtesy after his initial outburst, but this woman—his wife?—sounded presumptuous and demanding. Gina imagined she was used to getting her way. "This week belongs to my friend Carole, and she's letting *us* use it." She gave Alicia's shoulder a reassuring squeeze.

"She's crazy," the wife declared, giving her husband an aggrieved frown. "Tell her she's crazy."

"She's not crazy. There's been a mix-up, that's all." He smiled apologetically. Gina decided to absolve him for having said "hell" in front of Alicia. "I'm sure we can work this out, Ms....?"

"Morante. Gina Morante." Gina extended her hand.

The man shook it. His palm was dry. His face seemed to be drying off, too, as the air-conditioning did its work.

"Ethan Parnell," he introduced himself. "This is Kimberly Hamilton—" he gestured toward the blond woman, who pointedly did not extend her hand "—and her parents, Ross and Delia Hamilton," he concluded, indicating the older twosome, who remained near the door, looking supremely annoyed.

"And this is my niece, Alicia Bari," Gina said.

Alicia peered up at the younger pair. "I'm Ali the Alley Cat," she said, then hid behind Gina and wrapped her arms around Gina's hips.

"All right." Ethan Parnell drew in a deep breath. "Obviously, there's a problem here. We've just arrived from the airport and we're planning to stay in this condo for a week. My friend Paul Collins made the arrangements. I don't know who your friend is—"

"Carole Weinstock, and she told me this week was hers, and Alicia and I could stay here."

"Ali," Alicia murmured into the small of her back. "Ali the Alley Cat."

Gina reached around to give Alicia another squeeze, then stretched her smile as wide as it would go under the circumstances—which wasn't very wide. "As you say, there's been a mix-up. I'll phone Carole right now."

"Good idea," Ethan said with a nod. "Call your friend Carole."

The cheerleader whispered something harsh to him, but he waved her silent. Gina marched into the kitchen, Alicia still holding her hips and trotting behind her in awkward little steps. Was the cheerleader Ethan's wife? Gina wondered again. They had different last names, but that didn't mean anything nowadays. He'd introduced the older couple as her parents, not his in-laws, but that didn't mean anything, either.

Not that it mattered to Gina. She was going to talk to

Carole, get this mess straightened out and send these strangers on their way. This was her week with Alicia, her week to get the kid away from her squabbling parents, who needed the time to decide whether to file for divorce or give their marriage another try—and it would remove Alicia from all the tension. She deserved it, and Aunt Gina lived to make sure her niece got what she deserved.

Alicia abandoned her for the bag of chocolate-chip cookies that lay open on the counter. Gina didn't know if she'd already had a cookie, but right now she had more important concerns than Alicia's consumption of junk food. Besides, they were on vacation. Vacations meant extra cookies.

She dialed Carole's number back in New York and tried to ignore the faint long-distance hiss on the line. It occurred to her that Carole might not be home—but if she wasn't, Gina would try her cell phone. Carole *had* to be reached. They had to get this situation resolved.

Fortunately, Carole answered on the second ring. "Hello?"

"Carole, it's me, Gina."

"Gina! Is everything all right? Where are you?"

"I'm in your condo in Palm Point. Everything's fine—except there's this family here who say they've got the place for this week. They have a key and everything."

"Everyone who owns a share of the unit has a key," Carole reminded her. "Who are they?"

"Friends of someone named Paul—" she thought for a minute, then remembered "—Collins."

"Right, yeah. Paul Collins."

"You know him?"

"Not personally," Carole said. "But we traded

weeks. Remember when I went down to St. Thomas in January? That was his week.''

''So…you traded him this week?'' Gina felt her stomach tighten.

''Originally, yeah. But I was in touch with him after I got back from St. Thomas. I don't know, mid-February, maybe? And he said he wouldn't be using the condo in July. He was very definite about it, Gina. No way would he be using the condo.''

''Okay.'' Gina's stomach relaxed, but only a little. The definite Paul Collins had been true to his word; he was not using the condo in July. He'd apparently communicated something a little different to his preppy friends, however. ''We'll work this out,'' she told Carole, wishing she felt as certain as she sounded.

''I mean it, Gina. That place is yours for the week. I offered it to you after I talked to Paul, remember? Because he was very clear that he wouldn't be using the condo.''

''Right.''

''So don't let those people give you any crap.''

Gina laughed, which helped her stomach to relax some more. ''When do I ever let anyone give me any crap?''

''Right. Have a great week. And give Alicia an extra hug from me.''

''I will. Thanks, Carole.'' Gina hung up the phone, squared her shoulders and returned to the living room alone. The Hamiltons had moved farther into the room, checking out the bland, functional furniture, the trite seascape paintings on the walls, the spectacular view from the balcony. Gina didn't like the idea of them making themselves at home. ''Carole says,'' she announced, "that your friend Paul made it very clear to her—*very* clear—he wouldn't be using this place this week."

"He's not using it," Ethan retorted, his voice stern despite his polite veneer. "We are."

"If he wanted you to use it, he should have told Carole he was using it. He misrepresented his plans to Carole, and I booked my airplane ticket accordingly." And when the airline had alerted her to their "take-a-friend promotion," which would enable her to bring someone with her for only fifty dollars more, she'd booked a second airplane ticket. "He *misrepresented* himself," she repeated, savoring the word. "I'm afraid that means we'll be staying here, and you'll have to make other arrangements."

A flutter of protest arose from the Hamiltons. Ethan's jaw clenched, causing a muscle in his cheek to twitch. Great cheeks, Gina noticed—hollow but not sunken, drawing her attention back to his amazing green eyes.

He stepped toward her. She refused to back up—retreating to the kitchen struck her as tantamount to turning the condo over to him—but she had to admit that standing her ground against the tall, quiet man took a lot of guts. Fortunately, she had a lot of guts.

"Paul didn't misrepresent himself," Ethan said. "Your friend Carole misunderstood him."

"It was up to him to make sure she understood him," Gina argued, working hard to keep her voice as level as his.

"She already had her week here, in January. Did she think she was entitled to two weeks?"

"He said he wasn't going to use the place this week."

"He isn't. We are. You and the little girl will have to find another place to stay."

His gaze shifted, focusing on something behind Gina.

She spun around and saw Alicia standing in the doorway to the kitchen, a half-eaten cookie in her hand and a smear of chocolate on her lower lip. Her eyes shimmered with moisture. "Do we have to leave?" she asked in a tremulous voice. A fat tear slid down her cheek. "I want to go to the beach, Aunt Gina. We don't have to leave, do we?"

Gina wasn't sure how to answer. Carole and some ass named Paul Collins had crossed wires, and it seemed to her that Ethan and the Hamiltons had as strong a case for staying as she and Alicia did. But Ethan Parnell's case wasn't *stronger*. She and Gina had as much a right to be here as they did.

And the scale tipped slightly in her favor, because she had something they didn't have: Alicia. She had a niece for whom she would slay dragons, a niece who'd been through a hellacious few months as her parents' marriage deteriorated, and now she was crying, and Gina had promised they would go to the beach.

She turned back to Ethan and said, "We're not leaving."

CHAPTER TWO

"THIS IS OUTRAGEOUS," Delia Hamilton huffed. She set her purse on an end table by the sofa, as if staking her claim on the disputed territory. "They can't stay."

Ethan flashed her an impatient look. Delicate negotiations were necessary. Issuing ultimatums wouldn't help. "Mrs. Hamilton—"

"Delia's right," Ross piped up. "The woman and her daughter will have to go."

"She's my niece," the woman corrected him. "Not my daughter."

Ethan wished he could sit down, but that would put him at a tactical disadvantage. The headache that had seized him on the drive flared with renewed vigor, surging up from his neck over the top of his head and cresting at the bridge of his nose. Yes, the woman and her niece would have to go. There had been a monumental screwup, and it was her friend's fault, and unfortunately, she and her niece would be stuck paying the price.

New York City flowed in her veins—or at least, tripped along her tongue. She had a classic accent, all exaggerated vowels, harsh consonants and a sporadic absence of the letter *R*. Her straight black hair was chin-length and blunt-cut, her eyes dark, her nose a bit too long for her face and her cheekbones a bit too wide. Her complexion had a tawny olive undertone, making him wonder about her ethnicity. Morante—could be Hispanic, could be Italian. She wore a skintight black tank top covered by a sheer peach-hued shirt, short denim cutoffs that displayed long tanned legs, a black belt with an industrial-strength buckle and thick-soled leather sandals that made her feet look disproportionately tiny. His gaze strayed repeatedly to her feet. The skin of her insteps was unusually smooth and her toes were perfect little knobs tipped with pearl-hued polish. The second toe of her left foot sported a silver ring.

"I'm sure we can work something out," he said, although he was sure of no such thing. He forced his attention away from her feet and his gaze slid up those long legs again, the snug-fitting shorts, the black top that emphasized the swell of her bosom, her slender neck and pointy chin and those wide, sharp cheekbones. Silver hoops pierced her ears, two hoops per lobe. Nothing about her looked bland or boring—or safe.

She extended her arms to her niece, who obviously considered Gina the safest person in the room. The little girl ran into her aunt's embrace, sniffling and whimpering. "I don't want to leave," she sobbed into Gina's stomach. She had on a garish orange swimsuit, her hair was pulled into a lopsided ponytail and small gold dots adorned her ears. Gina Morante hugged her tightly.

How could the Hamiltons evict these women? Where would they go? Would Ross put them out in the street? Would Delia exile them to the airport?

"They can't stay here," Ross remarked, as if he felt Ethan needed a reminder.

"We can't just kick them out," Ethan retorted.

"Ethan." Kim's voice was like a stiletto, searching for the tenderest part of his headache and impaling it. "They can't stay."

"Excuse me," Gina said to Kim, her voice more of

a broadsword than a stiletto, whacking rather than stabbing. "This isn't for you to decide, honey. Alicia and I have every right to be here. Just because there are four of you and two of us doesn't mean you get to vote us off the island. We're here because your buddy Paul failed to communicate his intentions to my friend Carole. This situation is his fault, not mine and not Alicia's."

If Kim were a cat, she'd be arching her back and hissing. She was a woman, though, so she only crackled with electrifying anger, her upper lip twitching and her eyes narrowing on Gina. "Your friend Carole is obviously a complete imbecile. I'm sorry you don't have smarter friends, *honey,* but that's your choice. We're staying here this week. So get your things and clear out."

Ethan shook his head. He could tell just by looking at Gina Morante that she wasn't the sort of woman anyone could issue orders to. She pulled herself to her full height—a good three inches taller than Kim—and flexed her shoulders, which appeared inordinately powerful beneath the narrow straps of her skimpy tank top. Her eyes might be dark, but they flashed like lightning. "We're staying," she declared, her arms closing more tightly around her weeping niece.

"Okay." Ethan rubbed his temples and pinched the bridge of his nose in a futile attempt to massage his headache away. He glanced toward Kim, and was met with an indignant glower. Turning back to Gina, he saw steely resolve. "Either Paul or Carole screwed up. Or it was a joint screwup and they're equally to blame. It doesn't matter. We're going to have to come up with a compromise. It's off-season, right? There must be an available hotel room in the vicinity." He gave Gina a hopeful smile.

"You want us to move to a hotel room?"

"That would make the most sense."

"And we're supposed to pay for this hotel room how?"

He opened his mouth and then shut it. He had no idea what her financial circumstances were, but he supposed that even off-season, a week in a resort comparable to Palm Point was going to cost upward of a thousand dollars.

"I'll pay for the damn hotel room," Ross Hamilton interjected. "Find one and move out, for God's sake. I'll pay the damn bill."

"He's saying bad words," the little girl murmured between sobs.

"I don't want to move to a hotel," Gina argued. "I want to stay here. It's got a kitchen. We're entitled to stay here. This is Carole's week."

"Carole is an idiot," Kim snapped.

Gina glared at Kim. "Carole is a better person than you'll ever be. She's a pediatrician. She saves children's lives. How many children's lives have you saved lately?"

"Oh, for God's sake!" Kim retorted. "I don't care how many children's lives she saved. She's an idiot!"

"Enough." Ethan held up both hands like a cop halting traffic in all directions. He waited for both women to subside. Kim simmered. Gina remained just as she was, posture straight, head high, dark eyes shooting lightning bolts in Kim's direction. "Mr. Hamilton has generously agreed to cover the cost of a hotel. Ms. Morante, this is an extraordinary gesture. You really ought to—"

"He wants to pay for a hotel room? Great. Let him pay for it and stay there himself. I don't want to stay in a hotel. I want to stay here, where I can fix Alicia meals. I like the location. I like the setup. We're already un-packed here. We're not leaving.'' She sent a frosty smile Ross's way. ''Thanks for offering, though.''

''Your friend made a mistake,'' Ethan tried.

She turned back to him, and he nearly staggered under the force of her gaze. ''My friend or yours. Or they both did equally, like you said.''

He sighed. She was right. He could phone Paul, but even if Paul swore he'd made his plans for the condo clear to her friend Carole, it would only be a case of he-said-she-said. Without concrete proof, he couldn't assign the blame to one friend or the other.

''Why don't *we* stay at a hotel?'' Delia Hamilton sud-denly spoke up. ''Isn't there a Ritz-Carlton here on the island? Or something of that quality? Frankly, Ross, hav-ing to make my own bed isn't my idea of a vacation. If we go to the hotel, we'll have maid service, room ser-vice, all the amenities.''

''You want all four of us to go to a hotel?'' Ross frowned, his chiseled face contracting into a maze of creases. ''I offered to pay for one room, not three. We could do it in two rooms, I suppose, if you and Kimberly share one room and Ethan and I...'' He glared at Ethan and shuddered.

Trust me, Ethan wanted to say, *the feeling's mutual.*

''How about just you and me?'' Delia suggested. ''We passed several hotels not far from here. If one of them is nice enough and has a room, we could stay there. We'd be near the children. Kim could have the main bedroom here, Ethan was planning to stay on the sofa anyway and those two—'' she waved disdainfully at Gina and her niece ''—can have the other bedroom.''

"You'd want our Kimberly sharing an apartment with a total stranger?" Ross seemed horrified.

"Ethan will be here to protect her. And this woman says she's not leaving."

Ethan eyed Delia with newfound respect. Maybe she was a shopaholic. Maybe she was a frivolous club lady. But she'd come up with the solution Ethan had been contemplating but hadn't dared to voice. If he'd suggested it, Ross and Kim would have jumped down his throat. Delia they had to listen to, because she was their wife and mother.

"The woman *should* leave," Ross growled.

"The woman has a name," Gina reminded him. "And the woman has as much right to stay here as you do. But hey, your wife wants a hotel room. This ain't the Ritz."

Ethan shot her a look and saw a hint of a grin tracing her lips. He struggled not to grin back.

"Actually," Kim interjected, giving Gina a smile as authentic as a cubic zirconium solitaire, "I think Ethan and I could share this place with Ms. Morante and her daughter. Her niece, I mean." Her smile grew even brighter, expanding from one carat to two. "Dad, you and Mom could have a little privacy. If you're paying for the hotel anyway, you may as well get all the benefits of staying there. Why don't we see if we can get you a nice room at one of the hotels we passed?"

"Or you know, there might even be another empty unit here at Palm Point," Ethan said. "I'm sure there's a manager. We could see if anything's available here."

"Nonsense." Delia clearly had her heart set on maid service. And Kim, Ethan could guess, had her heart set on getting her parents out of the condo so she and Ethan could sleep together. He wasn't sure how he felt about that; cohabiting in the condo with Gina Morante and a melodramatic young girl might prove inhibiting. He had little experience with children. He couldn't even guess how old this Ali the Alley-Cat was. But he doubted he'd feel comfortable making love with Kim when there was a chance the kid might barge in on them.

Or Gina Morante.

If he could lock the bedroom door, maybe... But his gaze wandered back to Gina, her angular face and her geometric black hair and those wild, dark eyes. And for some unfathomable reason, he thought sleeping on the couch might be the best thing for him to do.

WHILE THE country-club people fluttered about, conferring, making phone calls and murmuring bad words, Gina emptied the master bedroom's drawers of her things and carried her suitcase into the second bedroom. It didn't have the beautiful ocean view the master bedroom boasted, and a twin bed wasn't a queen. But she couldn't come up with a better solution to their dilemma—except for kicking the country-club people out and sending them all to the Ritz-Carlton or whatever fancy hotel they wanted. Sharing this condo with two strangers wasn't Gina's idea of the perfect vacation.

Their friend had told Carole he wasn't going to use the condo this week. She knew Carole wasn't lying. Their friend had misrepresented his plans. But Gina couldn't prove it. So she was stuck.

She and Alicia would survive. She was good at making the best of bad situations. When she'd gotten expelled from Our Lady of Mercy in eighth grade for asking why, if God didn't want people to use birth control, he'd created human beings smart enough invent things like condoms and the pill, she'd quickly thrown together a portfolio of her scribblings and submitted them, along with an application, to the LaGuardia High School of Music and Art, which had seen enough talent in those scribblings—or enough chutzpah in Gina—to grant her a place in the freshman class. When she'd gotten cited for running a red light in Forest Hills a year and a half ago, she'd not only talked the cop out of giving her a ticket but wound up dating him for more than a year. And when he'd broken up with her, complaining that she spent too much time with all her weirdo friends, she'd phoned Bruno, the weirdest of her friends, and told him he would to have to escort her to every party she got invited to until she reached the point where she could think of Officer Kyle Cronin without either sobbing or cursing. It had taken more than a month, and a lot of truly awful parties, but by the time Gina had stopped sobbing and cursing, she'd talked herself into a job as Bruno's assistant. She didn't want to model sandals and mules for the rest of her life, after all. She wanted to *create* sandals and mules, and working for Bruno would give her that opportunity.

Right now, all she wanted to create was a wonderful week for Alicia. So it wouldn't be perfect. At least it would be good.

She carried her suitcase into Alicia's room, ignoring the quartet huddling in the kitchen. Alicia sat on her bed, knees tucked against her chest and arms hugging her shins. "When can we go to the beach?" she asked.

"As soon as I unpack."

"Are those people gonna leave?"

"Some of them. The older ones, I think. We'll just have to put up with the younger ones."

"I don't like the lady," Alicia said solemnly. "She's mean."

She's a first-class bitch, Gina wanted to say, but then Alicia would scold her for using bad words. "We can steer clear of her."

"The man is okay, though. He's very handsome."

"Is he?" He was a bit too clean-cut and conservative for Gina's tastes, his apparel obviously expensive and his attitude reeking of superior breeding and privilege. But she would have had to be blind not to notice how handsome he was. She bet his auburn hair would catch fire with red highlights when the sunlight struck it. And his eyes glinted with curiosity and—all right, call it sex appeal. And intelligence. He looked like the sort of person who spent a lot of time deep in thought.

Of course, that could be a pose. He could be a moron, the blonde's puppet. They were obviously a couple. Not married, though. Neither wore wedding bands. Besides, if they were married, the blonde's parents wouldn't be talking about his sleeping on the sofa.

Then again, Gina knew married people who slept apart. In particular, Ramona and Jack Bari, Alicia's embattled parents. Neither of them was wearing a wedding band these days.

Great. She'd brought Alicia to St. Thomas to get her away from her dysfunctional parents for a week. Was the poor kid going to wind up spending that week in the company of another dysfunctional couple?

"I'm almost done," Gina announced, pulling a pair of black jeans and a wraparound silk skirt from the suitcase and carrying them to the closet. She and Gina had both packed light, but they'd managed to fill every drawer in the dresser. "Let me put on a swimsuit, and then beach, here we come!"

"Beach, here we come!" Alicia echoed gleefully, shedding the last traces of her distress.

Gina carried her black bikini across the hall to the bathroom. The powwow was still going strong in the kitchen. Shutting the door, she looked around the small room. Her toiletries and Alicia's already took up most of the counter space. Well, Ethan and Blondie would just have to make do. They were getting the bedroom with the beautiful view; they could keep their toiletries on the windowsill, and they could admire the ocean while they put on their deodorant. And they'd better not hog the bathroom, either. They'd better not take erotic two-hour showers together. She glanced up at the showerhead and sighed, dismayed to see it was one of those adjustable pulsing spouts. Ideal for lovers, she thought sourly.

Her bikini on, she emerged from the bathroom, carrying two beach towels from the shelf above the towel rack. Ethan was entering the living room from the kitchen, but he froze in midstep when he saw her crossing the hall to her bedroom. She halted and stared back at him. "Something wrong?"

He swallowed. "No."

"Good." She continued into the bedroom, then glimpsed her reflection in the mirror above the dresser. Her swimsuit wasn't the most modest in the world, but everything that needed to be covered was covered. If he couldn't handle her walking around the condo in beachwear, he could move to the Ritz-Carlton with Blondie's parents.

"All set," she announced, tossing Alicia a towel and then pulling from the closet shelf the plastic bucket and shovel she'd remembered to pack. "Beach, here we come!"

"Beach, here we come!" Alicia yelled as she scampered out of the room.

HE'D FORGOTTEN the swimsuit part.

Well, he hadn't forgotten it. He just hadn't thought about it. And why should he? He'd gone to beaches before—the sandy Long Island Sound beaches at yacht clubs on Connecticut's south shore, the pebbly peaceful beaches of the lakes dotting the state's northwest corner, the high-surf ocean beaches of Cape Cod's National Seashore. Every beach he'd ever been on had included bikini-clad women among the bathers and sun worshipers.

But seeing a bikini-clad woman on a beach was far different from seeing one wandering around a shared apartment. And seeing any bikini-clad woman was different from seeing a bikini-clad Gina Morante.

Feature for feature, Kim had her beaten by a mile. Kim's beauty was of a quality that would cause the vast majority of heterosexual men to reel in astonishment. Her gently waving, corn-colored hair, her delicate little nose and softly curving lips, her body round in all the right places—she was a perfect ten.

Gina, on the other hand… Her revealing black bikini had made her legs look almost too long, and her breasts were kind of small in proportion to her hips, and her facial features were too pronounced. Yet if Kim was a beauty queen, Gina carried herself like a *real* queen, chin high, arms swinging, those wide strong shoulders held straight and proud. She radiated…*something*. He wasn't sure if it was confidence or sexuality or—damn it, *balls.* She was tough. Gentle with her niece but fierce with the world—or at least, with that small segment of the world that had tried to oust her from unit 614 for the week.

When she reemerged from her room with the kid, she had the decency to wear a lacy white cover-up over her bikini. It didn't hide much, but it distracted him from what was underneath. She sent him a smile that had a hint of teasing in it, and swung a bright green toy pail and shovel and a colorful tote bag as she guided her niece out the door.

"That's taken care of," Ross Hamilton announced, joining Ethan in the living room. He looked grim and patronizing, as if he considered Ethan an irredeemable loser, too inept to arrange a sensible vacation. "We've got our reservation. What a disaster."

"The reservation?"

"No—this entire situation. You'll convey our displeasure to your friend Paul, won't you?"

"I'll let him know," Ethan promised. "Do you want me to drive you and Mrs. Hamilton over to the hotel now?"

"I'd like to look around here first," Delia said as she trailed out of the kitchen with Kim. "We're not going to stay here, but we can at least check out the place. Because I don't know how much time we'll want to spend at Palm Point when those two—*people* are here," she concluded, uttering the word as though it were the worst sort of insult. "You may wind up spending most of your time with us at the hotel." She seemed distinctly cheered by the possibility.

Ethan couldn't imagine spending most of his time with the Hamiltons at the hotel. He'd rather hang out with a two strangers than with Kim's pompous parents. If he did ultimately decide to marry Kim, he'd make sure they never lived anywhere near Chevy Chase, Maryland—unless, of course, the Hamiltons moved to Nova Scotia.

"This bedroom is pretty. This is the one you'll be staying in," Delia declared as she and Kim wandered into the master bedroom. "Is it clean? Do they just shove the dust around, or do they do a real cleaning, with furniture polish?''

Not wishing to hear her assessment of the room's cleanliness, Ethan headed out onto the terrace. A breeze drifting up from the water fluttered the palm fronds and distorted the voices of the people enjoying the beach. Off toward the horizon, a rainbow-colored sail bobbed above the water. Closer to the shore, people waded in the water and floated on the surface, snorkeling gear strapped to their heads.

Ethan's gaze zeroed in on Gina and her niece as they set up shop in the shade of a palm. He told himself he'd spotted them instantly because of the Day-Glo brightness of the kid's swimsuit, but in fact Gina had attracted his attention. She'd shed the lacy cover-up, and even at this distance, he could see the curve of her back, the wind sifting through her hair.

''She's not very respectful,'' Ross Hamilton noted, sidling up beside Ethan and resting his hands on the railing. Ethan followed his gaze; it led him back to Gina. ''Obviously not well-bred. I don't like her attitude.''

''She probably just felt awkward,'' Ethan defended her. ''Her friend screwed up, and she was put on the defensive. She'll be all right.''

''Well, if it doesn't work out, we'll get another room at the hotel. But I must say, I'm not thrilled about this unexpected expenditure.''

''I'll talk to Paul about it.'' And say what? That Paul should reimburse Ross Hamilton for the hotel room? This wasn't Paul's fault, any more than it was Ethan's— or Gina's.

''Delia seems to be making the best of it,'' Ross said wryly. ''Give her room service and she's as happy as a duffer who's just gotten a hole in one. As for that woman…'' He gestured toward the beach, where Gina was now on her knees, scooping up sand with her bare hands. Ethan couldn't see her smile, but he could imagine it. ''I'd keep my things locked up if I were you.''

''You believe she's a thief?'' Ethan laughed.

''I don't know what she is. Neither do you. Don't let your guard down.''

Ethan wouldn't—but fear that Gina Morante would abscond with his money and credit cards wasn't his primary reason. What he had to guard against was the keen awareness she aroused within him. There was no good explanation for it, other than basic hormones, the typical male response to a woman strutting around in skimpy swimwear.

Gina wasn't his type. She was too urban, too gritty. He liked his women sweet and refined. Not pliant—Kim certainly wasn't pliant, but she was genteel. Ladylike. Gracious, except when her dander was up. She was elegant, subtle, the sort of woman who made him feel he was the most important man in the world.

So he had an ego. So he liked the way Kim stroked it. He wasn't going to apologize for being human.

A wisp of laughter spiraled through the air to the terrace. He had no way of tracing it to a particular person, but he suspected it was Gina's. Hers and her niece's. Their heads bowed and their knees touching, they dug in the sand, looking not the least bit elegant or refined or subtle.

They were obviously having a blast. And for one brief, incomprehensible moment, Ethan wished he were down there on the beach with them, digging.

CHAPTER THREE

WHEN GINA AND ALICIA returned to the condo, the country clubbers were gone. "Did they leave?" Alicia asked with what sounded like a combination of hope and dread.

Gina found several suitcases in the master bedroom, implying that the younger half of their group intended to stay at the condo with her and Alicia, as they'd said they would. They were probably gone only temporarily, moving the older half into a luxurious hotel room somewhere. "I think we're stuck with them," she told Alicia. "But we'll just go ahead and have our vacation as if they weren't here."

She made Alicia shower to wash off all the sand that dusted her arms and legs and clogged the cracks between her toes, then took a quick shower, too. She hadn't packed a bathrobe—she hadn't expected to need one—but when she peeked out around the bathroom door, she saw and heard nothing to indicate that Ethan and the cheerleader had returned. Wrapping a bath towel around her, just in case, she darted across the hall to the bedroom she and Alicia were now sharing. She was used to living alone in her studio apartment in Chelsea, where as long as the shades were drawn shut she could move around her home wearing as much or as little as she wished. Of course, she would have been discreet even if she'd been sharing Carole's condo only with Alicia.

Seven-year-old nieces should never be flashed by their aunts. But wearing a large bath towel was as discreet as she needed to be for Alicia.

She slipped into a light cotton shift, rubbed some moisturizing lotion into her cheeks and her legs and grabbed her purse. "There's a restaurant at the hotel just down the beach," she informed Alicia. "You ready for dinner?"

Unlike their housemates, she and Alicia lacked wheels. Fortunately, the restaurant she had in mind was a short ways down a path that was part boardwalk and part brick, lined with beach grass, sand and palm trees. Since she didn't have to drive home afterward, Gina happily indulged in a tall, frosty piña colada along with her grilled grouper and vegetables. Alicia wolfed down a burger, a basket of fries and a dish of vanilla ice cream with butterscotch sauce. However many cookies she'd devoured before they'd left for the beach, the snack hadn't interfered with her appetite.

During the early days of Ramona's marital crisis, Gina's sister had confided that Alicia wasn't eating much. The poor kid had lost a couple of pounds during the past spring, and she didn't have any weight to spare. But her appetite seemed fine right now. Even the invasion of strangers into their condo hadn't upset her enough to keep her from enjoying her dinner. Gina was grateful for that.

"I like the way it smells," Alicia said as they strolled back along the boardwalk toward Palm Point. She held Gina's hand and added a little skip to her step. "It smells hot."

"It *is* hot," Gina pointed out. "I think what you're smelling is the ocean and all the plants and flowers."

"This isn't the ocean," Alicia argued. "The ocean is gray."

"Up north it is. Down here it's turquoise. I guess this is actually a sea, anyway. The Caribbean Sea."

"The Carrybeaner Sea," Alicia said. Gina didn't bother to correct her. "Can we do that thing with the tubes tomorrow? What's it called? The thing with the masks and the tubes."

"Snorkeling. Sure." Gina pointed to a cabanalike building on the pool patio near the beach. "We can rent some equipment there."

"Is it hard?" Alicia peered up at her bravely. "I want to do it anyway, but is it hard?"

"No. It's really easy." Gina had tried snorkeling a couple of years ago, when she and a couple of friends had spent a long weekend at a lakeside inn in the Poconos Mountains of northeastern Pennsylvania. The most interesting marine life they'd seen through their masks had been minnows flashing past them and underwater reeds that billowed and danced every time had Gina kicked her flippered feet. It had been fun—and very easy. Alicia knew how to swim; snorkeling would come naturally to her.

Alicia sighed. "I love it here. Can we stay forever?"

Gina might have argued that Alicia hadn't been in St. Thomas long enough to fall in love. She suspected that what her niece loved was being far away from her feuding parents. "I wish we could stay here forever, too," she admitted. "No more work, and no more school for you—" a prospect that roused a cheer from Alicia "—and every day at the beach. And dinner at a restaurant every night. I could get into that."

"Then let's stay!"

"But we'd run out of money," Gina pointed out.

"And after a while you'd miss your friends." She didn't dare suggest Alicia would miss her parents. "And you'd never learn algebra."

"You can teach me. What's algebra?"

"It's a kind of math you have to learn in ninth grade." And then never use again, Gina thought, although she actually did use math a fair amount in designing shoes. Not algebra specifically, but she supposed all those years she'd spent in high school, learning trig and history and the periodic table, did her as much good as the classes she'd taken in design and sculpture and color theory.

They had reached the Palm Point pool, which gave off a faint whiff of chlorine. The sky stretched salmon pink above them, and the tide carried a constant breeze in on the waves. If Gina hadn't brought Alicia with her to St. Thomas, she'd probably be only just getting ready to go out now. She'd have located a club where she could stay until closing time, consuming fruity tropical drinks and dancing until she was sweaty and every muscle in her body ached. She loved dancing, especially with people who smiled, laughed and danced as enthusiastically as she did. She never went to clubs to pick up guys. She just wanted to enjoy the music with them.

But strolling through the humid tropical evening with Alicia had its own satisfactions, most of them at least as gratifying as dancing at a club would have been. Maybe she'd teach Alicia how to dance, and they could blast songs on the radio in the condo and dance around the living room.

No, they couldn't. Not with Ethan and What's-her-face sharing the unit.

Ethan and What's-her-face were still gone when Gina let Alicia and herself into the condo. They'd unpacked their things in the master bedroom, though. Gina was going to hate spending her week so conscious of them, alert to their presence and their absence, wondering when they would arrive and when they would depart. Alicia seemed more relaxed about the arrangement, however. She flopped onto the sofa, turned on the TV and flipped through the channels until she found a Spanish-language station. A variety show was on—lots of show-girls in skimpy outfits with fluffy feathers attached in strategic places, everyone speaking machine-gun-rapid Spanish. Alicia giggled. ''We get this channel at home,'' she said.

''Good. Maybe you'll learn some Spanish,'' Gina suggested, crossing to the kitchen for a can of soda. Swinging open the fridge, she spotted a six-pack of beer that hadn't been there before—a local brew with Bluebeard the pirate on the label—as well as a red-waxed sphere of Gouda and a jar of olives. Ethan and Blondie must have gone shopping. Their grocery list clearly differed from Gina's, which had included such gourmet delicacies as cornflakes, milk, peanut butter, bread and bananas.

The beer tempted. What would those people do if Gina helped herself to a bottle? Would they bill her? Short-sheet her bed? Toss her over the balcony?

She'd had enough roommates in her life—starting with her sister, Ramona, and including fellow students at the Rhode Island School of Design, a couple of apartment mates boasting various levels of neatness, consideration and integrity, and six other people one summer when a friend had talked her into participating in a group rental in Southampton. Every Friday, she'd spent two hours on an overcrowded train to reach their overcrowded bungalow three miles from the beach, where she'd slept on a mattress on the floor and argued with a ditzy platinum-blond wanna-be actress who was always leaving her shoes in the middle of the kitchen floor and a junior stockbroker who had loud sex with a different woman every night, and a social-climbing gay couple who bickered incessantly about which parties to crash. She still remembered the scream fest that had erupted when the stockbroker had helped himself to the gay guys' orange juice. World War Three would not be so cataclysmic.

No, Gina wouldn't take a bottle of beer. The last thing she wanted Alicia to witness this week was a fight.

She popped open a can of her own Diet Coke, wandered back into the living room, settled on the sofa next to Alicia and kicked off her sandals. She didn't want to watch Mexico's answer to the Rockettes, so she flipped through the channels until she found a nature show on yaks.

"This looks good," Alicia said, snuggling up to Gina.

Gina arched her arm around her precious niece and planted a kiss on Alicia's silky black hair. "It looks great," she said, settling back into the cushions and grinning.

ETHAN COULD COME UP with an extensive list of reasons for his insomnia: a strange bed, a strange room, a strange climate. Jet lag—although flying south and losing only one hour shouldn't have thrown him off that badly. Irritation with Kim's parents—that was a likely culprit. Irritation with Kim. Guilt over being in bed with her after implying to her parents that he would sleep on the couch. Guilt over being in bed with her and not wanting to make love.

Awareness of Gina Morante.

He felt guilt about that, too. Major guilt. Kim slept

soundly on her half of the bed, the familiar scent of her face cream wafting into the air around him. But he picked up a different scent, faint, almost subliminal. Gina's scent.

Kim hadn't seemed upset when he'd gently rebuffed her attempt to seduce him. ''I'm beat,'' he'd explained, a perfectly reasonable excuse. He'd endured a long flight with a ninety-minute layover in Atlanta, the stress of driving on the wrong side of the road, the much greater stress of behaving courteously toward Kim's overbearing parents, the hauling of luggage to the unit in Palm Point, the scaring up of a suitable hotel room at a resort down the road, more driving, stocking up on drinks and snacks, unpacking the groceries and the suitcases, dressing for dinner, enduring a three-hour meal with the Hamiltons, complete with aperitifs and a fifty-year-old bottle of wine, listening to Ross and Delia describe all the far superior resorts where they had vacationed over the years and bobbing and weaving through an interrogation concerning Ethan's politics, which were located a good few miles to the left of Ross Hamilton's. Ethan and Kim had dropped her parents off at their hotel and returned to Palm Point at around eleven. He hadn't been lying to her when he'd said he was too tired to do anything more than brush his teeth and fall into bed.

Falling into bed was easy. Falling asleep proved a much greater challenge.

He pictured Gina in her narrow bed across the hall. He pictured her niece in the other bed. What kind of woman vacationed with her niece? Gina seemed too funky to be an aunt. Aunts didn't wear toe rings, did they?

He tried to imagine Kim wearing a toe ring, then chastised himself for comparing her with Gina. They were two different women. Two *very* different women. Kim was a human resources executive at an insurance company in Hartford. Gina Morante looked like a chichi sales clerk at a SoHo boutique, or maybe a waitress at one of the trendier midtown restaurants. Kim wore tailored suits and dresses to work every day. The only kind of dress Ethan could imagine Gina wearing would be short, sheer or both. To hide those legs of hers would be a crime.

And he was a bastard for even thinking such a thing while his almost-fiancée slept beside him.

He drifted in and out of a slumber until sounds beyond the door alerted him that Gina and her niece had arisen. He remained in bed, thinking he might sleep more easily if they were in the kitchen, at the opposite end of the apartment. But when he closed his eyes, he was kept from sinking into dreamland by a memory of them as they'd looked from the balcony yesterday, digging in the sand, bowing their heads together and laughing.

Finally, unable to force himself to lie still any longer, he slid out of bed and moved silently to avoid rousing Kim. After donning a pair of khaki shorts and a polo shirt, he tiptoed out of the bedroom.

Their hushed voices rippled down the hall like a gentle current. The bathroom was empty, so he made use of it before heading to the kitchen.

The kid was seated at the small table, a heaping bowl of cold cereal before her. Gina stood leaning against the counter, holding a bowl of what appeared to be yogurt and sliced bananas. The room was filled with the soul-stirring aroma of freshly brewed coffee. He and Kim should have bought coffee yesterday when they'd stopped at a local convenience store to purchase beer, imported bottled water, macadamia nuts, cheese and other such necessities. Kim had insisted they wouldn't need coffee, since they would be meeting her parents for breakfast every morning. But right now, inhaling the fragrance of Gina's coffee, he realized that Kim had been wrong.

"Good morning," Gina greeted him. From her, the word came out *mawn-ing*.

"Good morning," he responded, rubbing his hand through his hair. He should have brushed it while he'd had access to the mirror above the bathroom sink, but he'd left his brush in the bedroom. Gina and her niece had monopolized the shelf space in the bathroom.

His eyes took a moment to adjust to the sunny brightness of the kitchen, and then went to work processing the sight of Gina, dressed today in a lime-green T-shirt and short white shorts. She was barefoot except for the silver ring circling one of her left toes. The sight of it jolted him in some way, and he lifted his gaze to her face. She'd pulled a hank of her hair back from her face and clasped it with a large barrette, the way a child might wear her hair. On her, it didn't look childish.

"I hope we didn't wake you up," she said. "We were trying to keep quiet."

"You were very quiet. Thank you." He gestured toward the hallway. "Kim's still dead to the world."

"You want some coffee?"

Desperately, but he should decline. If he drank her coffee, it would represent an unseemly mingling of their vacations. Yet when he watched her reach for the large ceramic mug on the counter beside her, lift it to her lips and take a sip, he couldn't resist. "I'd love some."

"Help yourself. The cups are in that cabinet." She gestured toward the cabinet above the coffeemaker. "I bought a pound of ground beans and there's no way I'm going to finish it all by myself in one week. So really, help yourself whenever you want some. I found a stash of filters in the cabinet with the napkins and paper towels.''

''I'm too young for coffee,'' the little girl announced as she patted the cereal flakes beneath the surface of the milk in her bowl. ''We're going snorkeling today.''

''Are you?'' Okay. He could handle this—drinking Gina's coffee and making small talk with her niece. Despite his lack of experience with children, he figured that discussing snorkeling with a spunky little girl couldn't be any harder than discussing politics with Ross Hamilton.

''Aunt Gina says it's easy.''

''Aunt Gina knows what she's talking about,'' he confirmed as he filled a mug with coffee for himself. The fragrance flooded him like an elixir, sparking inside him the notion that sharing the condo with Gina and the kid was actually a stroke of luck. If they hadn't been there, he would be having his first conversation of the day with Kim's father—after having spent the night on the couch.

''You could come snorkeling with us,'' the girl said.

He glanced sharply at Gina, who shrugged noncommittally. ''They rent gear at the cabana on the beach. There's milk in the fridge, by the way. No sugar, though. I don't use it, so I didn't buy any.''

He sipped his coffee, then shook his head. ''I drink it black. Thanks. It's wonderful.''

''They have good water here,'' she said. ''Coffee tastes different depending on the water you brew it with. This—'' she raised her mug toward him, as if proposing a toast ''—is delicious. Must mean the water is good.''

He thought of the bottled water Kim had insisted on buying, even after he'd pointed out that St. Thomas was part of the United States and he was sure its water had passed U.S. health standards.

"So, you wanna go snorkeling with us?" the child insisted.

"Ali, he's here on his own vacation," Gina reminded her. "He'll be doing things with the people he came with."

"They could come, too. They could get snorkeling stuff at the casino."

"Cabana."

"Yeah." The girl scooped a mound of cereal into her mouth, chewed and gave him a toothy grin. "Aunt Gina says we'll see fish. I wanna see an octopus."

"I don't know how many fish come to this beach. There's another beach about a mile up the coast that's supposed to be incredible for snorkeling," Ethan informed them.

Gina's dark eyes widened with interest. "Really?"

He felt absurdly proud of his knowledge. "Paul—the friend who owns a share of this unit—mentioned a beach to me. Coki Beach, I think it's called. There's even better snorkeling on St. John, but you have to take the ferry to get there."

"Coki Beach?"

She looked so interested, so grateful for his knowledge. His ego inflated a bit more. "Just a mile or so west of here."

"Can we go?" The girl twisted in her seat and gazed eagerly at her aunt. "Can we go there?"

"I don't know. We'd have to get a cab, I guess. Or there might be a public jitney."

"What's a jitney?"

"Kind of like a bus."

"I could—" Ethan cut himself off before completing

the sentence: *I could drive you there*. Maybe he could; maybe he couldn't. He'd rented the car for the convenience of the Hamiltons, not a strange woman and her niece.

Of course, if he and Kim went snorkeling with Gina and the kid, they could all drive there together, and leave Kim's parents to fend for themselves. Why not? The Hamiltons were residing at a luxurious hotel. They could get massages and drink Absolut vodka martinis while lounging by the pool. Or they could hit the links. Given a choice between snorkeling and golf, Ethan couldn't imagine choosing golf—and he couldn't imagine Ross Hamilton choosing snorkeling.

Maybe this whole time-share disaster would turn out to be a huge blessing. Ethan and Kim could do things with Gina and her niece and ignore Kim's parents. The time he'd spent with them on the flight to St. Thomas and last night at dinner was enough to convince him that an in-law relationship with them would never be a close, loving bond. He really ought to withhold judgment until he'd spent more than one day in their company, but where people were concerned, his instincts were usually pretty accurate. He'd known, within minutes of glimpsing Kim, that they would wind up in bed together, and that the experience would be spectacular. They had, and it was. And here he was, having spent a grand total of less than an hour in Gina Morante's company, and he knew…

He knew they would get along. Beyond that, he didn't want to know what he knew.

So they'd go snorkeling together. He'd sacrifice his evenings to Ross and Delia Hamilton, but surely he didn't have to sacrifice his days to them, too.

The sound of footsteps padding down the carpeted

hall caused him to turn. Kim, clad in a tennis skirt and top, her hair pulled into a bouncy ponytail, materialized in the doorway.

"Good morning," Gina greeted her in her distinctive New York accent.

Kim managed a cool smile, then turned to Ethan. "You aren't eating breakfast, are you? We're supposed to meet Mom and Dad at the hotel at nine."

"Just a cup of coffee," he said, then nodded toward Gina. "Gina generously offered me some."

Gina glanced toward the coffeepot, which was nearly empty. "I could make some more," she said.

"That won't be necessary," Kim assured her. "But thank you for offering."

"He's going snorkeling with us," the kid announced.

One of Kim's eyebrows ascended and the other dipped, enabling her to look simultaneously quizzical and skeptical. "Is he?" she asked, her elegant blue eyes boring into him.

"We were just talking about it," he said, refusing to succumb to her potent stare. Others quaked and quailed in the icy potency of her disapproval, but he never did—which, he suspected, was one of his main attractions for her. "Paul mentioned a place called Coki Beach, where the snorkeling is supposed to be phenomenal."

"We're meeting Mom and Dad for breakfast," she said.

"Breakfast isn't going to take the whole day. We could go snorkeling after breakfast."

"I was hoping we could go to Charlotte Amalie."

"Kim, we're not going to spend this entire week shopping." His voice was gentle, but he hoped she'd heard the warning in it.

She pursed her lovely pink lips, indicating that she

had. "I know that," she said crisply. "I thought we could go downtown today and get a feel for the place. We don't have to go snorkeling on these people's schedule." She waved her hand vaguely toward Gina and the kid.

Ethan knew she didn't intend to be rude. But the strangers they'd been accidentally thrown together with were irrelevant to her. They might as well not even exist, as far as she was concerned.

They existed for Ethan, though. He felt their warmth in the air, he heard the clinks of their spoons against their bowls, and he knew they were assessing Kim and giving her very low marks. He didn't blame them.

Yet, in a way she was right. Their schedule shouldn't dictate his and Kim's. He was under no obligation to drive them to Coki Beach or anywhere else. They could take the jitney.

And he'd be stuck with the Hamiltons.

It was enough to make him wish he were a jitney driver.

HE FINALLY MADE IT to the beach at a little past one-thirty. The sun was high and white, like an incandescent bulb in the sky. The beach smelled of coconut oil and sea salt, and the wind gusting off the water was warm.

Okay, so the Hamiltons wanted to shop. *He* didn't want to shop, and there was no reason on earth that he should have to. If he and Kim wound up married, he wouldn't be obligated to accompany her every time she went shopping. Why accompany her here?

After breakfast—another long, profusely caloric meal, this time lubricated by mimosas and spiced with a contentious debate on the current administration's environmental policies—he'd driven Kim and her parents into

Charlotte Amalie and arranged to meet them at five o'clock at a shaded kiosk by the wharf where all the cruise ships docked. During their initial excursion—"This is reconnaissance, not serious shopping," Kim had explained—they would scout out some interesting eateries, and when Ethan met up with them they'd choose a restaurant for dinner.

He'd agreed to everything Kim said. As long as he didn't have to do reconnaissance with her, he'd go along with whatever dinner plans her family wanted.

He did intend to do a little shopping at some point that week—not so much that preliminary recon was called for, though. If watches were as inexpensive as the guidebooks said, he might pick one up for his father. Maybe one for himself, too. But he couldn't imagine spending more than one day roaming the streets, alleys and arcades of Charlotte Amalie in search of bargains. It wasn't as if he and his father *needed* watches. And how could a person prefer shopping to lounging on the sand with a cold beer and a good book? Or snorkeling at Coki Beach.

He wondered if Gina and Ali had made it over to Coki Beach. If they hadn't found their own transportation there, it was probably too late for him to offer them a lift now.

He touched the cold surface of his beer bottle to his forehead and scanned the beach—looking for a spot to settle in the shade of a palm, not looking for a leggy, dark-haired tourist from New York. When he didn't spot her, he convinced himself he wasn't disappointed.

And when he did spot her niece, he convinced himself he wasn't elated.

Ali the Alley Cat knelt in the sand, molding and sculpting it with her hands. He watched from the walkway bordering the beach as she labored over what appeared to be a sand castle of some sort. She peered toward the water, then grinned and waved. Following the line of her gaze, he saw Gina striding across the sand, carrying a beach pail so full of water it splattered droplets with her every step.

Her bikini was as revealing as the one she'd worn yesterday. Today's was turquoise, the same color as the sea. The bottom was cut high and the top was cut low.

Kim is beautiful, he reminded himself, but that truth didn't seem particularly germane at the moment.

He ambled over the hot sand, figuring he'd just say hello and then find another location to settle. But when Alicia saw him, she eagerly waved him over. "Hey, come see what I'm making!" she hollered.

He reached Alicia the same time Gina did. She lowered her bucket to the sand carefully, and he tried not to stare at her bosom as she bent over. God, she looked great in a bikini. Ethan had never met a woman who didn't—any size, any shape, he happened to think women's bodies were wonderful—but Gina was definitely one of the most satisfying sights on the beach today.

"What are you making?" he asked. Up close, Alicia's efforts didn't resemble much of anything.

"The Brooklyn Bridge," she told him.

"That's a pretty ambitious project," he said, shooting a grin at Gina as she straightened up.

She grinned back. "You're standing in Staten Island, in case you were wondering."

"You can help," Alicia told him, her tone firm enough to convey that this was an order.

"Alicia, he came down to the beach to read," Gina chided the kid. "See? He's got a book. Let him be."

"No, I don't mind," he said, although he wanted to build the Brooklyn Bridge on a beach about as much as he wanted to shop for discounted liquor in Charlotte Amalie. He tossed down his book beside a pile of what he guessed was Gina's gear, propped against the base of a palm: the colorful canvas tote he'd seen her carrying yesterday, and mesh drawstring bags filled with snorkeling masks, tubes and flippers. Then he hunkered down next to Alicia. "What do you want me to do?" he asked.

"We have to dig," she said, pointing to a narrow trench she'd already carved into the sand. "This is the East River or New York Harbor. I forget. Aunt Gina says if we dig deep enough, the water won't disappear."

"You want me to dredge the harbor," he said, shooting Gina another look. She towered above him, her lanky body casting a long shadow across him.

"You don't have to do this," she called down to him.

Viewing her from his ground-level perspective, he couldn't imagine choosing his book over a few minutes with her—even if he had to pay for those minutes by digging in the sand with her niece. "I'll see how it goes," he said, refusing to commit to more than that.

"I'm dumping the water so Aunt Gina can get more," Alicia announced before emptying the bucket of water into the trench.

"Maybe you should get the water and let your aunt sit for a minute," he suggested, hoping Alicia and Gina wouldn't interpret his words as anything other than an attempt to earn a fellow adult a few minute's rest.

Alicia sprang to her feet. "Okay! You guys dig and I'll get the water!" Before Gina could object, the kid had grabbed the bucket and was racing down to the sea.

Gina lowered herself onto the sand, not too close to

Ethan. Her gaze remained on her niece. "She spills half the water," she told Ethan. "That's why we thought it would be better if I got it."

"This doesn't look anything like the Brooklyn Bridge," he commented, scrutinizing the span constructed of damp, packed sand above the trench.

Gina chuckled but refused to shift her attention from the little girl at the water's edge. "You've seen the Brooklyn Bridge?"

"I'm from Connecticut," he told her. "And you're from…Brooklyn?"

Still smiling, she shook her head. "Manhattan. I grew up in the Bronx."

He knew midtown Manhattan, where all the Broadway theaters and famous restaurants and office towers were, and the downtown business district. The Bronx was just a borough he passed through—and the punch line of jokes.

"I live down in Chelsea now," she told him. "You know the city?"

"Sort of." He smiled sheepishly and hoped she wouldn't quiz him. "I live in Arlington. That's in the northwest corner of Connecticut."

"Yeah. I know it." She used the plastic shovel to dig the trench deeper. A murky puddle of water lingered at the bottom. "So where's the rest of your group?"

"Shopping. I thought I'd come back and enjoy a little beach time." He glanced toward the snorkeling gear by the palm tree. "Did you visit Coki Beach?"

"Not today. We just snorkeled around here. They rent equipment for the whole week. The guy at the cabana said we should try to get over to St. John. There's this underwater snorkeling trail there. I can't imagine snorkeling along an underwater trail."

"It's supposed to be amazing." He wondered whether he'd be able to separate Kim from her Visa card long enough to take her snorkeling at Trunk Bay on St. John. Paul had told him he *had* to go there. He'd hate to go alone, though.

And he couldn't go with Gina. Not when she looked the way she did in a swimsuit.

"I'm figuring we'll try Coki Beach tomorrow. We saw some fish here. Not a lot, but Alicia was pretty excited."

Ethan did a little desultory one-handed digging while he sipped his beer. "You want some?" he asked, extending the bottle to her.

She flickered a glance toward the bottle, then zeroed in on Alicia again. "Thanks," she said, letting him place the bottle into her hand so she wouldn't have to look away from her niece. "It's hot out here. We brought some sodas down to the beach, but we finished them a while ago."

"Beer is better," he said. She smiled her agreement.

Down by the water, Alicia straightened up, clutching the rim of the bucket. Gina handed the bottle back to Ethan and watched her niece pick a path across the beach, sloshing water with each step. By the time she reached them, she looked upset. "I spilled too much of it," she said, a sob making her voice wobbly.

"That's okay, sweetie. Pour it in and I'll get the next one."

Ethan wanted to argue. He'd barely begun talking to her; he wasn't ready for her to run off. And he definitely wasn't ready to shoot the breeze with a little girl. But who would be the water carrier wasn't his decision to make. Gina rose, lifted the pail from Alicia's hands as soon as she'd emptied it into the trench, and stalked across the beach, her hips swaying as her heels sank into the sand.

Alicia threw herself back into the labor of digging. Ethan took another sip of beer and observed her. "We snorkeled today," Alicia told him as she flung sand to one side.

"Your aunt told me. She said you saw some fish."

"They were white. Kind of silvery. The color of angels," Alicia told him. "I wanted to snorkel forever, but I swallowed some water and started coughing, and Aunt Gina said we had to take a break."

"You've got a whole week," Ethan pointed out. "You can go snorkeling again tomorrow."

"Where's the lady?" Alicia asked.

He assumed she meant Kim. "She's in Charlotte Amalie. That's the big town on the other side of the island."

"Do they have snorkeling there?"

"No. What they have there is shopping."

Alicia wrinkled her nose. She obviously didn't think much of shopping. "Is she your girlfriend?"

"Yes," Ethan said, feeling noble and virtuous for having gotten that established, even if he hadn't established it with Gina. She'd surely figured it out. And now the kid knew, too.

"My daddy has a girlfriend," Alicia said, bringing him up short.

"Does he?" Perhaps her mother was dead, or her parents were divorced.

Or perhaps they weren't. "It makes my mommy very mad," Alicia said.

"I would imagine," he agreed faintly.

"I don't think she's as pretty as your girlfriend," Alicia continued matter-of-factly. "I haven't seen her, but the way my mommy talks about her... Sometimes my mommy uses bad words. I hate that.''

''I remember.'' Ethan recalled Alicia's howls yesterday when anyone uttered a *damn* or a *hell*. He toyed with the label on his bottle and searched the water for Gina, eager for her to return. Compared with this conversation, his political debates with Ross Hamilton had been a piece of cake.

''Aunt Gina is my mommy's sister,'' Alicia went on. ''That's what an aunt is—your mother's sister. Or your father's sister. Do you have any aunts?''

''Yes.'' He spotted Gina straightening up, clutching the replenished bucket. Good. In less than a minute, she'd be back to rescue him.

''Are they as nice as Aunt Gina?''

''No. Aunt Gina seems extra nice.'' Every step that carried her toward him made her seem even nicer.

''She is. Extra extra nice. Extra extra *extra*.'' She greeted Gina's arrival with a big smile. When Gina emptied the water into the trench, Alicia let out a whoop. ''Look, Aunt Gina! It's staying. We dug deep enough! The water isn't all soaking in!''

Ethan rose onto his knees and peered into the trench. A nice pool of water stretched below the bridge. ''Hey,'' he said admiringly.

''All right!'' Gina slapped Alicia's hand in congratulations, then slapped Ethan's, too. Her touch startled him. Her palm was slick and cool with water, her fingers slender, her wrist graceful. She wore a ring on her thumb, braided strands of silver in a pattern identical to the ring on her toe.

The brief contact obviously meant nothing. She was just celebrating their engineering feat. Because Ethan was there, she included him in the celebration. That was all.

Yet the cool texture of her skin and the exuberance behind her gesture stayed with him, long after she and Alicia had moved on to bolstering the bridge, decorating it with shells and strands of grass, analyzing the feasibility of importing some of those angel-colored fish to swim in their tiny version of New York Harbor.

Sipping his beer and listening to their bubbly chatter, Ethan felt the impact of Gina's hand against his and contemplated the tide as it tugged the sand, shaped the shoreline and left beach reconfigured, rearranged—almost unrecognizable. Tides could be dangerous, he thought. Extra extra *extra* dangerous. He'd better be careful.

Yet he closed his hand, as if he could hold Gina's touch inside it forever.

CHAPTER FOUR

EVER SINCE HER RUN-IN with the nuns at Our Lady of Mercy at the age of thirteen, Gina hadn't been particularly religious. But she believed in God—and if she hadn't, snorkeling at Coki Beach would have turned her into a believer.

The beach itself was nothing much, just a strip of sand, a few picnic tables, a man operating a kiosk from which he sold grilled sausages and citrus punch, and a couple of local women who'd set up a hair-braiding enterprise in the shade of a looming old tree. Alicia had asked if she could have braids done, and Gina had paid one of the women to add two delicate braids, tipped with beads the color of the sea, to the hair behind Alicia's right ear. Another kiosk offered snorkeling equipment for rent, but Gina had brought the gear they'd rented at Palm Point.

She'd also brought Ethan and Kim—or, more accurately, Ethan and Kim had brought her and Alicia. Grateful for the lift, Gina had packed extra peanut-butter sandwiches, fruit-juice boxes and grapes, happy to cater lunch for everyone in return for the free ride.

Kim hadn't seemed overjoyed with the plan, but she'd gone along with it. Her parents were apparently spending the day playing tennis and golf, and Kim had seemed torn about having to choose between those activities and snorkeling. Ethan had told her that whether or not she joined him, he intended to snorkel—"I can play tennis at the club in Connecticut, for God's sake," he'd argued, just loudly enough that Gina couldn't help overhearing him, even though he and Kim were in their ocean-view bedroom and Gina and Alicia were in the kitchen when this quarrel had taken place. By the time Kim had emerged with Ethan from their room, she'd been wearing a swimsuit and a resentful pout.

Once they'd arrived at the beach, though, she'd dutifully donned the mask and flippers Ethan had provided, and they'd gone into the water together. Gina had watched them kick away from the shoreline, then helped Alicia put on her equipment and followed them in.

The water was as clear as teal-tinted glass, and it swarmed with fish. Blue fish. Yellow fish. Violet fish. Iridescent fish that shimmered with all the colors of the rainbow whenever they swam through a wavering shaft of sunlight. Fish that skittered in and out of coral formations, ducked behind sea plants and sometimes swam right up to Gina's nose and stared at her, as if trying to determine whether she was one of them.

I am, I am! she wanted to shout—although she wasn't sure fish had ears. But she felt as if she were just another fish—a big, clumsy, gill-less one, but in some humble way a part of their magical world. Of course God existed, she thought. The tranquil beauty of all these fish letting Gina and a score of other humans snorkel in their territory proved it. How could a place this beautiful and peaceful exist if God hadn't created it?

She managed to keep track of Alicia while she swam among the glorious fish. Alicia wore her bright orange swimsuit, which made her quite visible in the water, and she frequently bobbed her head above the surface and hollered, "Aunt Gina! Over here! Look at this!" Her cries would invariably attract half a dozen other snor-kelers, who would all converge wherever Alicia was standing in time to see a vivid purple-and-orange fish scoot away, no doubt startled by the sudden crowd. Gina didn't mind, though. Whenever a few minutes passed without Alicia's giving a yell, Gina would surface and scan the inlet to locate Alicia and make sure she was safe.

Ethan seemed as taken by the underwater world as Gina was. He wouldn't yell to get her attention, but every now and then he would swim over to her, his feet pumping in his long black flippers, nudge her shoulder and point. Together they would watch a hole in the coral until some wondrously colored creature would emerge. Then Ethan would smile at her around his breathing tube and swim off.

He looked damn good in a swimsuit. Not that she noticed or anything.

Kim looked good in a swimsuit, too. Kim would prob-ably look good in a ratty bathrobe, torn stockings and hair rollers. Gina knew a fair number of models through work, but they tended not to be quite so beautiful. In person, they were often emaciated, and they also usually had some odd feature—knife-sharp cheekbones, perhaps, or a bumpy nose, or collagen-plumped lips. The New York fashion world loved slightly weird faces. Kim would never make it as a model; she was much too clas-sically pretty.

She left the water a good half hour before Gina, Alicia and Ethan were ready to break for lunch. Actually, Gina would have been happy to skip lunch and remain in the muted, glittery world of the fish, tasting salt on the rub-bery mouthpiece of her breathing tube and feeling her ears rush and pop with water. But eventually Alicia yanked on the strap of her mask and announced that she was starving, so Gina reluctantly abandoned her sacred fish for a sandwich.

She spotted Kim at one of the picnic tables, her wet hair combed back from her face and a book open in her lap. Gina wrestled out of her flippers, then helped Alicia off with hers. They stalked across the hot sand to the table, underneath which Gina had left her tote with the sandwiches, fruit and drinks. "We're hungry," Alicia declared.

Kim gave them a supercilious glance, then tucked a bookmark into her book. "Don't splash water on the pages," she chided Alicia. Gina glimpsed the book's title: *A Buyer's Guide to Diamonds.* Not exactly her idea of light vacation reading.

She wrapped a towel around Alicia, then draped a second towel over her own shoulders. Tugging off her mask and snorkel tube, she felt the snaggles in her hair. Had she thought to toss a comb into the tote? She didn't think so, but no big deal. She'd just be going back into the water after lunch.

"Wow!" Ethan's voice drifted toward her from behind. She glanced over her shoulder and saw him jogging up the beach, his mask perched on the crown of his head and his flippers dangling from one hand. His chest was sleek with water and lean muscle, and the wet fabric of his swimsuit lay pasted to his thighs and hips in a way that was just this side of obscene. Gina wished he would turn around so she could check out his buns. He belonged to Kim; she knew that. But a woman was allowed to look, wasn't she?

"Isn't it cool?" Alicia said, climbing up onto a bench. "Did you see those fish with all the colors on them? They *glowed!*"

"They were pretty special," Ethan agreed, sliding onto the bench across from Alicia and next to Kim, whom he gave a swift kiss. She shrank from him and held her book away, evidently worried that he would drip water onto it. His hair appeared as messy as Gina's felt, sticking out in all directions and spraying droplets of water every time he moved his head.

"All I've got is peanut butter," Gina said, unpacking the sandwiches from her tote. "And grapes. And lots of juice."

"I'm not hungry," Kim said. She hadn't done as much swimming as the others, and maybe she'd eaten a huge breakfast. Or maybe she was counting her calories, although her body, like the rest of her, appeared flawless to Gina. Then again, if Gina had packed a picnic of Brie and truffles, Kim might suddenly discover she had an appetite. Peanut butter was probably too déclassé for her.

She did help herself to a few grapes. Gina, Alicia and Ethan attacked the sandwiches and juice. "I couldn't find an octopus," Alicia said. "I wanted to, but I couldn't."

"Did you see all those coral formations?" Gina asked both her and Ethan. "It's amazing to think they're created by teeny little animals."

Alicia seemed troubled. "What teeny animals?"

"They're so teeny you can't see them," Gina explained. "I can't believe that snorkeling trail in St. John could be better than this. Thanks so much for bringing us, Ethan."

"Hey, I'm enjoying myself, too," he assured her.

Kim sniffed.

"You guys don't have to stay here on our account," Gina said, aware that Kim wasn't overly thrilled about the whole experience. "We can find our own way back to Palm Point, if you want to leave."

"I don't want to leave," Ethan assured her. Kim glared at him but said nothing.

Alicia tore off a sprig of grapes from the bunch at the center of the table. "I wanna go back in the water," she said between grapes. "And it's not true that you can get cramps if you go in the water too soon after eating. My friend Stephanie said her father said so. And he's like a scientist or something."

"Not that I want to cast aspersions on Stephanie's father," Gina said, "but it wouldn't kill you to stay out of the water a few minutes so you can digest your lunch."

Alicia frowned. "What are you going to cast?"

"Aspersions. And I'm *not* going to cast them."

"Excursions? What's that?"

.A hot wind rattled the palms overhead. Gina grinned and shook her head. "Never mind. If you can't sit still, you can collect shells for a few minutes. No snorkeling until I say so."

"I can go in myself!" Alicia had obviously figured out why Gina was preventing her from swimming. Cramps or no cramps, Gina wouldn't let her go in the water alone.

"No, you can't. It's a rule. Even grown-ups don't go in by themselves." Gina glanced toward Kim and Ethan, hoping for support, but they didn't say anything. Gina turned back to Alicia. "Why don't you collect some shells? Bring me back the prettiest shells you find, okay?"

Alicia made little attempt to hide her irritation as she slipped off the bench and stomped across the sand.

Kim leaned toward Ethan and whispered something.

Great. As if Gina didn't feel bad enough for having forbidden Alicia from returning to the water, now she was going to have to finish her sandwich while the lovebirds cooed and nuzzled each other.

It wasn't exactly nuzzling, really. Kim tucked her head close to Ethan's so she could murmur things to him, and he tilted his head to give her better access to his ear, but Gina didn't see any kissing. Not that she was looking closely. She was too busy choking down the last couple of bites of her sandwich. A few sips of juice, and she'd join Alicia on seashell patrol.

Before she could lift her juice box to her mouth, Alicia came racing back to their table, her feet churning the sand and the two narrow braids behind her ear dancing, the beads bouncing like blue bubbles against the dark background of her hair. "Aunt Gina! Aunt Gina! Guess what I saw?"

Gina was so grateful to Alicia for rescuing her from the lovebirds she lowered her juice box and struck a thoughtful pose. "An orangutan?" she guessed.

Alicia pulled a don't-be-silly face. "No! It's—"

"No, let me guess. A zeppelin?"

"A lizard!" Alicia told her. "A big green lizard!"

"I bet it's an iguana," Ethan said.

Gina eyed him, surprised. She hadn't realized he'd been listening.

"It's really big and funny-looking," Alicia announced, yanking on Gina's hand as if she could pull Gina's attention back to her. "Hurry, Aunt Gina, come look at him before he runs away."

Gina had never seen an iguana before—and she wasn't sure she wanted to see one now. But she bravely stood and let Alicia drag her across the beach. A shadow stretched beside her, and when she glanced to her left she saw Ethan loping to catch up to them. "Kim's a wimp," he said, "but I want to see the iguana."

"How do you know it's an iguana?" Alicia asked. "It could be a dinosaur."

"I don't think so." He flashed a smile at her. "Iguanas are indigenous to the region."

"What does that mean?"

"They live here," Gina explained.

Alicia halted. "It's right over there," she said, lowering her voice to a near whisper as she pointed toward an outcrop surrounded by scrubby beach grass and ferns. Perched upon the rock, basking in the sun, was a large lime-colored creature, as grotesque in appearance as the fish had been beautiful. Its skin reminded Gina of textured vinyl, its head was circled in green fringes that resembled the collar a court jester might wear in a Renaissance castle and its tail draped over the rock, long and wiry.

Gina flinched. It was truly a vile-looking beast. Now that she'd viewed it from only a few feet away, it would probably be starring in her nightmares for years to come.

"Yuck," she muttered, then pivoted on her heel and stalked back to the picnic table, at which Kim sat with her book spread open but her gaze on the rock where Alicia had discovered the monster. Her smile was quizzical as Gina collapsed onto the bench and hugged her arms around herself. "That was the ugliest thing I've ever seen."

"Really?" Kim laughed, but she seemed sympathetic. "I don't like insects. I figured I wouldn't like iguanas, either."

"It was scary. Ugly enough to creep me out." Gina gave a shudder, then reached for her abandoned juice box. She took a deep sip through the straw and wished the apple juice were applejack, or something even stronger, something to help her recover from the sight of that horrid lizard.

By the rock, Ethan had hunkered down to eye level with Alicia. Gina could see his mouth moving, but he was too far away for her to hear the words. "He's an environmental nut," Kim said. "He runs the Gage Foundation, an organization that gives grants to protect habitats."

Gina nodded, impressed. She wouldn't have figured him for that kind of career. He seemed like such a white-bread businessman, as upper-crust as Kim and her snotty parents.

"He actually thinks insects are interesting." Even wrinkling her nose, Kim looked adorable. "I guess I'll have to get used to his weird interests once we get married."

"You're engaged?" Gina asked, eyeing Kim's left hand. No ring, but she *was* reading that book about diamonds.

Kim wiggled her fingers. "We'll probably pick a ring out down here. The jewelry stores offer fabulous discounts. And of course everything's duty-free. That was the main reason I jumped at the chance to come to St. Thomas. I mean, St. Thomas in July?" She wrinkled her nose adorably again. "But I figured the shopping would be great."

"I guess." Gina enjoyed shopping well enough. She wasn't a diamond sort of girl, though. She liked her jewelry funky, and if she ever had a lot of money to blow on earrings and necklaces, she'd go for handcrafted Native American designs. She was a real sucker for silver-and-turquoise.

"Actually..." Kim slid closer to Gina on the bench.

She glanced sidewise, then focused once more on Ethan and Alicia, down near the rock, deeply engrossed in their conversation. Gina couldn't count on them to rescue her as Kim struck an intimate pose. "I should apologize for the way I've been behaving."

Gina agreed; Kim should apologize. But she didn't want to have to listen while the beautiful blond woman bared her soul and sought forgiveness.

Kim was going to make her listen anyway. "It wasn't just the shopping. I was hoping this trip would be a chance for Ethan to bond with my parents, to bring us all together as a family. And when you and your niece refused to move out of the time-share, well, that dream went splat. Know what I mean?"

"Sure." Gina's dream of having a peaceful week in the tropics with Alicia had gone splat, too.

"My parents are wonderful people. I want Ethan to love them as much as I do. I thought it would be so perfect, the four of us living together in Paul's condo, cementing the relationship."

Gina shrugged, her gaze drifting back to Alicia and Ethan huddling near the rock. The sun must have dried his hair, which looked tawny, shot through with red highlights in the afternoon light. If he'd been boring Alicia with his lecture on iguanas, she'd have let him know. But she was clearly enthralled by what he was telling her, nodding at regular intervals. Maybe living in Paul's—correction, in *Carole's*—time-share had cemented the relationship between Ethan and Alicia.

No, of course it hadn't. There was no relationship, other than whatever existed between strangers brought together by a disaster. And perhaps a shared love of snorkeling. Or iguanas.

Still, Kim seemed determined to make amends. "So

when our plans didn't work out the way I'd hoped, I blamed you and your niece. I realize it's not your fault. Well, it is, in a way, but that's not the issue. The issue is that I didn't behave well, and I'm sorry."

"Forget about it," Gina said, wishing *she* could forget about it. Across the beach, Alicia clamped her hand around Ethan's sun-bronzed forearm and said something to him. Gina would bet his skin was warm, his bones thick and hard beneath firm muscles. Alicia shouldn't be touching him—it struck Gina as much too personal—but she was seven years old and didn't know better. And Ethan, kind soul, didn't pull his arm away.

If Kim noticed Alicia's forwardness, she didn't comment on it. Gina wasn't sure why she was so aware of that touch. Her family were touchers. Her mother, in particular, used her hands to talk and loved touching whomever she was talking to, as if the words were being imparted through her fingers as well as her mouth. Gina and her sister, Ramona, had picked up that habit, although they were not as bad as their mother, and Alicia was Ramona's daughter, so she, too, must have inherited the touching gene. Gina would have to explain to her that it wasn't a good idea to touch someone unless you felt really comfortable with him and you sensed he wouldn't mind—although it appeared that Ethan didn't mind. He just kept talking to Alicia, pointing out parts of the iguana with his free hand while the leathery green monster sunned itself on the rock. Maybe Ethan was so glad to have a willing audience for his habitat lecture that he'd endure a few minutes of Morante touching.

Then again, perhaps the reason Gina was so fixated by Alicia's touching him was that he was Ethan, a tall, athletic, undeniably sexy guy. Kim's guy, yes, but even with his swimsuit dried out and no longer clinging to his butt, he had a magnificent body. Maybe some small part of her wished *she* could put her hand on his forearm, or his shoulder, or the taut surface of his chest.

Not that she would. Not that her awareness of him as a man would play into her life in any significant way. Under Gina's moral code, messing with another woman's man was a major, major sin—which was why she hated the lady her brother-in-law was having an affair with as much as she hated her brother-in-law.

"So have you set a date yet?" she asked Kim, partly because Kim had been nice enough to apologize for acting so bitchy toward her and Alicia and partly because she needed to establish clearly in her mind the fact that Ethan and Kim were a couple—and if Ethan had chosen a woman like Kim, he would never have had any interest in a woman like Gina, anyway. She and Kim were practically polar opposites, after all. Kim was refined; Gina had grown up in the Bronx. Kim was a gorgeous blonde; Gina's best feature was her feet. Kim read books on gemstones; Gina read books with sex in them. She'd bet *A Buyer's Guide to Diamonds* didn't have a single sex scene in it. If Ethan's taste in women ran to specimens like Kim, he'd probably think having his forearm touched by someone like Gina would be on par with having his forearm touched by his grandmother, or maybe the nurse taking his blood pressure at his annual physical.

"Not yet," Kim said. "I'd hoped that this week we could start working out all the details for our wedding."

"Just because Ali and I are sharing the condo with you doesn't mean you can't work it out. We're doing our best to stay out of your way."

Kim didn't thank her for that, although Gina felt a little gratitude would be appropriate. "Well, I'd hoped my parents would be able to participate in the discussion. But they're off playing golf, ~~and~~ Ethan and I are here. If they were staying with us, we'd have that much more time to talk about what kind of ceremony we wanted and where to hold the reception. And setting the date, too, of course.''

If and when Gina got married, she wouldn't want her parents in on the discussion. Tony and Rosa Morante were wonderful people, arguably among the greatest parents in the world, but Gina had no intention of letting them plan her wedding for her. She'd always figured she and the lucky guy would present everything as a fait accompli to her parents: "Hi, folks, this is Ethan, and we're getting married at St. Anthony's the third Saturday in May, and afterward we'll host a dinner party at Rossini's in Riverdale." Or, "Hi, folks, this is Ethan, and we're going to have a nice civil ceremony followed by champagne and cake at the Botanical Gardens." Of course, his name wouldn't be Ethan, but just for example. Her parents would be fine with that, also. They'd planned Ramona's wedding with her as if they were five-star generals plotting a critical military campaign. No detail had been too small, from the centerpieces to the color of Ramona's garter, from the boutonnieres to the sueded upholstery in the bridal limousine. And ten years after all that meticulous planning, Jack Bari, the son of a bitch, was having an affair.

"Are you involved with someone?" Kim asked.

Did she want to be Gina's confidante, or was she just trying to make conversation? Gina tried to shake off her resistance to Kim. The poor woman was miles from home, in a bizarre housing arrangement with her fiancé and two total strangers. True, her parents were at a hotel just down the road, but maybe Kim needed someone her own age to pal around with.

Gina wasn't going to pal around with her if it meant they had to go shopping. But she could force herself to be sociable. It would make the bizarre housing arrangement a bit easier. "I broke up with a guy six months ago," she said.

"Men," Kim said, sighing profoundly. "Can't live with them, can't live without them."

Actually, Gina could do both just fine. But she gave Kim a sisterly nod.

At long last, the intrepid lizard observers abandoned the rock and returned to the picnic table. Gina's spirits lifted as Alicia raced over to her. "Ethan knows everything," she reported, her voice charged with excitement and awe. "He told me all about how iguanas lay eggs and how if their tail falls off they can grow another one."

Gina hoped the laying-eggs part of his lesson hadn't been too graphic. "Lucky animals. If I lost my tail, I'd want to grow a second one."

"You don't have a tail," Alicia pointed out, giving Gina another of her don't-be-silly looks, which dissolved into a giggle. "Can we go snorkeling now?"

"Absolutely. Fish, here we come!" Gina said, grateful to Alicia for rescuing her from having to indulge in girl talk with Kim. She reached for Alicia's mask and slid the strap over the little girl's head. Then she grabbed her own mask.

"Fish, here we come!" Alicia cheered, lifting her flippers and charging toward the water.

CHAPTER FIVE

ANOTHER EXCRUTIATING dinner, this time at the hotel where Kim's parents were staying. The restaurant was nice enough—elegant and expensive, just the way the Hamiltons liked it—and the wine list was large enough for Ross Hamilton to pontificate on its strengths and weaknesses. He also pontificated on the inferior quality of the golf clubs he'd had to rent that day, the absence of morality in the films Hollywood was currently churning out and the extremism of environmentalists who panicked about the melting of the polar ice caps.

Ethan suspected Ross had raised that final subject solely to bait him. The old man knew Ethan's work for the Gage Foundation involved funding projects designed to protect and improve the environment. He was saying provocative things to test Ethan. Ethan didn't feel like being tested.

He drank his wine, ate his grilled conch and told Ross Hamilton that global warming was a significant problem, and that when—not if, but when—the polar ice caps started melting, the planet would be drastically altered. Ross pointed out that by the time the problem became significant, he would be dead, so it was hard for him to care about the threat. Ethan suggested that he might show some concern for the world his grandchildren would inherit, and Delia Hamilton let out a delighted cry, beaming her approval at Ethan and Kim at the mention of potential grandchildren.

Three hours of Ross lecturing, Delia glowing and Kim sending him warning looks that he chose to ignore did not constitute a pleasant dinner. He'd had a hell of a lot more fun discussing iguanas with Ali the Alley Cat that afternoon.

On the drive home, Kim said, "We have to talk."

"All right," he agreed, aware that no matter how much her parents annoyed him, he owed them a modicum of respect, if only because he'd been dating their daughter for the past six months. "I'm sorry. I shouldn't have enumerated the flaws in your father's reasoning on global warming. But he was saying those things because he wanted a reaction. I gave him the reaction he wanted."

"That's not what we have to talk about. Look out," she added, pointing to a goat ambling along the side of the road. The goats of St. Thomas weren't as visible after the sun set, especially because Ethan was still in the habit of checking the right and not the left shoulder of the road.

"I see it." He swerved slightly to avoid the goat.

"We have to talk about why we're not having sex," Kim announced.

Wonderful. That was exactly what Ethan wanted to talk about after a painful evening with her insufferable parents.

"If it's because those people are sharing the apartment—Gina and the little girl—"

"No, it's not." He shot Kim a glance. She looked skeptical, but he was being honest. And he might as well continue being honest. "Kim, we planned this vacation in part so we could get away from all the demands of our jobs and just be together. Right?''

''Well, don't blame me that you spent yesterday at the beach alone instead of with me.''

''That's just it,'' he said, not bothering to tell her that he hadn't been alone at the beach. He'd been with Gina and Alicia, building the Brooklyn Bridge out of sand. But there was a limit to how much honesty Kim needed. ''You wanted to go shopping yesterday. You wanted to go shopping again today, but I twisted your arm and you came snorkeling with me, instead. If I hadn't insisted, you would have gone shopping.''

''I would have gone golfing with my parents—and *then* shopping,'' she corrected him. ''But I compromised for you, Ethan. I went snorkeling because you wanted to. I met you more than halfway.''

''It shouldn't have to be a compromise,'' he tried to explain. ''It's not that I expect us to do every single thing together. But when we come to a place like St. Thomas, with some of the most spectacular snorkeling in the world—''

''*And* spectacular shopping,'' she reminded him. ''Plus, my dad said the golf course was good, even if the rental clubs weren't.''

''The thing is, you and I want to do different things. It's like a big deal for one of us to do what the other one wants. A noble compromise. Maybe we just don't share many interests.''

Kim reflected on that possibility for a bit. ''We don't have this problem back in Connecticut,'' she noted.

''Back in Connecticut, we both work long days. If we get together after work, we eat dinner and zone out in front of the TV, or review work that we brought home from our offices. Then we go to sleep, because we're exhausted. It's not as if we share that many activities at home, either.''

"I always thought one of the interests we shared was sex,'' she said.

True enough. But this trip was supposed to be about more than sex. It was supposed to be about peering into the future and finding out if that future might include a Kim-and-Ethan lifetime commitment. He'd been peering since he and Kim had met her parents at the airport in Atlanta, and he just didn't see a lifetime commitment with her up ahead. And without a commitment, sex would just be sex. Which he wasn't opposed to, but he and Kim couldn't go back to that, not after she'd been browsing through the jewelry shops of Charlotte Amalie in search of duty-free diamond solitaires.

"The thing is, my parents aren't staying at the apartment with us. We maneuvered things so we could share a bed. I think we're wasting a major opportunity here.''

The opportunity couldn't be all that major if it didn't tempt him. "Look, Kim— I'm sorry,'' he said. This time the apology came from his heart. He turned onto Palm Point's entry drive and navigated carefully over the speed bumps, weighing each word as he steered along the narrow driveway. "I've got a lot on my mind. I know it's not fair to you, but right now I need to think some things over.''

"In other words, we're not going to have sex tonight, either.''

He sighed, wishing she hadn't reduced their situation to such a primitive level. But if she thought the only problem between them was that they weren't having sex, then the real problems between them were clearly enormous. "No,'' he said quietly. "We're not going to have sex tonight.''

"Great," she grunted, offering a pretty little pout. "Fine, Ethan. You want to think some things over? Be my guest." She barely waited for him to stop the car at Building Six before shoving open her door and leaping out.

He locked up the car and followed her inside. She was truly gorgeous, all elegant curves and delicate features. Yet he felt nothing when he looked at her—not resentment, not anger, not frustration. Definitely not lust. Not tonight.

The only light in the condo came from the recessed ceiling spotlight in the hallway leading to the bedrooms. Gina and Alicia's door was closed, and as soon as Kim entered the master bedroom, she closed the door, too. Was she expecting Ethan to sleep on the couch? Forget that. If she didn't want to share a bed with him, *she* could sleep on the couch.

He stared at the closed door for a minute, then stalked through the living room toward the kitchen, deciding to do his thinking on the terrace, armed with a cold beer. Halfway to the kitchen he paused, aware of a silhouette on the terrace, visible through the sliding-glass doors. He moved closer and realized Gina was sitting on one of the molded plastic chairs, staring out at the beach and the ocean beyond it, and the night-dark sky above.

He should have been annoyed by the realization that women were occupying every decent think-things-over locale in the condo. But far from annoyed, he felt a twinge of anticipation. He could think things over in Gina's company if he had to. Maybe he could even talk to her in a way he couldn't talk to Kim. If his buddy Paul were around, Ethan could bounce his thoughts off him. But here in St. Thomas, miles from home, he was friendless.

Perhaps Gina could be a friend.

He continued to the kitchen and pulled two beers out of the fridge.

A COOL, constant breeze rose off the water and drifted up to the balcony, soothing Gina as effectively as a full-body massage. She had tucked Alicia into bed a while ago, told her a story about a fish that owned magical reverse-snorkel gear that enabled it to swim in the air, and sat with her until she fell asleep. But it was only ten, and Gina wasn't ready to go to sleep herself yet. She was physically tired but mentally wide-awake.

So she'd settled herself on the balcony. She didn't need a book or a TV show to entertain her. The velvety night sky, lit with stars and a hazy half-moon, and the rhythmic whisper of the wind through the palms, and the salty-sweet smell of the sea were better than any sitcom or HBO movie.

St. Thomas was glorious. Compared with New York it was so peaceful, so tranquil. No car horns, no crazy people shouting on street corners or sitting on stoops and bickering, no buses rumbling down Seventh Avenue or delivery guys on bicycles zipping along the sidewalk, scattering the pedestrians. No sour smells of auto exhaust, no gusts of searing heat blasting up through the subway vents, no flattened cigarette butts and scraps of trash lining the sidewalks. She loved the city, loved its noise and energy and humanity—but man, she'd developed a whopping crush on this serene tropical island.

She leaned back in her chair and propped her bare feet up on the terrace railing. The wind ruffled her hair and she sighed contentedly. No heartbroken sister in St. Thomas, she thought. No schmuck of a brother-in-law.

No infidelity, no divorce. That whole mess was a thousand miles away.

She recalled Alicia's innocent question their first evening here: "Can we stay forever?" If only.

She heard the rattle of a door behind her, a squeak as it slid open. So much for peace and tranquillity, she thought, bracing herself for the invasion of Ethan and Kim. Glancing over her shoulder, however, she saw that Ethan was alone.

Well, not technically. He was accompanied by two bottles of beer, one of which he extended toward her. "Mind if I join you?" he asked.

She didn't have the right to mind. The terrace, like the rest of the condo, was shared territory. But since he'd come bearing the gift of beer, and he had such an endearingly tentative smile, and his hair looked so soft as the breeze fluttered through it… "Make yourself comfortable," she said, gesturing toward the chair beside her.

Ethan lowered himself into the chair and handed her the bottle, which was icy, fresh from the refrigerator. He had on khakis and an oxford shirt that was far too crisp and formal for vacation attire; his initials were monogrammed above one of the cuffs. He set his own bottle on the floor, freeing both hands so he could roll up his sleeves. Then he kicked his feet up next to hers. He had on preppy leather deck shoes without socks. Nice ankles, she observed before steering her gaze back to the black water below.

"Is Alicia asleep?" he asked.

"Probably on her second dream by now." Gina took a sip of beer, determined to accept Ethan's presence casually, as if she actually knew him. With his sleeves cuffed up to his elbows, she noticed that his wrists were as nice as his ankles. His skin looked tan in the moonlight, the hairs on his forearms glittering in coppery strands in the misty light of the moon. A thin gold watch circled his left wrist and his fingernails were clean and square. She remembered how Alicia had touched his arm that afternoon when he'd been teaching her about iguanas, and how Gina had wished she could touch his arm, too.

Just a playful fantasy, she assured herself, just her imagination having a little fun. He was Kim's fiancé. She would never touch any part of him.

"Where's Kim?" she asked, more to shut down her fun-loving imagination than because she actually wanted to know.

"She's having a snit," he said, as nonchalantly as if they were old friends who shared confidences all the time.

If he could act as if they were old friends, she could, too. "Did she lock you out?"

He shrugged and took a sip of beer, apparently unperturbed about the whole thing. "I haven't tried the doorknob yet. Alicia won't freak out if she finds me sleeping on the couch tomorrow morning, will she?"

"Alicia's cool. She won't care."

"She *is* cool." He ran his thumb along the edge of the label on the bottle. Long thumbs, she noted. Long tanned fingers. That he and Kim were having a quarrel shouldn't free Gina to be so conscious of his strong, graceful hands, but she couldn't help herself. She was only human, and he was one hell of a good-looking guy.

"You think my niece is cool?" Keeping a seven-year-old girl at the center of their conversation was an effective way to steer her mind away from Ethan's sex appeal.

"I think…" He let out a breath. "Never mind. It's none of my business."

"What?"

Ethan studied Gina for a long moment. She resolutely stared at the water and tried to ignore the fact that he was scrutinizing her. Finally he spoke. "She mentioned something about her father."

Gina's breath caught. She turned to him, wary. "What did she say?"

"He has a girlfriend?" Ethan asked rather than stated it.

Gina swore under her breath, then sank lower in her chair. "Yeah. The asshole. Ali's parents are separated. Things are pretty screwed up at home, so I thought I'd take her away from all that for a week."

"Poor kid." He sounded genuinely sympathetic. "I don't know much about children, but…it must be hard on her."

"That's an understatement." Gina sipped some beer, letting the sour bubbles dance across her tongue. "Thanks for being so patient with her today, talking to her about that ugly green lizard."

"Iguanas aren't ugly."

"Yeah, right."

"They probably think human beings are ugly."

"Then they're ugly and blind," she said.

He laughed. For someone destined to sleep on the living-room sofa instead of with his girlfriend, he was in a pretty good mood.

"Kim said you work for some environmental organization."

"The Gage Foundation," he told her.

"I've never heard of it. What does it do?"

"It's a charitable trust set up by the Gage family fifteen years ago,'' he explained. ''Back in the nineteenth century, the Gages ran fabric mills throughout Connect-icut. They made a fortune but polluted a few rivers. Their descendants decided to create an endowment to redeem their tainted souls by protecting the environment. I'm the foundation's executive director.''

''So you—what? Give money to do-gooders?''

''I evaluate applications, monitor the investments and, yes, fund do-gooders.'' He swallowed some beer and sighed. He seemed so relaxed Gina couldn't help but relax, too. ''How about you?'' he asked. ''What do you do in the real world?''

''I design shoes.''

He shot her a look, then laughed. ''Really?''

''Someone's got to do it.''

''I guess.'' His gaze strayed to her feet, her toes curled around the wrought-iron rail. ''I probably shouldn't say this, but…has anyone ever told you you've got beautiful feet?''

It was her turn to laugh. ''Oh, yeah, a few people have told me that. I worked my way through college as a foot model.''

''A foot model?''

''Modeling shoes, mostly, for magazines and catalogs. Sometimes modeling stockings, sometimes foot-care products, but mostly shoes. My feet are a perfect size five and a half B, which is kind of weird since I'm taller than average. Most women my height would wear around a size eight or nine. But I've got a real tiny base. It's amazing I don't fall over.''

He grinned, his gaze lingering on her feet. ''It's not just that your feet are small,'' he explained. ''They're shaped so perfectly.''

''And they aren't bony, and I don't have veins showing through the skin. Body-part models have to fit really restrictive specs. But the pay wasn't bad, and it was nothing like full-body modeling, you know, where eating a cookie or sprouting a zit might cost you a booking. There isn't a huge demand for foot modeling, but it was enough to keep me in peanut butter and pizza.''

"So, you went from foot modeling to shoe designing?"

"More or less.'' Crickets hummed in the shrubs beneath the terrace, and as the mist cleared, the moon's reflection spread across the water like a spill of silver. "I majored in fabric design in college. It was an art school,'' she answered the question glinting in his eyes. "Rhode Island School of Design. I thought I wanted to be a painter, but then I got sidetracked into patterning and fabric stuff. After that, I went back to New York, did more foot modeling and trekked around to designers with my portfolio. I got a job offer to design bed linens, but it was down in North Carolina and I didn't want to leave New York. And in the meantime, I always had to take care of my feet, keep the skin smooth and callus-free, avoid stubbing my toes, the pedicures, the whole thing. When you're that conscious of your feet, you become conscious of your shoes. There are an awful lot of really uncomfortable shoes being designed and produced. Anyway, I was doing some modeling for Bruno Castiglio, who designs shoes—you've probably never heard of him, but he's a pretty big name in the shoe world—and I talked my way into a designer position with his company. This can't possibly be interesting to you,'' she concluded, realizing she was talking way too much about herself.

"I'm fascinated,'' Ethan said.

She turned to him and found not a hint of sarcasm or

boredom in his expression. His gaze wandered back and forth between her face and her feet. She wondered if he approached everything so intently—iguanas, the environment, Gina's insteps. But he didn't approach his relationship with Kim intently. He seemed pretty lackadaisical about that.

"It's none of my business," she began, "but—"

"I've already said things that were none of my business," he reminded her. "You owe me one."

"Well, just that if you're going to marry Kim, you really ought to learn how to kiss and make up after an argument. I mean, locking each other out of the bedroom doesn't seem…I don't know." It really was none of her business, just as her sister and brother-in-law were none of his business. But she'd hate to think of Ethan and Kim having a child someday, and then indulging in knock-down-drag-outs while the child got so tense she lost her appetite the way Alicia had last spring. Parents simply shouldn't do that to their children.

"I don't believe I'm going to marry Kim," he said, then drank some beer.

The plot thickens, Gina thought. "She told me you two were engaged."

"Well, we haven't…" He exhaled. "She assumed we came down here to plan our marriage. I assumed we came down here to see if we had what it takes. I don't think we do."

"You'd better clue her in." Gina felt a twinge of sisterly loyalty. Men who kept women in the dark about their intentions lost points in her book.

He nodded. "What's you opinion, Gina? Should I tell her now, when we've still got four days left in our vacation? Or should I wait until we're heading for home?"

"If you tell her now, you'll ruin the vacation," she

pointed out. "On the other hand, dishonesty isn't a good policy."

"Still, her parents are here. If I break up with her, her father might come after me with a golf club."

"He's probably already pissed because he had to pay for a hotel room."

"Yeah. Although his wife was pleased about that. She likes room service." He gazed out at the water. "They say women turn into their mothers. I wonder if in twenty-five years Kim will be demanding room service."

"If you want to find out, you're going to have to marry her." Gina sipped her beer, the cool curve of the bottle pressing against her lower lip. "But I don't think that's true—that women turn into their mothers. Some, maybe, but there's no guarantee. I haven't turned into my mother—who happens to be a really terrific lady— but I'm not going to turn into her."

"How are you different from her?"

"By the time she was my age, she'd been married six years and had three kids—me and Ramona and my brother, Bobby. Her whole life was running loads of laundry, cooking, dragging us kids off to church and sitting around the kitchen table with her girlfriends, gossiping and drinking lemonade. She loved that life, never felt her horizons were limited, never missed the nightlife. All she ever wanted was to make a good home for my dad and us kids, and she did. I'd go crazy if I had to live that kind of life, but it was right for her."

"But now, with her kids grown and gone, doesn't she want more?"

"No. She and my dad still live in the row house I grew up in. She still cooks for him and goes to church and gossips with her friends. Of course, she's a grandma now. That's as much fun as being an aunt. Maybe even more fun.''

"Alicia is your sister's child?''

"Right.''

"Does your brother have any kids?''

She shook her head. "Bobby is the baby of the family. He's twenty-four, a New York City cop and a devout bachelor.''

"A cop? Wow.'' He looked impressed. "That's dangerous work.''

"Yeah, I guess.'' She chuckled. Bobby was hardly the fearless macho type. He was an energetic guy, funny and talkative, a toucher like Ramona and Gina and their mother. "He walks a beat, does a lot of community outreach, gets homeless people into shelters and picks up shoplifters. About the most dangerous part of his job is all the women throwing themselves at him. Women seem to think cops are heroic studs. Especially when they're young and have a few dimples.''

"I don't know about the stud part, but they are heroic,'' Ethan argued, his eyes remaining on her. "How about you? Are you a devout bachelorette with men throwing themselves at you?''

She snorted. "The only thing I'm devout about is being Ali's aunt. As for men throwing themselves at me, sure, it happens all the time. Sometimes there are so many I have to beat them back with a stick.''

His smile lingered, but he didn't laugh. "I'm not surprised.''

That he took her seriously was flattering, but it also made her uncomfortable. Never in her life had she been forced to beat men back with a stick. "There are a lot of foot fetishists in the world,'' she joked, figuring a little humor would remove the strain she was suddenly feeling as he continued to study her. "Lucky for me I've got a cop in the family if I need protection from the weirdos."

He shifted his gaze to her feet once more, and she wondered if he was a foot fetishist. Doubtful. He seemed too straight-arrow for anything that kinky. She couldn't even picture him slumming at the downtown clubs she liked to go to with her friends, or shopping in the vintage clothing boutiques, or sitting in a café until 4:00 a.m., sipping iced chai with vodka and arguing over whether punk music would see a resurgence before the end of the decade.

Sucking on a woman's toes? No way. Not Ethan.

Which was fine with her. If a man ever sucked on her toes, she'd kick him in the teeth. She wanted her kisses where they'd have the greatest impact—her mouth, her face, her breasts, her... Well, never mind. She shouldn't be thinking about such things while sitting next to another woman's fiancé, even if the lovebirds were feuding.

"So, you're a devout aunt," he said. "What does that mean? You worship your niece?"

"I don't worship her, but I spoil her rotten," Gina said, aware of the boastful lilt in her voice.

"She doesn't seem rotten to me."

"I guess I'm not spoiling her enough."

He chuckled, then tilted his chair back, balancing it on its two rear legs. "She's going to remember this week for the rest of her life."

"So will I," Gina said. A fresh breeze washed over her, fragrant with the perfume of the tropical flowers blooming in beds along the walkways below. She would never forget that smell, and the balmy air, and the moonlight draped over the water. She'd never forget the fish at Coki Beach, and the hot, powdery sand, and the iguana, who was grotesquely ugly no matter what Ethan said. She'd never forget the feel of Alicia's small, soft hand in hers, and the infectious music of her laughter as she scampered across the beach.

Gina suspected that she would also never forget this handsome, quiet man who was so easy to talk to, even though once their vacations were over he would go back to his life, with or without Kim, and Gina would go back to hers, and they'd never see each other again. This week, this night, this conversation, this unexpected closeness would be nothing more substantial than a dreamy memory—but it would stay with her forever.

CHAPTER SIX

KIM HADN'T LOCKED the door. In truth, Ethan would have been surprised if she had. Barring him from the bedroom would have been too public. No matter how angry she was, she'd never want Gina and Alicia—two veritable strangers—to discover him asleep on the living-room sofa the next morning, because then they'd know he and Kim were on the outs. Kim felt very strongly about maintaining appearances and convincing everyone that her life was just peachy-keen.

Ethan was grateful she'd left the door unlocked for him, if only because convertible couches were rarely as comfortable as beds. He managed to slide under the covers without waking her. The glowing red digits of the alarm clock on the night table indicated that midnight had come and gone a few minutes ago, and after all the snorkeling he'd done during the day, he ought to have been exhausted. But sleep eluded him. He couldn't get his mind to settle down.

Why was it so easy to talk to Gina? For hours, he'd sat with her on the deck, enjoying sea breeze and the conversation. He'd learned that her mother was Italian, her father's family from the Azores, "but he converted to Italian when he married my mom," Gina had joked. Her father owned a hardware store, and she'd grown up somewhere between working class and middle class. She didn't have much time to paint anymore—or

much room, given the minuscule dimensions of her studio apartment in Manhattan—but she did still play
around with watercolors, which she could work with at
her kitchen table or even outdoors, propping a pad on
her lap. She believed Jackson Pollack was grossly over-
rated and Georgia O'Keeffe was a goddess. She'd never
been to the northwestern part of Connecticut, where
Ethan lived, but she'd traveled the coastline plenty of
times, either on the interstate or by train, in her journeys
to and from her art school in Rhode Island. She was
twenty-eight years old and she hoped someday to live in
a house or apartment big enough for a dog to share her
home with her. "I like mutts," she'd said.

He hadn't been surprised. She seemed like a mutt-type
person, the exact opposite of Kim, whose childhood pet
dog, one of those breeds with long elaborate hair and a
pudgy little face, had taken ribbons at regional dog
shows. Ethan had seen photos of Kim's dog and he'd
thought that if dogs could talk, this one would have had
a voice like Betty Boop.

Beside him Kim sighed and shifted against her pillow.
Her hair spread fluid and golden around her face. At one
time, just the sight of her hair would have made him
hard.

Now he felt no excitement, no arousal, nothing but
restlessness. He could have slept more easily sitting upright on that terrace chair, next to Gina.

A veritable stranger. An unexpected friend. A sharp,
funny, utterly unselfconscious woman who loved snorkeling as much as he did and had the most beautiful feet
he'd ever seen.

AT SOME POINT he must have fallen asleep, because
when he opened his eyes daylight was seeping under the

drawn drapes and into the bedroom. Rolling away from the window, he discovered that Kim was gone.

He glanced at the clock on the night table. Eight-fifteen.

If Kim had been given to high drama, her absence might have concerned him. But she tended to be stable and staid, and again, deeply devoted to maintaining appearances. He doubted that she would have fled to her parents' hotel, not only because she couldn't very well go crying to Mommy and Daddy about the lack of sex in her life but also because she'd be hesitant to drive on the left side of the road.

She was probably in the kitchen, drinking some of Gina's coffee. Or she was sitting on the terrace, in the chair Ethan had occupied last night, and enjoying the view. Maybe Gina was out there with her, chattering away. Maybe Kim found Gina as easy to talk to as he did.

He wondered if he could persuade Kim to travel to St. John today, so they could go snorkeling at Trunk Bay Beach and see that spectacular sea life. She hadn't been thrilled about yesterday's snorkeling. Maybe if they swam together, had a little fun together, shared an exotic experience together, they could find their way back to, well, togetherness.

Not likely, but he really wanted to visit Trunk Bay. He heaved himself out of bed, made a halfhearted attempt to smooth the blanket and fluff the pillows and donned a pair of shorts and a polo shirt. Barefoot and rumpled, he left the bedroom and headed down the hall, following the sound of female voices and the aroma of coffee.

They were in the kitchen. Kim looked surprisingly chipper, considering that yesterday had ended with enough hostility that he and she hadn't even said good night to each other. She wore a peach-hued blouse-and-shorts outfit, and her hair was pinned back from her face with matching peach-colored barrettes. Alicia had on blue denim shorts and a shirt with glittery threads running through it. Gina wore white shorts and a sleeveless top. Her exquisite feet were naked except for the silver ring circling one toe.

He let his gaze slide up her body. He hadn't looked at her face much last night, mostly because they'd been sitting side by side and staring out at the horizon, but also because he hadn't wanted to acknowledge her unique beauty while he was in the throes of a major problem with Kim. But he looked at her now. Her features were too strong, too angular for her to be beautiful the way Kim was. Her eyes were as dark as the coffee steaming in the glass decanter, and they were too wide, too intense, too challenging.

God, he could stare into her eyes forever.

He quickly turned to Kim, who smiled blandly at him. "Good morning," he said.

"Guess what?" Alicia blurted out, lowering her spoon into the bowl of cereal before her. "There's this store that sells stuff that changes color in the sunlight, and we're going there!"

"A store?"

"In Charlotte Amalie," Kim said coolly. "We're going shopping—Gina, Alicia and me. My mother, too."

"We're going to have a ladies' day," Alicia bragged, obviously proud to be thought of as a lady.

"Oh, so I don't have to go? Phew!" He pretended to wipe his brow in relief at this near miss.

"No, you don't have to go shopping," Kim confirmed. "You'll be playing golf with my father."

Ethan opened his mouth to object that he didn't play golf, he didn't like it and he wouldn't do it. But he held his words. If he wanted Kim to travel to Trunk Bay Beach with him, he supposed he'd have to compromise when it came to golf. Although it didn't seem like a fair compromise, since all he was asking her to do was experience a natural phenomenon renowned for its visual splendor, while she was asking him to spend several hours hiking across crew-cut lawns, whacking a little white ball and enduring the company of her father. In the time it would take to complete an eighteen-hole round, Ross Hamilton would be able to lecture him on the glories of unfettered capitalism, the irrelevance of the hole in the ozone layer and the necessity of making Delia Hamilton happy by producing grandchildren for her. He'd also probably find a few spare minutes to discourse on Napa Valley varietals.

But Ethan wanted to snorkel at Trunk Bay. And he wanted what remained of this vacation week to go pleasantly, even though he and Kim were drifting apart. If Trunk Bay and pleasantness hinged on his playing golf with her father, he'd play golf.

The sudden ringing of the telephone jolted him, resonating painfully inside his skull, much too loud for someone who hadn't yet had his morning coffee. "That's probably my father now," Kim said, "calling to find out when to reserve a time at the links."

"Right," Ethan grumbled, lifting the receiver from the wall unit. "Hello?"

After a brief pause, a woman's voice came on the line: "I'm sorry, I must have the wrong number." Not just a woman's voice—a woman's voice with a profound New York accent.

"Who are you trying to reach?"

"Gina Morante?" The woman asked more than stated it.

"She's right here." He extended the phone in Gina's direction. "It's for you."

Eyebrows rising in surprise, Gina carried her mug around the table and took the receiver from Ethan. Their fingers brushed as he handed it over, a whisper of sensation that reverberated in his solar plexus—and lower. Her feet might be her most gorgeous appendages, but her hands weren't far behind.

That he could respond so strongly to such a fleeting touch from her troubled him. Perhaps it was just as well that he'd be golfing with Ross all day. Just as long as he wasn't with Gina, swimming with her, talking with her, doing anything that might lead to another touch. A miserable game of golf in the merciless heat, with a boring companion, might be just what he needed to get his head straightened out. Or it might leave his mind permanently warped.

Either result was better than for Ethan to spend more time with Gina, trying to think of excuses to touch her.

"HELLO?" Gina said into the phone.

"Gina? Who was that man?"

"Ramona!" She recognized her sister's voice right away. Her delight immediately transformed into wariness. Ramona wouldn't have phoned unless something was wrong. "What's up?" she asked carefully, not wanting to alarm Alicia, who had dropped her spoon into her cereal bowl, spraying droplets of milk across the table, and shrieked, "It's my mommy!"

"Nothing. I just need to talk to you. Who was the man who answered the phone, Gina? Did you pick some guy up or something? With Alicia right there, I swear to God—''

''It's a long story,'' Gina cut her off. ''We're sharing the condo.''

''Mommy!'' Alicia hollered, bouncing in her chair.

''You want to talk to Ali?'' Gina asked Ramona. ''She definitely wants to talk to you.''

''Of course I want to talk to her. But listen, Gina, when I'm done talking to her, I need to talk to you. Privately, if you know what I mean.''

Gina did. ''Sure,'' she said, then gestured toward Alicia, who scrambled out of her chair. ''I'll put on Alicia first.''

''Mommy!'' Alicia bellowed, grabbing the phone. ''Mommy! I went snorkeling! It was so great! And I saw this iguana! It was really creepy-looking. Ethan taught me all about iguanas....''

Gina backed away from the phone and glanced at Ethan and Kim. The condo had a second phone extension in the master bedroom. Gina had as much right to use that extension as Ethan and Kim did, but it was their room—the room Ethan hadn't even been sure Kim would let him into last night.

She'd let him in. Whatever their quarrel, they'd apparently made up. Kim had seemed cheerful enough that morning when she'd joined Gina and Alicia in the kitchen, and Ethan, while scruffy and uncombed, didn't seem terribly upset with the state of his life. Spending the night together in the master bedroom must have led to a reconciliation.

''I need to use the extension in your room,'' she whispered, hoping not to distract Alicia as she babbled into the phone about her collection of seashells and the various restaurant meals she'd consumed.

"No problem," Kim said. Ethan agreed with a nod.

Gina nodded back, then mouthed to Alicia, "Let me know when you're done." After giving Alicia's shoulder a squeeze, she strode out of the kitchen, across the living room and down the hall to the master bedroom, trying not to let Ramona's unexpected call roil her. Her sister wouldn't have interrupted their vacation unless she had bad news to deliver, but she'd sounded okay. And she'd said nothing was up.

She'd also said she needed to speak privately with Gina.

Something was up.

Sighing, Gina swung through the doorway into the master bedroom. The first thing she noticed was the bed, sloppily made, the blanket wrinkled—and a foot-wide gap between the two pillows, both of which looked lumpy, as if the people using them had tossed and turned.

Some reconciliation.

Gina turned away, ashamed that a peek at their bed had led her to analyze Kim and Ethan's sex life. Whether they reconciled was none of her business.

Determined not to think about the bed, she moved toward the window. She gradually became aware of a faint, slightly flowery scent in the air. Kim's perfume.

Although the bed wasn't tidily made, the room was neater than hers and Alicia's, which was strewn with shells, beach toys, the dolls and books Alicia had brought with her and an invisible dusting of sand that made the carpet feel gritty against her bare soles. Neither Ethan nor Kim appeared to be a major slob. No clothes lay draped over the furniture or heaped on the floor. The only shoes visible were a pair of elegant white leather sandals, protruding from underneath the bed. Most of the toiletries cluttered atop the dresser and windowsill were Kim's, not Ethan's. Gina moved to the window—to admire the view, not to snoop, she told herself—and took note of Ethan's things: aftershave, antiperspirant and a thick, wood-handled hairbrush with a few strands of tawny hair trapped in the bristles. Very few, she noted with satisfaction. He wasn't going bald.

"Aunt Gina?" Alicia yelled from the kitchen. "Mommy wants to talk to you!"

"Okay, thanks!" Gina yelled back before lifting the receiver from the phone on the night table. She lowered herself to sit on the bed, then stood, then thought *the hell with it* and dropped back onto the mattress. Just because this was Ethan's bed didn't mean she had to remain standing while she talked to Ramona.

"I'm on," she said into the phone.

A click signaled that Alicia had hung up the kitchen extension. "So who's this Ethan?" Ramona asked. "That's all Ali could talk about. Ethan went snorkeling with her. Ethan built the Brooklyn Bridge with her."

"I told you, we have to share the condo," Gina said, wishing Ramona would let it lie but knowing she wouldn't. "There was a scheduling snafu. This other couple—Ethan and Kim—are in one bedroom and Alicia and I are in the other. We're all getting along. It's no big deal."

"Who are they?"

"Friends of someone who owns a time-share here. Their friend told them the place was empty this week, just like Carole told me. So we all wound up here together."

"How cozy."

"As I said, we're getting along. Ethan knows about iguanas and Kim knows about shopping. Ali and I are learning a lot from them." She decided that was all the explanation her sister needed. "Now, tell me why you called, Mo."

"Why I called." Ramona sighed heavily. "Jack moved out."

Gina grunted in acknowledgment. She would have cursed, but she wasn't sure Jack's leaving the house was the worst thing in the world. At the very least, she ought to find out how Ramona felt about the situation.

"I thought we were trying to work on things," Ramona said. "This week, while Ali was away, this was our chance to work with the counselor, you know? Bare our souls, clear the decks, get down to brass tacks. So last night after a session with the counselor, he says to me that if I want him to keep seeing the counselor, fine, but he has no intention of breaking up with his tootsie. He loves her, she makes him feel like a new man and nothing the counselor says is going to change that. So I told him, if he loves her so much, he can get his things out of my house and go live with her. And the son of a bitch said, 'Okay.'"

"Okay," Gina echoed, then winced to think she'd used the same word that might have slipped past the son of a bitch's mouth just last night. A tight knot of pain lodged in the center of her forehead and she pinched the bridge of her nose to stave it off. Bad enough she had to go shopping with Kim today—she would have declined the invitation, but when Kim started telling Alicia about some shop in Charlotte Amalie that sold shirts, caps, tote bags and nail polish that changed color in the sunlight, Alicia had pleaded with Gina to go. And since the kid's father was a dickhead, the least Gina could do was buy her a shirt that changed color in the sun. She could even tolerate a day with Kim and her mother, if it would make Alicia happy.

"You knew this was a possibility," she reminded Ramona.

"It's not like I'm devastated," Ramona said, although her voice wavered. "Yeah, I knew this might happen. So it's happening. He's moving out. When Ali gets home, there's going to be no daddy jackets in the coat closet, no ratty sneakers in the garage, no *Sports Illustrated* on the coffee table, no Mike's Hard Lemonade in the fridge. It's all going."

Good riddance to trash, Gina thought, though she didn't say it.

"What I want," Ramona said, "is for you to tell Alicia, so she doesn't go into shock when she walks in the door."

"You want me to tell her you booted her father's sorry ass out the door?"

"Maybe come up with a different phrasing. I've worked real hard to make sure Alicia doesn't use coarse language. You should hear some of the kids in her school. They say *ass* and *damn* and worse, all the time."

Gina checked the impulse to use a few words coarser than *ass* and *damn* right now. "We're on a vacation, Mo! What am I supposed to do—grab her in the middle of snorkeling and say, 'Oh, by the way, your daddy moved out'?"

"Over dinner, I was thinking. After she's had a nice meal. She's eating okay?"

"She's eating fine. And I'm not going to spoil a nice meal by telling her her parents haven't worked things out and won't be getting back together."

"*Someone's* got to tell her," Ramona argued.

"Yeah. You and Jack."

"For me to tell her, she'd already be home. She'd know. She might be hysterical, Gina. I'm asking you to help me break the news to her, all right? If not over dinner, while she's on the beach, or when you tuck her into bed, or whatever. Sometime when you can talk calmly and answer her questions."

"How am I supposed to answer her questions? Am I supposed to tell her the truth? Should I say you kicked Jack out because he loves his tootsie better than you?"

"Gina." Ramona took a deep breath. "You're smart. You're obviously smarter than me. I was stupid enough to marry the bastard, right? So you're the smart one. And you're down there in paradise with Ali. You'll know what to say to her. Just something to prepare her for what she'll find when she gets home. You love her, right? Do this for her."

Ramona might think Gina was smart, but she was pretty smart, too. She knew Gina would do anything out of love for Alicia. "Okay," she conceded. "I'll figure something out."

"Thanks." Ramona's voice trembled, a sob nibbling at the edges of it. "I'm sorry I'm making you do this."

"Forget it. I'll take care of it."

"I love her. I just don't want her getting upset."

Gina could think of no way to tell Alicia this news without upsetting her. But she would be as gentle and tactful as she could. She wouldn't call her brother-in-law a dickhead. "I'll take care of it," she said again. "You take care of yourself."

"Okay." Ramona was weeping openly now. "I'll see you Sunday."

"Right. Stay mellow, Mo. The worst is behind you. This is as bad as it's going to get."

"I know," Ramona said through her sniffles. "I've

got a real tough lawyer ready to roll. We're going to put Jack through the wringer.''

Gina smiled. Even distraught, Ramona had her priorities straight.

She said goodbye, lowered the phone and muttered a few words that would qualify as exceptionally coarse. How could she break this ghastly news to her beloved niece? Once Alicia knew her parents' marriage was irredeemably over and her father had moved out, she'd never want to leave St. Thomas. She already didn't want to leave it, without knowing what a mess she'd be returning to. Once she knew the mess, she'd be even more adamant about staying. And who could blame her? Gina wouldn't want to leave paradise to return to a broken home, either.

But she'd promised Ramona she would tell Gina, and she would.

On the plane home, maybe. That way she could avoid spoiling what was left of Alicia's vacation with the looming shadow of bad news. She'd tell Alicia—in proper language—when their glorious week was over, when the time had come for them to return to real life.

The headache she'd tried to fend off blossomed between her eyes, spreading like an ink spill on blotter paper. Groaning, Gina flopped back on the bed. Her head hit a pillow and she smelled not Kim's scent but Ethan's, a spicy, sexy fragrance.

She bolted upright. The last thing she needed was to get all swoony over the thought that his head had recently nestled into the pillow her head was currently nestled into. She couldn't afford to waste time acting like a teenager with a crush, dreaming about his gemlike eyes, his windswept hair, his lean body clad in swim trunks and nothing else—or his spicy, sexy fragrance, or his pillow. She had to focus solely on Alicia, on making the next few days the best in that little girl's life, so that when reality reared up and slapped her in the face, she would be strong enough to take it.

Gina swung her legs off the bed, straightened her spine, forced the corners of her mouth upward and left the bedroom. Ethan was hovering in the bathroom doorway, straddling the threshold. As soon as their gazes met, his brow furrowed. "Is everything okay?" he asked.

"Everything's fine," she said, straining to keep her smile alive.

His frown deepened.

"It shows, huh?" she murmured, abandoning the effort to look happy.

"It shows," Ethan confirmed, tracing a fingertip along the curve of her lower lip. "Not in your smile but in your eyes."

She told herself the brush of his finger meant nothing. He was only pointing out how phony her smile had looked. That her mouth tingled in the wake of his caress was irrelevant. He and Kim had reconciled.

Sort of, she amended, recalling the gaping distance between their pillows.

Well, he wasn't making a pass at her, anyway. He wouldn't. He and Kim had their own mess to deal with, one nowhere near as disastrous as Ramona's mess with Jack but one Gina wanted to steer as far from as possible. If Ethan could flirt with her when she'd clearly just finished a troubling phone call, he was a jerk. And she didn't think he was a jerk, so she had to assume he wasn't flirting. Just expressing concern—and warning her to overhaul her attitude before she confronted Alicia.

She drew in a breath, and her smile this time was

genuine, even though sadness washed through her.
"Damn. I don't want Alicia to know."

"Give yourself a minute." He stepped out of the bathroom and waved her inside. As soon as she'd entered
the narrow room, he closed the door behind her.

She felt another tingle, not on her lips but deeper, in
the place where affection and gratitude and a bunch of
other emotions she didn't care to examine lived inside
her. If he'd been flirting, he wouldn't have sacrificed his
turn in the bathroom to offer her a moment of solitude.
He was being a nice guy, that was all. Nicer than most
of the guys she knew—but she didn't want to think
about that, either.

She did need a minute to pull herself together. Squinting at her reflection in the mirror above the sink, she
noticed what he'd seen: the anger and frustration shad-
owing her eyes and the tension tugging at her mouth.
She splashed some cold water onto her face, washing
away the lingering effect of his touch, and rehearsed a
few smiles in the mirror, wishing one would look natural.

Alicia's toothbrush was propped in a glass at the edge
of the sink, bright pink, with small, soft bristles. She
was so young. She didn't deserve to have an ass like
Jack for her father. Maybe it was just as well that he
was clearing out of the house. The less Alicia had to
deal with him, the better.

Gina didn't really believe that, but the notion gave her
comfort.

After squaring her shoulders and inspecting her reflection one last time, she swung open the bathroom
door. Ethan was leaning against the wall, watching for
her, and when he saw her he straightened. "Better?"
she asked.

"Much." He motioned with his head toward the kitchen. "Go buy her some stuff."

"That's what God invented credit cards for," she said, pleased that she was able to joke. "Hey, Ali!" she called out as she marched down the hall and through the living room. "Ali the Alley Cat? Did you enjoy talking to your mommy? Did you tell her we're going shopping today?"

"I want to buy her a shirt that changes colors, too," Alicia announced as Gina joined her in the kitchen. "Can we buy her one?"

"You bet," Gina promised. "A shirt that changes colors is just what she needs."

CHAPTER SEVEN

"No, THAT ONE'S not right for you," Delia Hamilton told Alicia.

Gina sighed. Alicia had already picked out a shirt for herself with a tropical bird that changed color in ultraviolet light, a shirt with a palm tree that changed color for her mother and a duck-billed cap with a grotesque iguana that changed from lemon yellow with orange highlights to lime green with brown highlights for Gina. But before Gina could pay for the selections and escape from the store, Alicia's gaze had snagged on a display of nail enamels that also changed color in the sunlight. UV lamps around the store enabled Alicia to observe the color changes: a bottle of green polish turned mauve, a bottle of white turned taupe. Glittery gold turned coppery brown. That was the bottle Alicia had settled on.

The choice had inspired Kim's mother to intervene. Apparently, she viewed herself as an expert on color. "Your skin has golden undertones, sweetie," she explained, wresting the bottle from Alicia's fist and placing it back on the shelf. "You want to find a color that enhances your complexion, not one that clashes with it."

"But it doesn't matter what color it is," Alicia argued politely. "'Cause it changes color."

"Yes, but you want to find colors that will complement, not overstate. Do you know what *complement* means?"

Alicia nodded. "Like, 'that's a pretty dress.'"

Delia smiled and, in spite of herself, so did Gina. She'd spent three hours in the woman's presence so far, trailing her into liquor stores and jewelry stores and liquor-and-jewelry stores, listening to her expound on the nuances differentiating Stolichnaya from Absolut and the visual properties of natural versus lab-created emeralds. Along the way, she'd arranged to have a case of Absolut shipped to her home in Maryland and debated at length with Kim over the merits of two emerald tennis bracelets, both of which, the shop owner assured her, were made with only natural gems.

Alicia had been a real trouper throughout Delia's forays into the shops lining Charlotte Amalie's Main Street and the alleys that branched off it. Gina's chest was swollen with pride over her niece's exemplary behavior. Most seven-year-olds wouldn't have the stamina or the patience for the full-bore shopping style of the Hamiltons. But Alicia hadn't whined or squirmed or tugged on Gina's hand and whispered that she wanted to go to the beach, not once.

It helped that there were so many interesting sights to take in: quaint stucco-and-brick buildings with towering arched doorways flanked by ancient shutters; shelves of tacky souvenirs—dolls and bongo drums, plastic mugs and paperweights shaped like Bluebeard's Castle— looming above showcases of exquisite jewelry, elegant leather goods, perfumes and designer scarves. Friendly clerks at several of the stores offered everyone—even seven-year-old girls—sips of exotic liqueurs in shot-size paper cups. In one alley, a kiosk displayed steel drums, and Gina let Alicia bang on a few before they continued down the walk. A closet-size store embedded into a wall sold straw hats that smelled like a zoo, Alicia declared. Gina didn't argue; zoos often had cages lined with straw.

If the hectic scenery of the bazaar-like shopping district hadn't been enough to keep Alicia in line, Kim's mother would have. When she wasn't occupied ordering booze or eyeballing bracelets, she doted on Alicia, regaling her with stories about the pirates who used to roam the alleys of the city three hundred years ago and the Danish merchants who traded with them. "It was kind of like money laundering," she explained. Gina wasn't sure Alicia knew what that meant, but she took it all in, wide-eyed and rapt.

They'd eaten a lunch of sandwiches and lemonade in an open-air snack shop through which rare, warm breezes wafted. Once Alicia had slurped the last of her lemonade, she'd asked, "Can we go to the store with the shirts that change color in the sunlight?" Another child might have been cranky from the heat and traffic, all the walking and browsing on the crowded, narrow sidewalks of the city. But she didn't seem the least bit worn-out.

Before they left the snack shop, Gina had pulled Alicia's hair off her neck into a scrunchy to keep her from getting overheated. The two narrow braids she'd had woven into the locks yesterday dangled playfully behind her, adorned with their turquoise beads. "I don't know if the Hamiltons have other shopping to do," she'd said, "but you and I can go to the store, okay?"

"Oh, we'll all go," Delia Hamilton had insisted, looking as fresh as the cool lemonade frosting the surface of Gina's tumbler. "I didn't want to go there too early, because I just know you're going to want to buy things there, and if you'd bought things there this morning, you'd have had to lug those shopping bags around all day. Trust me, Alicia—'' she'd covered Alicia's hand with her own and gave a little squeeze ''—when it comes to shopping, strategizing is essential.''

Gina supposed she would be defining *strategizing* along with *money laundering* for Alicia that evening. And *complement,* she added as Delia went on about which shades of nail polish most effectively brought out the subtle undertones of Alicia's coloring.

Kim had spent most of the day subdued. Gina wondered if she was stewing about her spat last night with Ethan, or maybe she resented that her mother was devoting the bulk of her attention to Alicia. The elegant blond woman who had been so appalled at the thought of sharing a condominium with Gina and Alicia seemed all but ready to adopt the kid.

''She wants grandchildren,'' Kim murmured, watching as Delia held various bottles of nail polish against Alicia's cheek, sometimes sighing happily and sometimes shaking her head.

''Ali's already got a grandma,'' Gina said, using the singular because she wasn't sure whether Jack's mother still counted as a grandmother now that her schmuck of a son had chosen to leave his wife and child and move in with the Other Woman.

''Well, knowing my mother, she's just trying out the grandmother role, giving it a dry run with your niece. If she likes it, she'll set her sights on becoming a grandmother as soon as possible. If she doesn't, she'll back off. But Alicia is making the whole thing seem awfully pleasant.''

Did she hope her mother would back off? Gina wondered. Or did she expect to make up with Ethan and get their engagement on track once more? ''Alicia's usually not so pleasant,'' Gina said, though she didn't mean it.

In her eyes, Alicia was damn near perfect. "I don't think anyone's ever discussed nail polish colors with her in such detail before. It's a whole fashion thing. Ali's getting into it." She shot Kim a measuring glance. Like her mother, Kim displayed no effects of the heat—no sweat, no droopy hair, no wilted clothing. She'd seemed more animated in the jewelry store, even though the discussion had focused on emeralds rather than diamonds, the subject she'd been reading up on yesterday. Clothing and nail polish that changed color obviously didn't excite her.

Or maybe she was stewing because her mother was having such a grand time testing out her grandma routine.

"My sister was only twenty-three when she had Alicia. It's hard, especially when you're that young," Gina said. "A lot of work. I want to have kids someday, but I've got to admit, being an aunt is much more fun."

"It's too late for you to have kids that young," Kim remarked, in a supercilious tone that insulted Gina. She was hardly an old maid. She wasn't even "of a certain age" yet. In fact, she might well be younger than Kim. Not that it mattered; they weren't in competition.

"Okay," Delia said, then released a grand, satisfied breath. "We've settled on these three bottles."

Three? Well, what the hell. Alicia's father had walked out on her. The least she deserved was as many bottles of nail polish as she wanted.

Gina carried all the items to the counter and handed the clerk her credit card. Next month when the bill arrived, she would probably go into cardiac arrest. But she'd pull through. Nail polish was practically a necessity, anyway. Before they left St. Thomas, she would give Alicia a manicure. And a pedicure. She wasn't as

fanatical about moisturizing her feet and keeping the
skin smooth and supple as she'd been during her foot-
modeling days, but she remembered how to give a good
pedicure. She might need to buy a little bubble bath for
soaking Alicia's feet, but she had scissors, files, cuticle
clippers and all the rest. Maybe this evening, after their
ladies' day, they could have a ladies' night. Shopping
and then spa. She'd smear facial cream on Ali's cheeks
and massage a leave-in conditioner into her hair, and
they could gossip about all the girls in Alicia's Brownie
troop.

"Now," Delia said, her matronly authority reminding
everyone that she was in charge. "Shall we go back and
make a decision on the emerald tennis bracelet?"

"I was thinking I might want a watch, instead," Kim
announced. "One of those Chopard watches. You know
the ones with the happy diamonds floating under the
crystal."

"I suppose we should look at them before making any
decisions," her mother agreed.

The last thing Gina wanted to do was look at watches
with happy diamonds floating inside them. "I'm thinking maybe Ali and I will head back to Palm Point," she
said. "We can grab a taxi—"

"Oh, no, I wouldn't think of it," Delia silenced her.
"We're supposed to meet Ethan and Ross at five at that
old restaurant—what's it called?"

"The Hotel 1829," Kim answered.

"Right. It's just a few blocks from here. We'll all
have dinner together."

"But we can't all fit in the car," Gina pointed out.
"Ali and I are going to have to take a taxi home, one
way or another. So we may as well—"

"Of course we can all fit. You can put Alicia on your lap. She's small."

Gina would have declined, but Alicia piped up. "I wanna see the happy diamonds, Aunt Gina. Can we go see the happy diamonds?"

Her father was scum. Of course she could see the happy diamonds.

So off they went, back to this jewelry store and that, down an alley called Drake's Passage and up an alley called Raadets Gade. Along the way, they stopped at a store filled with expensive tchochkes, where Delia and Kim debated the relative merits of various figurines and Gina held her breath the entire time they were in the store, fearful that Alicia might accidentally bump into a shelf and break a two-hundred-dollar porcelain rendering of a glum-faced clown. Who would want all these dust collectors in their homes, anyway? Obviously someone who didn't live in a tiny studio apartment. She barely had room for her clothes and books in her home. Shelf space, like every other kind of space, was at a premium.

Wasn't it F. Scott Fitzgerald who'd said, "The rich— they're different from you and me"? The rich, as far as Gina could tell, obsessed over whether Orrefors crystal was better than Lalique. Normal people, like her and Alicia, bought novelty T-shirts and hats with ugly iguanas on them. And nail polish in three colors—or six, depending on the available sunlight.

After purchasing a set of crystal candlesticks—Baccarat, not Lalique or Orrefors—the Hamilton women led on to the watch store, where Alicia gawked at the bejeweled timepieces. "Can I get a watch?" she asked Gina.

Her father might be scum, but Gina had her limits.

Or, more precisely, her credit card did. "You've got a perfectly good watch."

"It's got a plastic strap," Alicia noted.

"With the Power Puff Girls on it. It's a fine watch."

"I guess," Alicia said uncertainly.

Gina wanted to give her lecture on the worth of things. But this store, with its display cases of Patek Phillipe, Rolex, Breitling and, yes, Chopard watches with floating diamonds beneath their crystals, didn't seem like the right environment for such a speech. All she said was, "You can get the same information from a Power Puff Girls watch as from a happy-diamonds watch. Either one is going to tell you the time. You don't get better time from a fancy diamond watch."

Alicia considered that, then conceded with a nod. "Is Mrs. Hamilton going to get a watch with happy diamonds?"

"Kim might." Thousands of dollars, she thought. Tens of thousands of dollars for a watch. How many hours of modeling mules and sandals would it take her to buy such an object? Thank goodness she didn't want one.

The rich were different. And it occurred to her, as Kim had the salesman remove several watches from the locked showcase so she could drape them around her wrist, that no matter how easy talking to Ethan was, no matter how comfortable she felt with him, no matter how much fun she'd had in his company last night, tossing back a beer and feeling the Caribbean night settle over them, he was one of the rich. Whatever the current status of his relationship with Kim, she was the woman he'd come to St. Thomas with, the woman who called him her fiancé. He was one of *them*.

ETHAN SHOULDN'T have been so glad to see Gina and Alicia waiting at the restaurant along with Kim and Delia Hamilton. He shouldn't have felt a rush of elation at the thought of Gina having dinner with him. Actually, he shouldn't have had the energy to feel much of anything.

Ross Hamilton had put him through the wringer on the golf course that day. The sun had beaten down on them, relentlessly hot and glaring, but Ross had insisted that they walk the links rather than rent a cart. "Exercise," he'd said, puffing from hole to hole like a recently retired colonel trying to whip a recruit into shape. "That's the beauty of this sport. If you do it right, you learn patience, you develop skill and you tone up the cardiovascular system."

"I belong to a health club in Arlington," Ethan had muttered, tramping along behind Ross, the weight of his rented bag of clubs pressing down onto his shoulder. "I tone up my cardiovascular system on a treadmill." In air-conditioning, he wanted to add. With a TV set tuned to CNN right in front of him.

"After you and Kim settle down, you'll need to join a golf club," Ross had informed him, then teed up, swung his driver and sent his ball soaring. "I'll arrange to have you join my club. I know it sounds impractical, given that you live in Connecticut and the club is in Maryland. But I'm sure you and Kim will be coming down to visit whenever you get the chance, and you'll want access to the club then. Besides—" he watched critically as Ethan lined up to drive his ball, and pursed his lips in disdain when Ethan's ball failed to reach the fairway "—it's a very selective club. They don't accept just anyone. If I sponsor you, of course, you're in. And that will ensure our family's legacy at the club for generations to come."

Ethan had gritted his teeth and mopped the sweat off the back of his neck with a handkerchief. If anything could be more disagreeable than playing golf that afternoon with Ross, on a day when the brilliant turquoise of the Caribbean Sea was visible beyond the rolling lawns of the course they were playing and he couldn't stop thinking about how much he'd rather be swimming, snorkeling or boating, it was the notion of joining Ross's golf club in Maryland and having to play more golf with him.

But he'd gotten through the eighteen holes somehow. He'd soldiered on, keeping his mouth shut, letting Ross vent about the ineptitude of unskilled workers, the intricacies of the sprinkler systems required to maintain golf courses—"It's amazing how much water they need! This course alone probably consumes more water in one week than the island's population uses in a month"— and the prospects for a Kim-Ethan union. "Kim is a remarkable young woman," Ross had pointed out. "You're not the first man who ever wanted to marry her. But if you win her hand, you will be the luckiest man who ever wanted to marry her."

I will never marry your daughter, Ethan had wanted to announce, but he'd seen no reason to spoil Ross's vacation. Kim was indeed a remarkable woman, and he had no doubt some other guy would win the title "Luckiest Man"—and would cherish that title in a way Ethan never would.

Actually, the longer the game had dragged on, the more Kim had risen in Ethan's esteem. For her to have evolved into a smart, strong and generally good-natured woman after growing up in the overbearing presence of Ross Hamilton was nothing short of miraculous.

Once he'd turned in their rented equipment, he'd been forced to endure a "nineteenth hole" drink—iced tea for him, bourbon and water for Ross. Then he'd dropped Ross off at his hotel and enjoyed a blessed hour of solitude, during which he'd showered, donned fresh clothing and lounged on the terrace, remembering how relaxed he'd felt last night while he'd been shooting the breeze with Gina.

So perhaps it was no surprise that he was thrilled to have her and Alicia joining them for dinner. The two of them looked weary but not too bedraggled after their long day in town, and Gina carried only one plastic shopping bag. Kim and her mother juggled numerous bulging bags and bubbled with energy, as if shopping fueled rather than drained them. No one was sulking, no one sniping. He could only assume their ladies' day had been more successful than his gentlemen's day.

"We had such a wonderful time today I insisted that Gina and Alicia have dinner with us," Delia said as the group gathered outside the restaurant's entry. "I hope you don't mind."

"I got three nail polishes that change color," Alicia boasted. "And we saw happy diamonds, too."

"Alicia is a fine little shopper," Delia praised Alicia, giving her a pat on the head. Alicia beamed.

Gina discreetly rolled her eyes. "It's okay if you want it just to be family, though," she said, addressing him directly. "We can get a taxi. I don't want to barge in on your dinner."

"No, no, by all means, have dinner with us," Ross said gruffly, before Ethan could tell Gina how welcome she and the kid were. He hoped his expression conveyed that message. She continued to study him, skepticism twisting her mouth and something that might have been worry or amusement lighting her eyes. He nodded and touched her elbow, urging her ahead of him into the restaurant.

It occupied a historic building and had a broad dining porch that overlooked Charlotte Amalie's harbor. Kim had read about the restaurant in a guidebook and made a reservation for four, but the host quickly moved their party to a larger table on the porch, from which they could see rooftops and narrow alleys and at least five cruise ships, illuminated by strings of sloping lights, retreating from the port to the open sea.

Ethan wound up seated between Kim and her mother; Gina sat directly across from him. Her blunt-cut hair looked almost bluish in the twilit evening, and her face glowed like polished bronze in the light from the candle at the center of the table. When she opened the menu the waiter presented to her, Ethan noticed her shoulders twitch.

He shouldn't be so attuned to her, but he couldn't help it. He'd seen her reaction and understood it at once: the prices had shocked her. "I'm treating," he said abruptly.

"Oh, that's not necessary," Ross argued.

It *was* necessary. The restaurant was obviously more expensive than Gina had expected. She'd been coerced into this dinner party, and Ethan couldn't allow her to blow her budget just because Delia considered Alicia a "fine little shopper." "Please. I insist." He shot a quick look at the pile of parcels behind Delia's chair and added, "Given the power shopping these ladies did today, I may be the only solvent person at this table."

He meant it as a joke, but it took Ross a full minute

of harrumphing before he managed a smile. "Very well, then. Be a sport," he grumbled.

Gina apparently wasn't as easily persuaded. Her lips pursed, she paged through the menu, emitting waves of tension. "I don't know, Ethan—"

"I insist," he said firmly, his tone leaving no room for debate.

Her eyes met his above the menus, and he was again unable to define the emotions he saw churning in them. Pride, perhaps—she didn't want his charity, and he couldn't blame her. Discomfort at being included in an event that was beyond her means. A mixture of anxiety and defiance. "All right," she finally said, but it sounded more like a dare than a concession.

Ross, who had appropriated the wine list, waved over the waiter and ordered a bottle. "I hope you don't mind," he belatedly said to Ethan.

Ethan was the host; he should choose the wine. He glanced at the list to see what Ross had ordered. A seventy-dollar bottle—not the most expensive on the list, but definitely not one of the cheaper ones. "Sure," he said not wanting to get into a pissing contest with Ross over the wine. "Alicia, what would you like to drink?"

"Can I have milk *and* soda?" she asked Gina in a stage whisper.

"Just milk," Gina told her. "It'll give you strong teeth."

"I want strong teeth," Alicia said in a louder voice, including the others. "Stronger than an iguana. Did you see any iguanas today, Ethan?"

"Not a one."

"Me, neither." She seemed amazingly poised, seated among so many adults, a lone milk drinker surrounded by wine sippers. Her shirt had a dark spot on it—something must have dripped onto it earlier in the day—and her hair was frizzy and disheveled except for the tight bead-adorned braids tucked behind her ear. But her spirits were high and she wasn't even squirming.

He wondered what bad news Gina had gotten from her sister that morning, news from which she'd wanted to shield Alicia. Obviously she'd succeeded in keeping the kid ignorant. Ali the Alley Cat didn't seem to have a care in the world.

A sommelier approached their table with the wine and poured some for Ross to taste. He studied, sniffed, chewed a mouthful and, after several ponderous moments, nodded his approval. Glasses were filled, orders placed. Alicia asked if she could have a hamburger, and the waiter told her she could have ground sirloin grilled over an open fire and served on a wheat roll with a garnish of mesclun and tomato. "That's essentially the same thing as a hamburger," Gina explained, and Alicia smiled and ordered it. Everyone else selected from the elaborate list of entrees. Ethan visualized the bill and let out a slow breath. He could handle the cost, and he considered the expenditure worth sparing Gina's feelings.

Why did he care so much about sparing her feelings? Why was he so keenly aware of the deep darkness of her eyes? Why did she have to be seated directly across from him, so that every time he lifted his gaze it collided with hers?

"I've been wondering," Ross said, turning to her. "What kind of accent is that?"

"What kind of accent is what?"

"*Your* accent."

"I don't have an accent," she said, smiling sweetly.

"She's from New York," Alicia offered.

"I've known New Yorkers who don't have quite so pronounced an accent," Ross pressed Gina.

"I guess you know the wrong New Yorkers, then," she said with obviously fake sympathy. When Ethan caught her eye, she flashed him a wicked grin. He couldn't help but smile back.

She must have sensed his approval, because he saw her relax, her posture losing its rigidity and her grin lingering, teasing her mouth. God help them all, she was going to have fun with Ross. She was going to puncture his pomposity. This dinner could turn out to be a disaster—the most entertaining disaster Ethan had ever witnessed.

She more than lived up to his expectations. When the waiter delivered baskets of bread to the table, she launched into a description of her uncle Rodolfo—"Like that guy in the opera, you know which one I mean? The opera where she dies of TB."

"TV?" Alicia asked, her eyes round. "You can die from TV?"

"Only if you watch the wrong shows," Gina had joked. "You know Uncle Rodolfo, right? Gramma's brother?"

"He makes pizza."

"That's right," Gina confirmed. "Anyway, he makes rolls out of leftover pizza dough and sells them to gourmet restaurants. People think his rolls are fantastic, and all they are is pizza dough. What do you think, Ali? Are these rolls pizza dough?" she asked as she passed Alicia a flaky, buttery biscuit.

And later, when the salads were brought out, she poked her fork through the mixed greens and said, "You know what this looks like? Those weeds that grow through cracks in the sidewalk in the city. I hope it doesn't taste like weeds. Then again, I have no idea what weeds taste like. Mr. Hamilton, you're a man of the world. Have you ever tasted weeds?''

''No,'' he said, his voice dissolving into a cough. Kim sighed heavily and her mother's lips pinched as she prodded her weedy salad with the tines of her fork.

Over their entrees, Gina described some of her favorite eateries in the Bronx neighborhood of her youth. Alicia chimed in, mentioning some of her favorite restaurants in White Plains, where she lived. They concurred that Happy House had the best waffles, although Alicia complained that the syrup bottles were too sticky. ''That's because they don't wipe them off,'' Gina explained, before detouring to the subject of her boss. ''He designs shoes,'' she said. ''More accurately, *we* design shoes, since I'm on the design staff. I'm learning so much from Bruno. The man's a genius. He knows everything you'd ever want to know about leather.''

''I can imagine,'' Ross grunted.

''He's got the face of a pre-Raphaelite angel,'' Gina said. ''I majored in art—I know pre-Raphaelite, and Bruno fits the bill. Isn't that the way it always is?'' she asked Kim conspiratorially. ''The best-looking ones are always gay. Present company excluded, of course,'' she added, indicating Ethan and Ross with a sweep of her hand. ''Bruno's last boyfriend could have passed for Pierce Brosnan's twin. I'm telling you, he was gorgeous. Why couldn't the guy have fallen in love with me?'' She shrugged, then shot Ethan another mischievous grin.

He wasn't sure why she was treating him as her accomplice. Possibly because he was the only one at the table who realized she was teasing. Like her, he took pleasure in watching Ross Hamilton shift uncomfortably in his chair, jaw clenched even as he tried to chew, throat laboring to swallow. Ross was a snob. He deserved to have his feathers ruffled, and Gina was a wonderful feather ruffler.

She saved her best ruffling for last. With coffee—and cognac for Ross, which Ethan was sure he'd ordered only because it was so damn expensive, and a dish of vanilla ice cream for Alicia, because she'd been so well behaved—Gina said, "I just don't get golf, Mr. Hamilton. Maybe you can explain it to me. Why would any sane person want to play it?"

He glowered. Ethan could practically hear him rumbling like threatening thunder. "I'm sure it's probably too refined for you to understand, my dear," he muttered.

"It tones up the cardiovascular system," Ethan said helpfully.

Ross aimed his menacing frown at Ethan. "The pleasures of golf extend far beyond its health benefits."

"Isn't jogging better, cardiovascular-wise?" Gina asked. "Plus, all you need to jog is a pair of running shoes—which is an area I think Bruno should extend into. Sports shoes in general. I don't understand why jogging shoes have to look so dorky. Gotta admit, though, they're a hell of a lot more attractive than golf shoes. You ever see those golf shoes that look like old-fashioned saddle shoes, with the fringed flap over the laces? I mean, yuck." Even Delia chuckled at that.

Ross seethed. Ethan could guess the style of the old guy's golf shoes at home. He was still struggling to suppress his smile when he handed the waiter his credit card.

Over Gina's protests, he managed to fit everyone into the huge rental car. Gina was slim enough, and Alicia small enough, that they could sit side by side with the seat belt stretched around both of them. Kim looked squeezed, stuck in the middle seat in back, and her lush mouth settled into a halfhearted pout. If she weren't so ticked off at him, he suspected she would have been amused by Gina's performance over dinner. True, she loved her father and felt a loyalty to him, but she did have a sense of humor. Or at least she'd had one in Connecticut. If her mother could laugh over Ross's golf shoes, surely Kim could.

Maybe she couldn't laugh at anything because she and Ethan weren't having sex. Maybe she couldn't laugh because their relationship was unraveling. Maybe she couldn't laugh because he'd failed to accompany her to a jewelry store in town to pick out an engagement ring.

He felt bad about that—but not bad enough to buy her a ring. He'd feel a lot worse if he pretended they were on track for marriage, if he closed his eyes to the obvious lack of love between them. Over the past few months they must have been in some kind of love—the wild-infatuation kind, the hot-sex kind—but this trip had been their chance to discover if they were also in the kind of love that carried a couple happily into old age together. And they weren't.

He was relieved to have recognized that essential fact before it was too late. He wished Kim could accept the truth and share his relief. But she'd really, really wanted him to buy her a ring, duty-free.

She'd just have to come to terms with the reality that marriage, commitment, the whole till-death-do-us-part thing was never duty-free.

CHAPTER EIGHT

WHEN THEY ARRIVED back at Palm Point, Alicia wanted to watch TV. So, unfortunately, did Kim. "I am not going to shut myself up in the bedroom," she said imperiously, once she'd returned to the living room after dumping all her purchases in her and Ethan's bedroom. "We're paying just as much as *they're* paying for this apartment."

Everyone was paying zero for the apartment, but Gina didn't mention that. The fact was, her watch read nine-fifteen, and no show appropriate to a seven-year-old would be on at that hour anyway. Tugging Alicia away from the television set, she said, "How about let's let Kim watch TV and I'll polish your nails for you?"

"With my new nail polish?"

"With whichever of your three new nail polishes you want."

The promise of a manicure was enough to entice Alicia. She raced eagerly down the hall ahead of Gina, ceding the television to Kim.

Gina and Alicia ended up in the bathroom, which wasn't huge to begin with but seemed even smaller with the two of them in it. It contained what Gina needed, though: bright lighting, water and hard surfaces to lean on. Since she hadn't brought any bubble bath to St. Thomas, she improvised, fetching a large bowl and some liquid dishwashing soap from the kitchen and creating a warm pool of suds for Alicia to soak her hands in.

"I want the polish that turns from purple to blue," Alicia requested. "On my toes, too, okay?"

"Claws and paws," Gina confirmed. "You're getting the works. You were such a good girl today! I was getting cranky by the end, but you were a champ. Didn't you feel tired?"

"No," Alicia said, settling herself on the floor and removing her sandals. "Shopping's fun." She looked much more comfortable than Gina felt on the unyielding tiles. The bathroom was humid, the air tinged with a vaguely familiar scent.

Ethan's shampoo, she identified it. She hadn't been aware of sniffing his hair—but damn it, she couldn't help noticing things about him. Like the way his eyes had constantly sought hers during dinner, and the way his mouth had twitched as though he was struggling not to smile while she ran old man Hamilton through the wringer. Like the way he'd stabbed his food with his fork, and the way he'd held his wineglass. Like the way he'd helped her fit the seat belt around both Ali and her, his hands smoothing the band over her hip…and the scent of his hair.

Alicia appeared as fixated on shopping as Gina was fixated on Ethan—and neither was a healthy fixation. "I liked the way the stores smelled," her niece babbled. "Except that store with the straw hats in it. But the other stores—some of them smelled like perfume. Remember the store that had all that crystal in it, and there were rainbows in all the glasses? It smelled like perfume. Maybe I should've gotten perfume for Mommy."

Perfume was the last thing Ramona needed right now—or maybe it was the second-to-last thing, the last thing being a shirt that changed color in the sunlight. "Perfume can be hard to buy for other people," Gina told her as she pulled the cuticle stick from her manicure travel kit and nudged Alicia's cuticles. "Sometimes a perfume smells good in the bottle, but then it doesn't smell good on the person."

"That's silly!" Alicia giggled.

"No, it's true. A perfume that smells just fine on one person will smell bad on another. It has to do with body chemistry."

Through the closed door, she heard muffled voices. Kim and Ethan, arguing. "I bet Ethan would know about chemistry," Alicia said. "He's so smart."

"I'm smart, too," Gina boasted, although her knowledge of chemistry was pretty much limited to paints, dyes and solvents. She dried Alicia's hands off, then smoothed her short nails with a file, more for show than because they needed to be shaped.

Another swell of voices rose from the living room again. The words were muffled and muddled, for which Gina was grateful. She didn't want to hear what Ethan and Kim were quarreling about—especially if their fight concerned Gina's needling of Kim's father throughout dinner, and Ethan's tacit encouragement of her.

"They don't like each other very much, do they?" Alicia said in a deafeningly loud whisper that echoed off the glossy tile walls.

"I think," Gina whispered more softly, "they're just having some problems."

"Like Mommy and Daddy?"

Gina busied herself shaking the bottle of purple nail enamel. Ramona and Jack were having some problems the way Placido Domingo had some voice. But she wasn't going to tell Alicia that now. She wasn't going to spoil Alicia's manicure—or her vacation. "Your parents are married," she noted. "Ethan and Kim aren't."

"I don't think they should get married," Alicia said somberly. "I think Ethan should marry you."

"Me?" Gina laughed, but for some reason her laughter got stuck in the vicinity of her diaphragm. "Ethan and I have nothing in common."

"You both like to snorkel," Alicia pointed out.

"So do you. Why don't you marry him?"

"I'm too young." Alicia's frown conveyed that she considered her aunt extremely foolish even to suggest such a thing. "But you're old. You should marry him."

"I don't want to." Gina tried to force another laugh, but it wouldn't come. She busied herself dabbing polish onto Alicia's nails, one finger at a time.

"Why not? I bet he's rich."

"See? There you go—he and I have nothing in common. He's rich and I'm not. Now, hold that hand flat and don't move it. Give the polish a chance to dry."

Alicia laid her hand carefully on her knee and extended her other hand to Gina. "If you married him, you'd be rich, too."

"Why are you so eager to marry me off?" Gina asked, pretending indignation. "I like my life fine the way it is. I don't have any room in it for a husband. I don't have any room in my apartment for a husband, either."

"You could get a bigger apartment," Alicia suggested.

"Big apartments are too expensive."

"If you married Ethan, you'd be rich."

Gina painted a final dot of polish onto Alicia's pinkie, then capped the bottle. "Let them dry, and then I'll do a second coat," she instructed Alicia, then leaned back against the wall and shifted her butt so it wouldn't go numb. "I'm in no hurry to find a husband. And in any case, I don't want you mentioning to Ethan that you think he and I should get married. He's got to work things out with Kim, and we should mind our own business."

"But—"

"And even if he and Kim don't work everything out, he's all wrong for me, Alley Cat. He's too fancy. Know what I mean? He's a Connecticut kind of guy. And I'm a New York kind of girl."

"He could learn to like New York."

"Sure, he could. But it wouldn't be in his blood, the way it's in yours and mine." Hearing herself say the words convinced Gina of their resounding truth. Ethan might be handsome. He might have a subversive sense of humor. He might be breaking up with Kim. He might even be flirting with Gina, if she was willing to let her imagination stretch that far.

But he wasn't her kind of guy.

AN HOUR LATER, Alicia was sound asleep, her fingers and toes tipped in shimmering purple polish. The fighting between Ethan and Kim had long since ended, and when Gina emerged from her bedroom, after telling Alicia her own version of "The Ugly Duckling," making it about a Bronx pigeon's egg that wound up in a suburban robin's nest, and fumbling her way through the song "Under the Sea" from *The Little Mermaid*—"because that movie is like snorkeling," Alicia had explained—the TV was off and the door to the master bedroom was closed.

Gina should probably go to bed, as well. But she was too wound up. All day long she'd deferred thoughts about her sister's disintegrating marriage. Now, without Alicia to distract her, worry and anger inundated her.

She'd liked her brother-in-law at one time. Jack Bari had been staggeringly handsome, and he'd doted on Ramona, and he'd called Alicia his princess. He'd also been kind of a jerk, laughing too loud at things that weren't funny, like the Three Stooges or broadcasts where they showed baseball players getting hit in the groin by line drives. He'd been lazy around the house, tossing his jacket onto a chair rather than hanging it in the closet, and leaving dirty dishes in the sink rather than stacking them in the dishwasher. He'd insisted on his nights out with the boys—although, in retrospect, Gina wondered whether some of those nights out might have been spent not with the boys but with his sweetie pie.

Yet he'd seemed like a pretty typical guy. Gina had yet to meet a man who was diligent about cleaning up after himself. Her father was truly one of the best men she knew, but he never managed to get his dirty laundry into the hamper, and the concept of making a bed was alien to him. Kyle used to keep his uniform impeccable, but the minute he took it off he turned into Officer Slob, dressing in frayed jeans and torn T-shirts, splattering coffee all over the counter and never bothering to wipe the spills. She recalled the overall tidiness of the master bedroom that morning when she'd taken Ramona's phone call, but for all she knew, Kim picked up after Ethan.

What was she going to tell Alicia? How was she going to break the news to her magnificently manicured niece that King Jack had deserted his princess and abdicated the throne for a little extramarital nookie?

Maybe some fresh island air would clear her head. She padded barefoot through the silent living room to the sliding-glass door—and saw Ethan seated out on the terrace by himself. Just as he'd found her last night.

She pushed open the door. He glanced around and his face broke into a spontaneous smile. "Hey," he said softly.

"Mind if I sit out here awhile?"

He gestured toward the empty chair next to him. "You're paying as much as I am," he joked, then lifted the beer bottle he had in his hand. "Would you like one?"

"No, thanks. I'm stuffed from dinner and tanked on wine. Thanks so much for treating us, Ethan. That was awfully generous of you."

He shrugged. "If you can get tanked on a glass and a half of wine, you must be a cheap date."

All right, she wasn't tanked. She didn't want a beer, though. She didn't want anything more than what she had right at that moment: the starlit sky above her, the murmur of the ocean below her, the tangy air around her. And Ethan beside her.

She shouldn't want that.

He, too, was barefoot, his feet propped onto the railing. The hems of his trousers slid up just enough to expose his bony ankles. The breeze toyed with his shirt, causing it to ripple against his chest. His hair was mussed, his forearms tanned, tendon and muscle tapering down to his large, strong hands.

She shouldn't want this.

Neither of them spoke for a while. Ethan sipped his beer. She leaned back in her chair and listened to the wind and the water. Finally, he broke the silence. "So, what was the phone call about?"

She might have been annoyed that he'd reminded her of that unpleasant subject, except that she hadn't really needed a reminder. Concern about her sister and Alicia was stuck like a piece of food in her throat. She was going to have to swallow it down or cough it up if she didn't want to choke on it.

She decided to cough it up. "My sister kicked her husband out of the house," she said. "He's going to be gone by the end of the week. I'm supposed to explain all this to Alicia before we get back to New York, so she'll be prepared."

"Ouch." Ethan reached over to pat her hand, which rested on the arm of her chair. He left his long, warm fingers draped over hers, a gesture too casual for her to read meaning into but too comforting for her *not* to read meaning into. She moved her hand experimentally, but he didn't draw his away. His touch felt good, so she relaxed and let herself accept it. "I gather you haven't told Alicia yet," he said.

"How'd you guess?"

"She's too happy." He sipped some beer. "Is she close to her father?"

"She thinks he makes the sun rise. God, he's such a bastard."

"These situations are never simple, Gina. There may be good guys and bad guys, but no one is ever all good or all bad."

Was he giving her moral instruction? Or perhaps working through his own "situation" with Kim? "The son of a bitch stepped out on my sister," she grumbled. "Are you going to defend him?"

Ethan eyed her and laughed. "And turn you into my enemy? No way." He held up both hands in surrender.

Gina laughed, too, although she wished he hadn't removed his hand from hers. It was just as well that he did. The more she desired the contact, the more she ought to avoid it. "You make me sound dangerous."

"I saw what you did to Kim's father this evening. You *are* dangerous."

"I wasn't really that bad, was I?" She'd only been teasing the guy, trying to pluck some of the stuffing out of him.

"You were great. I was cheering you on the whole time."

"Is Kim mad at me?"

"Kim is mad at the world right now." He sighed and let his hand settle back over hers. Maybe this time he was seeking comfort rather than giving it. She arched her hand so she could slide her fingers between his, and he responded with another gentle squeeze that sent a charge through her. She'd never been turned on by holding a guy's hand before. And she wasn't really holding Ethan's hand—and she wasn't really turned on. But…*damn.* The heat of his palm, the protective curve of it and the strength in those fingers… It all felt much, much too good.

"I bet it's just you she's mad at," Gina said, as if to convince herself that she shouldn't like him, that maybe *he* was one of the bad guys. "You broke her heart."

"I don't think it's broken." His thumb moved lazily along the outer edge of her pinkie and he stared out at the horizon. "Kim's a terrific woman. I like her. She's going to make some man very happy someday." He sighed. "Unfortunately, I'm not that man."

"You told her that?"

He pondered the question for several long seconds. "Pretty much," he said.

"Meaning what? You were vague, you left the door open, you're hedging your bets?" She knew guys who kept their options viable, stringing along several women at once and insisting to each one that he'd stopped seeing the others. One of her classmates at RISD, a sculptor with a buff build and bedroom eyes, had been a master at that game. For a while, she'd been one of the several women he'd strung along. Eventually, before she'd gotten too involved with him, she'd figured out that the line he was handing her—"I've ended things with the others. You're the only woman who matters to me"—was the same line he was handing a photography grad student and a premed from Brown University, just up the road from the art school.

"Meaning," Ethan said, "I told Kim I was never going to marry her."

"And she heard you clearly? Sometimes…" She didn't want to say anything against Kim—or against women in general. Much as she relished his hand clasping hers, he *was* a man, which meant he didn't automatically deserve her trust.

"Sometimes what?" he prodded her.

"Men don't make themselves as clear as they need to be," she said, placing the blame where it belonged.

He stared at her. "We don't make ourselves clear?"

"You know. Like maybe you told her you weren't going to marry her, but you still felt close to her and wanted to be in her life because she's a terrific woman and blah-blah-blah. And you're holding my hand here, just kind of testing the waters, but you've got Kim warming the bed for you. That kind of thing."

He lifted his hand from hers, letting his fingers slide across the back of her hand in a farewell caress. "I'm sorry. I didn't think you'd mind."

She minded *not* having his hand there, but she wasn't going to tell him that. "I don't even know you, Ethan.

And I'm not in the market for one of those vacation romantic fantasy flings, okay? I'm here in St. Thomas with my niece.''

"And I'm here with the Hamiltons. Don't worry. I won't touch you again.''

Talk about breaking someone's heart. She was proud of herself for doing the right thing, but her hand felt cold and abandoned. "We have nothing in common,'' she reminded him, just as she'd reminded Alicia earlier that evening.

He stared at her again, his gaze curious, tinged with amusement. "Nothing at all,'' he said, a bare hint of sarcasm coloring his voice.

"You know what I mean.''

"I'm not making a pass at you, Gina. I wasn't making a pass at you when I took your hand. It was just a gesture of friendship.''

Oh, God, had she just made a total ass of herself? Had she read more into his touch than he'd ever intended? Her cheeks tingled as embarrassment flooded her. "All right, well, I don't know what I'm talking about,'' she mumbled, pushing herself to her feet. "It's past my bedtime. I'm going inside.''

He grabbed her hand once more, and pulled her back into her chair. "Hey,'' he murmured. "It's there, Gina. We both know it's there. I'm not making a pass at you, but…'' He pulled her hand toward him, close enough so he could peer at her fingertips, close enough that he could kiss them if he'd wanted to. He looked as if he wanted to. But he placed her hand back on the arm of her chair and released it, then took a long slug of beer. "I'm not your brother-in-law. I'm not the kind of guy who takes his girlfriend on a vacation and—what's your expression? Steps out on her?''

"Good." Her voice sounded rusty and she swallowed.

"Not that I don't want to. Make a pass at you, I mean." He addressed the horizon. "But I won't."

"I think that's the best thing." She had to force out the words, even though she believed them fervently. What she wanted, what he wanted—it wasn't the best thing. The best thing was to pretend neither of them wanted anything.

"Do you hate me for being honest?" he asked.

"Are you kidding? You get points for being honest." Without his hand to clasp, she fidgeted, tapped her fingers together, picked at a thread on her shorts. "Whatever it is between us, Ethan, it's meaningless. It's just the ocean and the heat and the Caribbean moon. You go someplace exotic, and you get thrown together with a stranger, and it distorts everything. I'll bet if we met under different circumstances, we'd never even notice each other."

"I'd notice you," he said simply.

"Well, yeah. Guys notice anything with breasts."

"Actually, it was your feet that caught my attention." He gazed at them, and she wondered whether she should tuck them underneath her so he wouldn't have to see them. "Your feet and your eyes," he added.

"My eyes are nothing special. My feet, okay, no argument. But my eyes are just—"

"Wide and dark and full of spirit," he said. "And shining with love for your niece. They're wonderful eyes."

"Oh." She'd never felt comfortable receiving compliments. Even when people gushed about her feet, a reaction she'd grown accustomed to, she always wanted to deflect the flattery with a joke. But she couldn't think of any jokes to defend herself from Ethan's flattery. In a way, this entire conversation was hysterical—but not necessarily funny.

"I'm sure your breasts are fine, too," he added. "They just haven't been my primary focus."

"I think I'm relieved." A tiny laugh escaped her. "Anyway, Ethan, my point was, if you met me in New York City, say, and I was wearing closed shoes, you never would have given me a second look. We would have been two strangers passing each other on a crowded sidewalk."

"Depends on how crowded the sidewalk was."

"Get real. You probably wear suits to work every day."

"I'm expected to. It's that kind of job."

"And I dress in all black. Or I dress funky. I'm probably the only one of all my friends who doesn't have a tattoo—and that's only because I'm afraid of needles."

"Thank God for that. I hate tattoos."

"Okay, so that's my point. We have nothing in common."

"We have plenty in common," he argued. "I hate tattoos, and you don't have a tattoo."

She laughed again, more easily this time. "You're a white-bread businessman, Ethan. I bet you went to prep school."

"Only because my father was on the faculty," he told her. "He teaches classics. As his son, I got a free ride."

Free, schmee. She'd hit a bull's-eye. "Okay, so you're a preppy. Probably went to an Ivy League university, too."

"Amherst College."

"Same thing. I bet you don't know how to eat pasta with a spoon."

"With a fork and spoon together? I've seen it done. I've never done it myself, but—"

"And you know your way around sailboats."

"Well—growing up in Connecticut…"

"And you think New York City is dirty and noisy and full of the great unwashed, and when you go into the city it's to see a Broadway play or some concert at Lincoln Center, and then you flee back to Connecticut right after the final curtain call."

"I…" He shut his mouth, thought for a moment, then spoke again. Keeping his voice level was apparently a struggle. "I don't get down to New York that often," he said. "Believe it or not, we've got plays and concerts in Connecticut. When I go to New York, it's usually for business. I take care of the business and then I go home." He glared at her. "How often do you go to Connecticut?"

"Why would I want to go to Connecticut? I've got everything I want in the city."

"Rolling hills? Clean beaches? Forest ponds? Ponds in Connecticut are complex ecosystems. What have you got in New York—that reservoir in Central Park? It's man-made and it's dead. There are no fish, no algae, not even any insects living in it."

"It's probably got cockroaches. They're everywhere." She smiled, hoping to soften his criticism of her beloved city—and her criticism of his precious, ecosystem-filled corner of southern New England. "I'm sure Connecticut is very nice. All I'm saying is, if it weren't for my friend Carole and your friend—what was his name?"

` "Paul."

"Your friend Paul," she continued, "we never would

have crossed paths. It's only because of some mixed signals that we met.''

"But we did meet. It doesn't matter how.''

"And we have nothing in common.''

He returned her smile. She held her breath, stunned by the sheer male beauty of his smile, the hint of dimples, the startling white of his teeth, the searing flash of confidence in his eyes. "We both like to snorkel,'' he said.

Hearing Alicia's observation coming from his mouth disoriented her even more. "That's only one thing,'' she said, sensing a hint of defensiveness—or maybe desperation—in her tone.

"I'm going snorkeling at Trunk Bay Beach on St. John tomorrow,'' he told her. "I've asked Kim to join me, but I don't know if she will. I'd be happy to take you and Alicia with me. If it's half as amazing as Paul told me it was, you'll want to come.''

She definitely wanted to go, and not just because Trunk Bay Beach was reputedly an amazing place to snorkel. She wanted to go because Ethan would be there and they'd share the one thing they had in common. They'd revel in the sights, surface to compare notes, swim together trailed by streams of bubbles and examine coral formations and schools of fish. She wanted to go because Alicia would find it thrilling, and Alicia deserved every wonderful experience Gina could pack into this week for her.

She wanted to go because Ethan thought she had wonderful eyes. Which was just about the worst reason in the world.

"Ali and I wouldn't miss it,'' she said.

CHAPTER NINE

TO HIS SURPRISE, Kim opted to accompany Gina, Alicia and him to Trunk Bay Beach the next morning. Maybe he shouldn't have been that amazed—her only alternative might have been golf with her father. Compared with that torture, enduring a day at one of the world's preeminent snorkeling sites must have seemed more tolerable to her. Or maybe she'd believed him when he'd said all those things Gina had accused him of saying: that she was a terrific woman; that he was genuinely fond of her; that he didn't regret their relationship, even though it was never going to conclude in a marriage proposal. Clichés, maybe, but he'd meant every word.

Or maybe she'd come along to St. John with the rest of them because she wanted to keep an eye on Gina and him. Not that there was anything to keep an eye on. He'd meant every word he said to Gina, too—but he wasn't going to take action. She didn't want him to. And with Kim around, and the kid, it wouldn't be right. And...

He just wouldn't.

On the other hand, Gina's breasts did rank right up there with her eyes and her feet as parts of her anatomy worthy of worship. She was wearing a swimsuit, of course—a black one-piece that looked as though it had been painted onto her. Maybe she'd worn it instead of a bikini to hide her body from his view, but if that was her plan, it was a monumental failure. The suit outlined the roundness of her bottom, stretched snugly across her belly, nipped in at her waist and swelled over her breasts. When she waded into the water, her nipples hardened.

Terrific breasts, really. Not big, but her feet weren't big, either. Size had never impressed him as much as shape and proportion, and when it came to shape and proportion, Gina Morante was spectacular.

And he was a shallow bastard for thinking about her that way.

Alicia was all pumped up about her nail polish. "Look, Ethan!" she shrieked as they assembled at the water's edge to don their snorkeling gear. She waggled her hands under his nose. "My nails were purple inside, but now they're blue! They change color like magic!"

He tried to fake some enthusiasm for her manicure. Kim's excitement seemed authentic. "Oh, Alicia, your nails came out so nice! Did you polish them yourself?"

Alicia gave her a look that shouted, *What a stupid question!* "Aunt Gina did them for me. She gave me a pedicure, too." She lifted one flippered foot off the packed, wet sand. "She knows all about pedicures. She's a foot professional."

"I'll bet she is." Having apparently exhausted that subject, Kim turned to Gina. "I'm not as good at this snorkeling stuff as you are," she said, studiously ignoring Ethan. "I hope you don't mind if I stick by your side."

"Sure. We should all stay together, anyway. No swimming alone, right, Ali?"

"That's your rule." Alicia clomped into the water, then lifted her feet and started swimming, her flippers transforming from implements that made her walk clumsily to graceful extensions that made her swim like a stingray.

He watched Gina and Kim dive in beside her as he adjusted the straps of his facemask. One woman he didn't want; one he couldn't have. One had claimed she was perfect for him—they could have been handsome together, and upper-class, and they could have joined her father's private golf club and raised children who would know the difference between an iron and a mashie, who would prep not because their father was on the faculty of a private school but because Hamilton offspring always prepped. They could have drunk Absolut martinis together—the very thought made his stomach lurch—and been smugly content with all their blessings.

The other dressed in black and embraced New York City and hung out with tattooed people and *tawked* instead of talked. And he couldn't stop thinking about her.

Alicia surfaced and waved him in. "Come on, Ethan! It's great!" She was probably the only one of the three females who didn't object to his company.

All right. He'd come here to explore the marvelous underwater world of Trunk Bay, not to drown in pointless ruminations on women. He tucked the end of his breathing tube into his mouth and pushed off.

The underwater world was indeed marvelous. The coral formations and shimmering schools of fish were enough to take his mind off the women in his life—or the women *not* in his life, which seemed a more accurate description of both Kim and Gina. He lost track of them, although every now and then he spotted Alicia, her shorter flippers kicking and leaving swirls of sunlit bubbles in their wake. More than once she swam over to him, tugged on his arm and pointed out a vivid anemone or a conch half-buried in the undulating sand beneath them. When he finally surfaced, he saw no sign of Kim or Gina at all. Alicia hovered near him, her hair slick and black, her two skinny braids so tight and smooth they resembled cable wires adorned with turquoise beads. She spit out her breathing tube and yelled, "Isn't this great?"

"Where's your aunt?" he asked, looking around. The water was full of swimmers and snorkelers, but he didn't see a woman in a sleek black swimsuit and fluttering black hair among them.

"She and Kim went in. They said I could stay out here if I stuck by you."

He nodded, thinking that it would have been nice for someone to inform him he'd been assigned baby-sitting duty.

Actually, he didn't mind baby-sitting Alicia. She was a good kid with a broken home awaiting her at the end of the week. She seemed curious about the names of the fish—before coming to St. Thomas, he should have brushed up on tropical ichthyology—and the questions she asked implied that she cared about his answers.

In the six months they'd been together, Kim had never asked him a single question about ecology.

As he and Alicia treaded water, he acknowledged what was really bothering him right now: the prospect of Kim and Gina off on their own, bonding in sisterhood, or antimanhood, or anti-Ethanhood. He wanted Gina to be *his* friend, but maybe she and Kim were developing a friendship, as well, one in which they could gossip about him, compare notes and enumerate every caddish, selfish, sexist thing he'd ever done to either of them. He tried to perform a quick mental inventory of all those things: Breaking up with Kim. Holding Gina's hand. Smirking while Gina punctured Ross Hamilton's pomposity over dinner. Letting Kim believe, as recently as a week ago, that she had a future with him. Deluding not just Kim but himself.

He was a vile specimen, and Gina and Kim were no doubt collaborating like colleagues in the D.A.'s office, constructing an airtight case against him. His only character witness would be Alicia, a seven-year-old girl with bluish-purple fingernails.

Her fingers, he noticed, were also bluish-purple. "I think it's time to leave the water," he suggested. At her pout, he added, "Just for a little while. Then we'll come back in."

"Okay," she grumbled.

They swam together until they were near enough the beach to walk. Ethan looped an arm around Alicia's skinny waist and scooped her off her feet so she could pull off her flippers. She giggled and shrieked, and he impulsively swung her in a circle before setting her down again. She didn't weigh much to begin with, and in the buoyant water she felt absurdly light.

He tugged off his own flippers, then took her hand and helped her wade through the water, which was knee-high for her and barely covered his ankles. Near the water's edge, she slowed and scanned the beach, which was fairly crowded with swimmers, divers and sunbathers. He searched the beach, too, and spotted Gina and Kim in the shade of a couple of palms, at the picnic table where they'd left their outerwear and gear bags.

"There they are." He pointed them out to Alicia.

She came to a complete stop, apparently reluctant to join them. "Do you like Aunt Gina?" she asked.

In more ways than I can tell you. "Sure," he said, keeping his tone casual.

"'Cause she's not married, you know."

He peered down at the little girl. Was she playing

matchmaker? Did she know how unnecessary that was—and how futile? "That's her business, don't you think?"

"I'm just saying." Alicia dropped one of her flippers, picked it up and tried to wipe the sand off with her fingers. Ethan eased it out of her grip and dunked it into the sea to wash it off. When he handed it back to her, she resumed speaking. "'Cause she'll probably get married someday, so if you liked her, I mean, she isn't married this minute."

"I know." Before this week, he'd never in his adult life had a sustained conversation with anyone under the age of fifteen. Now, here he was, discussing Gina's availability with a pushy little girl. He wanted to explain to Alicia that she was way out of her depth, that forces far beyond her ability to manipulate were in control of whatever did or didn't or might or might not exist between him and Gina. But if he said anything like that, she probably wouldn't understand. And in any case, he didn't feel comfortable discussing the subject.

"My uncle Bobby isn't married, either," she said calmly, slipping her hand back into his. "But he doesn't matter, 'cause he's a guy."

"Your aunt Gina mentioned him to me," he said, eager to change the subject.

"He has lots of girlfriends. But Aunt Gina doesn't have a boyfriend. She used to, but she doesn't anymore. I don't know why."

"I don't, either," he said, half to himself. She ought to have dozens of boyfriends, hundreds of them, lining up for the opportunity to win her heart. Perhaps she did. Perhaps she chose—wisely, he thought—not to share this information with her blabbermouth niece.

"I met Aunt Gina's old boyfriend a few times," Alicia said, bristling with self-importance. "He was a policeman like my uncle Bobby."

"Really." Ethan tried to envision Gina kissing a cop. The picture stayed resolutely out of focus.

"He was very handsome. But he wasn't rich like you."

Ethan's mouth slammed shut. What did Alicia know about his personal finances?

"Anyway, I just thought you'd like to know," she said, then abruptly broke from him and trotted across the sand to the table where Gina and Kim sat. He took a minute to collect himself and assess the girl. Gina couldn't have coached her to say these things to him. If she'd wanted to encourage his interest, she'd had the opportunity last night.

No, this was something the kid was doing on her own. Ethan would bet that if Gina knew what Alicia had said to him, she'd throttle her beloved little niece. Grinning, he strode across the sand to the table in the shade.

By the time he reached it, Gina was gone. Alicia and Kim sat at the table, Kim thumbing through a glossy booklet called *Where to Shop on St. John* and Alicia resting her chin in her hands. "Aunt Gina went to the snack bar," she announced. "She's getting us food."

"Food is good." Ethan dropped his snorkeling gear near the table and gazed toward a concession stand not far from their table. "Do you think she needs some help?"

"She said she's paying, because you paid for dinner last night."

"I meant help carrying the food back."

"You're such a gentleman," Kim said dryly, barely glancing up from the booklet. "Go lend her a hand."

Was Kim deliberately pushing him onto Gina? He

didn't know—and he didn't care. If Ross had been at the concession buying food, Ethan would have gone over to help him. He *was* a gentleman.

Alicia's eyes shone eagerly at him. Avoiding her hopeful gaze, he loped over the hot sand to the snack bar and wove through the small crowd to reach Gina, who was up at the counter placing an order, her wallet in her hand. "Hey," he said.

Startled, she turned toward him. "Oh—hi, Ethan. I'm getting hamburgers for everyone. I hope that's okay."

"Sure. I just came to help."

"Help?" She smiled. "I guess those hamburgers can get pretty heavy." She turned back to the counter, where an attendant had wedged four lidded soft-drink cups into a tray with circles cut out of it. While she watched the slender young man assemble her order, Ethan watched her. Her shoulders were nearly horizontal, their bones and hollows unnervingly alluring. Equally sexy was the ridge of her spine, visible above the deep U-shaped back of her swimsuit. The skin of her back had a golden undertone, and it looked as smooth and soft as velvet.

He was taking a crazy chance, and he didn't care. Her nape was calling to him, the sleek shadows of her shoulder blades, the expanse of tawny skin. He slid his hand under her wet, thick hair, then trailed his fingers down the narrow chain of vertebrae to the edge of her swimsuit. Her back was as soft as he'd imagined, but much warmer.

She went very still, her eyes remaining on the food clerk, her hands motionless on the counter. For a moment she seemed to stop breathing. Then she whispered, "Ethan."

He let his hand drop, but stopped himself before apologizing. He wasn't sorry. And anyway, she hadn't snapped at him to bug off and behave himself. All she'd done was say his name, which could have been an invitation as much as a warning.

"Anything else, miss?" the clerk asked in a lilting accent as he balanced four small bags of potato chips atop the burgers.

"No, that's all," she said in a cool, controlled voice. She handed him some money and glanced at Ethan. "If you want to make yourself useful, you could take the potato chips back to the table. They're going to fall off the tray."

"You take the potato chips," he said, piling the bags on the counter and lifting the heavier tray. "I'll carry this."

He didn't wait for her, but instead turned and walked back to the table. The tray was constructed of stiff cardboard, yet he barely felt its rough edges against his palms. His hands felt only the memory of Gina's warm, sexy back.

ONE MORE DAY, she thought as she stuffed her change into her wallet and gathered the bags of potato chips. She paused to grab napkins and straws from the dispensers at the end of the counter, then continued toward the table, watching Ethan up ahead. He had a firm, confident stride, not the sort of swagger she saw in some men but a limber gait, his long legs devouring the distance between the food stand and the picnic table. His wet trunks clung to his butt just enough to make her want to cup her hands around that part of him and squeeze, to see if his muscles were as hard as they looked.

Well, there was an idiotic idea, she thought. She was *not* going to fondle Ethan's butt. She wasn't even going to think about it. She was going to enjoy the rest of today and tomorrow—her last day in the Virgin Islands with Alicia. Sometime during the next forty or so hours, she was going to break the news to Ali that her father had vacated the family homestead, and she was going to comfort Ali and assure her that everything would be all right, even though she had no way of knowing that was true. Sometimes love meant having to lie a little, or at least make baseless assertions.

After she broke the news, she and Ali would fly home—and Ethan, his erstwhile almost-fiancée, her superblond mom and her windbag dad would vanish from Gina's life forever. In two days she'd be back in New York, a city teeming with men who boasted rock-hard butts.

Yeah, right. Before she and Ethan had clashed over the condominium at Palm Point, she'd been in New York City, and none of the rock-hard butts she'd seen there had ever seized her imagination the way Ethan's did.

"Potato chips!" Alicia yelled as Gina neared the table. "Can I have potato chips?"

"Everyone gets a bag," she told Alicia as she distributed them. "They came with the burgers."

"You can have mine," Kim said, pushing her bag across the table to Alicia.

"You don't want them?" Alicia appeared shocked. She obviously couldn't conceive of anyone not wanting potato chips.

"They're fattening. Not that you have to worry about that," Kim said with a smile.

Fattening, hell. Gina tore open her bag and popped a crunchy, salty chip into her mouth. As she chomped down on it, her eyes met Ethan's. He was smiling—and damned if his smile wasn't vastly more enticing than his rear end. He had those luscious dimples. Of course, for all she knew, he might have luscious dimples on his other cheeks, too. The thought made her laugh.

Ethan's smile deepened. If he knew what she'd been thinking, what lewd notion had stimulated that laugh, he'd lose his smile fast enough. Or else he'd smile even more, and run his hand along her back again, and make her sigh as her body shivered in the wake of his touch...

She hadn't been aware of how steamy the midday air was. Actually, it hadn't been as steamy a few minutes ago as it was now. She rearranged herself more comfortably on the bench across the table from Ethan and he brushed one of his feet against one of hers in the sand under the table, his gaze meeting hers to let her know that contact wasn't accidental.

She pulled her foot back. He was playing with her, playing with fire. Last night he'd promised he wouldn't make a pass at her. He'd said he wouldn't touch her again. And here he was, breaking his promise.

To her great discredit, she was glad. Because the thought of never being touched by Ethan was truly depressing.

AFTER LUNCH, Kim announced she was going to take a cab to Cruz Bay to shop. She would meet them at the dock in time to catch the four o'clock ferry back to St. Thomas. She tied a chic, gauzy skirt around her waist, slapped a straw hat onto her head and allowed Ethan to walk her to the beach's entrance to find a cab for her.

Gina contemplated whether to wait for him before heading back into the water with Alicia. If she waited, he might interpret that to mean she welcomed his advances—and his interpretation might be right. But even though his caress by the snack bar had aroused her to a ridiculous degree, she'd have to be crazy to let him think she wanted him to push for more.

Yet if she and Alicia returned to the water while he was up at the road with Kim, that would be rude. Besides, Alicia ought to digest her lunch before she resumed swimming. Gina wasn't sure whether the belief that swimming immediately after eating caused cramps was a myth, but better safe than sorry.

Alicia didn't seem in any rush to go back into the water, anyway. "Do you want to snorkel some more?" Gina asked her.

"Of course I do! It's great." Yet Alicia sat patiently, swinging her feet under the bench and gazing up into the shifting palm fronds above her head.

"So how come you aren't nagging me to go back into the water?"

"I'm digesting."

The last time they'd snorkeled, Alicia hadn't wanted to take the time to digest. "You want to wait for Ethan, right?" Gina guessed.

Alicia giggled. "He's so nice, Aunt Gina. I really think you should—"

"I can't, honey, okay? After tomorrow we're never going to see him again." She needed to convince herself as much as Alicia.

"People see each other all the time," Alicia argued. "If they want to, they can make a plan."

"Well, I don't know that I want to. We'll be leaving St. Thomas on Saturday, and Ethan'll go back home to his home and we'll go back to ours." *And yours will be a disaster,* Gina thought, sighing. "But if you want, we'll wait for him today."

"'Cause we don't want him to come back and not

find us here, and then he'll go snorkeling all by himself, which is dangerous. No swimming alone—that's the rule."

"Then we'll definitely wait. We don't want him breaking any rules." *We most certainly don't,* Gina added silently.

Within a few minutes Alicia spotted him strolling back to the table by himself. "There he is!" she hollered, not bothering to hide her delight. Gina felt a weird flutter in the pit of her stomach as he approached. He looked better from the front than from behind, his chest beautifully muscled, his eyes squinting slightly in the glaring sunlight, his hair a touch lighter than it had been the day, nearly a week ago, when he and the Hamiltons had tried to evict her and Alicia from the condo. His movements had an elegance about them, the sort of refinement Gina credited to a prep school education and a Connecticut address.

"We waited for you," Alicia announced as he drew near.

"That was very nice of you," he said, then glanced at Gina.

"Ali didn't want you swimming alone," she explained, hoping he wouldn't go searching for any other reason.

"So let's swim together," he said, gathering up his snorkeling gear.

They went together, the three of them staying close as they followed the underwater trail of markers and ogled the coral formations and sea life. The water was balmy and the fish were friendly. Ethan freely touched Gina as they swam—her arm, her shoulder, a tug on her hand to get her attention so he could point out a blossoming plant she might have missed. He touched Alicia, too, guiding her around outcroppings and other swimmers. Maybe he was just a toucher, like her.

Gina tried to recall him touching Kim. No, he wasn't a toucher. He must simply feel close to her and Alicia, and comfortable with them. He touched them because it was a way of sharing.

They had snorkeling in common. That afternoon, it was more than enough.

CHAPTER TEN

SHE WANTED that last day for just herself and Alicia—a fact Ethan could appreciate. He respected her wishes, even though respecting them meant he couldn't spend *his* last day with her. But then, what was the use of attaching himself to her? After they left Palm Point tomorrow morning, their roads would diverge, just like in the Robert Frost poem. Gina would be nothing more to him than a slowly fading memory. Years from now, he and Paul would still be laughing about the crazy mix-up with the time-share, and he'd have to struggle to remember her name.

He respected Kim's wishes for her last day on St. Thomas, too. Considering that this vacation wasn't what either of them had hoped for, she'd weathered the situation with poise. For all he knew, she was as relieved by the outcome as he was. If he had come to realize that she was all wrong for him, she'd probably come to realize that he was all wrong for her.

And it could have been worse. They could have come to their realizations while sharing the condo with Kim's parents. Ethan would always be grateful to Gina for having spared him that disastrous fate.

In this deeply respectful mood, he agreed to drive with Kim to Charlotte Amalie for the day. While there, he'd buy a watch for his father, a bottle of rum for his secretary and what the hell, maybe even something for himself. And something for Kim, whatever she wanted—as long as what she wanted wasn't a diamond solitaire.

They drove over the winding mountain roads, beneath a blue sky flocked with cotton-ball clouds. Ethan had grown used to driving on the left side of the road, and he was beginning to recognize some of the goats that grazed along the shoulders. His fingers no longer clamped reflexively around the steering wheel when a jitney or a motorcycle rumbled past them on the right. He no longer tensed when he had to steer the car down a thirty-degree slope or around a hairpin turn. In fact, he'd grown extremely fond of the island, not just for the swimming and snorkeling but for its picturesque roads, its relaxed pace, its friendly citizens—and yes, its goats. Maybe he ought to consider buying a time-share on the island. You never knew whom you might meet through a time-share.

To his right, Kim sat quietly. Occasional glimpses of her reminded him of how incredibly gorgeous she was. He recalled with nostalgia the first time he'd seen her. His first thought had been *God, she's beautiful.* Nothing more, nothing less, nothing complicated. The same notion filled his mind when he saw her today, six months after that first meeting. She really was that beautiful.

And they'd had a decent run, he reflected as he maneuvered the car around an acute bend in the road. He and Kim had given each other their best shot. When they got back to Connecticut, he would likely never see her again, and that understanding made him wistful. It really would have been great if things had worked out. But they hadn't.

Gina had nothing to do with anything.

After wedging the car into a parking space on a narrow, sloping lane a few short blocks from Main Street, he gave an extra yank on the parking brake and sent forth an unvoiced prayer that the car wouldn't roll down the road while they were shopping. Not surprisingly, Kim knew her way around Charlotte Amalie's shopping district. She hustled Ethan up sidewalks and down alleys, zeroing in on this shop for perfume, that boutique for a belt, this kiosk for a mother-of-pearl hair clasp, that outlet for a scarf. Ethan insisted on buying her the scarf, a Hermès rectangle of silk featuring a simple pattern. When she looped it around her neck and asked him what he thought of it, he was once again stricken by her astounding beauty.

"I'm sorry," he said abruptly.

Her perfectly shaped eyebrows flexed, and she studied her reflection in the mirror above the counter. "About what? The scarf doesn't work?"

"The scarf is fine. It's very nice. Let's get it."

"Then what are you sorry about?" she asked as she handed the scarf back to the clerk to ring up.

Ethan passed the clerk his credit card, then turned Kim to face him. She looked placid yet determined, someone used to getting what she wanted. Maybe, once she'd analyzed things, she'd recalibrated her goals—skip the wedding proposal, get the Hermès scarf—and she'd achieved those new goals.

However, he had to finish the apology he'd begun. "I'm sorry this vacation didn't turn out the way we'd planned."

"Well." She shrugged and accepted the shopping bag from the clerk as Ethan signed the charge slip. "My mother got to stay in a luxury hotel and my father played plenty of golf. Things could have been worse."

Did she think he was apologizing for the screwup with Paul's condo? "I meant, I'm sorry our…" No, he wasn't going to use the word *relationship*. It was one of those terms men preferred to avoid. "I'm sorry this isn't ending with wedding bells. That was what you wanted, wasn't it?"

"Oh, don't worry about me. I turned down two other marriage proposals while you and I were dating. I'm sure there'll be many more." She hooked the bag's handles over her wrist and sashayed out of the shop, leaving Ethan blinking in confusion.

Two other marriage proposals? Had she been seeing other guys while she'd been dating him? Was he supposed to be flattered that she'd declined their offers of marriage?

Shaking off his shock, he hurried out of the shop and searched the pedestrians crowding the sidewalk. He spotted Kim half a block away at the center of a milling throng, using her hand to shield her eyes from the glare as she stared through a window at an array of jewelry. He worked his way through the crowd to her. "Tanzanite," she said.

"What?"

"This jewelry is all tanzanite. These are fabulous prices."

He'd never even heard of tanzanite. "Do you want to go in?"

She shook her head. "I think I shot my load with the Chopard watch."

She stepped away from the store, but he grabbed her hand before she could get too far ahead of him. "Kim. Who was proposing marriage to you while we were dating?"

"Nobody you know," she said blithely. She started down the sidewalk and he fell into step beside her. "Men ask me to marry them all the time, Ethan," she explained. "You're probably the first man I've ever been involved with who *didn't* ask me to marry him. That made you very special to me."

"I see." So if he'd given her the proposal she'd been angling for, would she have turned him down and gone off in search of someone more special?

"There will be others. There are *always* others." She paused again at another window. "Ooh. Cartier."

He stood by patiently while she scrutinized the jewelry. After a minute, she sighed, straightened up and resumed her walk. Ethan adjusted his stride to remain even with her. "I do wish we hadn't wasted the opportunity for sex," she went on. "Once my parents were no longer staying in the condo, we could have had a good time."

"Yes, but—" He sighed, aware of how old-fashioned he was about to sound. "Once I saw that we weren't going anywhere with our…" Again he choked on the word *relationship*. "That we weren't going anywhere," he said, "I thought sex would be…I don't know."

"It would have been good. It was always good, Ethan."

It wouldn't have been loving, though. It wouldn't have included the emotional component, the intimate connection. It just would have been…sex. Not that there was anything wrong with sex, of course. But Ethan wanted intimacy along with physical pleasure. He wanted to look into his lover's eyes and see more than mere satisfaction in them. He wanted a woman who laughed with her whole body, who considered coral reefs more precious than coral jewelry, who let passion seep into everything she did.

He wasn't sure what Kim wanted, but he had no doubt she would find it. That understanding eased his mind.

She didn't need to hear how sorry he was; she didn't seem to care. He was done apologizing.

"How about a drink?" he offered.

She flashed him a smile—a breathtakingly pretty one. "As long as it has rum in it," she said.

THE DAY WAS SUBDUED. The sun didn't shine as brightly as it had earlier in the week, and puffy clouds drifted across the sky. The beach at Palm Point was less crowded than usual, the waves gentler, the breezes muted. St. Thomas seemed to be toning itself down, preparing to say goodbye to Gina and Alicia.

Gina considered it miraculous that she could hold her own in her conversations with her niece while her mind kept wandering off. It traveled, alternately, down two paths. She'd capture it and drag it back from one path only to have it escape down the other.

The first path led to thoughts of the ghastly news she had to break to Alicia. *Sweetie, you know that prick Mommy married? Right, the asshole you call Daddy. Well, he's gone. Bye-bye, ciao, sayonara.* No, that wouldn't do.

Alicia, your father loves you more than life itself, but he just couldn't stay home anymore. For your sake, because he loves you so very, very much, he had to leave. Alicia would see through that bull without having to squint.

Alley Cat, your mother loves you madly, and I do, too. And so do your grandparents. Things could be worse. That might work.

"I said," Alicia broke into her ruminations, "I'm going to fill the bucket with water and I'll be right back. I'm not going in the water by myself, except maybe my feet."

"Okay," Gina said, giving her head a sharp shake. "Up to your ankles. I'll keep an eye on you."

She watched Alicia scamper down to the water's edge, swinging her bucket, and her mind strayed down the other path, the Ethan path.

He would have chosen to spend the day with her and Alicia. She'd known it without his having to ask. The desire had glowed in his eyes and whispered in the curve of his mouth when he'd smiled, in the brush of his hand against hers as they'd both reached for the coffee decanter at the same time that morning. All yesterday afternoon when they'd snorkeled together, she'd known. Last night, after she'd washed up and was crossing the hall to join Alicia in dreamland, and he'd stepped out of the master bedroom at the same time, and their gazes had collided, and they'd both stood motionless, watching each other while the minutes stretched like taffy....

The yearning was there.

But nothing would come of it. She didn't *want* anything to come of it. This vacation was for her and Alicia, a week away from all the crap in Alicia's life. And even if Alicia hadn't been with her, Gina wouldn't have chosen to start anything she couldn't finish—especially with a representative of the blue blood elite.

So she and Alicia spent the day by themselves on the beach, building sand castles, digging moats, constructing bridges. "This can be the Frog's Neck Bridge," Alicia declared as she molded the damp sand above a moat.

"The *Throgs* Neck Bridge," Gina corrected her.

"How come they named it that?" Alicia asked. "It's a silly name."

"It's a pretty bridge, though. Have you ever driven over it?"

Alicia shook her head. "I don't think so. It goes to

Long Island, and we never go to Long Island. I wish it was called the *Frog's* Neck Bridge. That would be so funny." She didn't laugh, though. She worked diligently, solemnly, as if compelled to finish her bridge before the clouds thickened and covered the sun.

They would cover it, Gina thought sadly. Even if the sky cleared, the clouds of tomorrow loomed on the horizon. Alicia would be going home to a broken family, and Gina would be going home to a life without Ethan.

Which was a really stupid thing to be upset about, since a week ago she'd never even heard of him.

At four o'clock they rinsed off the bucket and shovel, shook the sand out of their towels and climbed the hill to building six. Once inside the apartment, they took turns showering, got dressed and headed off for dinner at the restaurant just down the beach, where they'd eaten the first night. Like that night, Alicia ended her meal with a butterscotch sundae. She smiled as she ate it, but her eyes looked worried, as if she knew the evening wasn't going to end well.

They walked back to Palm Point on the brick path that edged the beach. A bench near the path beckoned, and Gina led Alicia over to it. They sat and stared at the water, an expanse of deep blue in the dwindling light. "I don't want to leave," Alicia said, just like that first night. "I want to stay here forever."

"So do I," Gina admitted. "But we've got to go home."

Alicia leaned her head against Gina's shoulder. "This has been the absolutely best vacation in my life, Aunt Gina."

Gina arched her arm around the girl's shoulders and pulled her close. "Ali, I've got to tell you something. I don't want to, but I have to. Okay?"

"Okay." Alicia peered up at her.

"When we go home tomorrow, your daddy isn't going to be at your house."

"Does he have to work? Sometimes he has to work on weekends."

Yeah, right, Gina nearly blurted out. *He says he's working, but he's really spending the weekend with the Other Woman.* "I don't know if he has to work," she said honestly. "What I know is, he won't be living in your house anymore. He and your mommy decided it would be best if he moved out."

"Why?" Alicia's eyes glistened. "Because of his girlfriend?"

Gina nodded. "It's called being separated. Your parents are going to be separated now."

"When will he come home?" Alicia asked in a quivering voice.

"I'm sure he'll come over to the house so he can see you." Gina was sure of no such thing, but she had to offer Alicia some hope to cling to. "The thing is, I don't think he and your mommy are going to stay married."

"They're getting a divorce?"

"I think so."

Alicia started to cry. Tiny sobs shook her and she buried her face against Gina's breast. "I don't want them to get a divorce."

"I know, Ali. It stinks, doesn't it?"

"I want everybody to be together. I want us all to live at home."

Gina ran her hands over Alicia's soft, dark hair, ferreting out the narrow braids and fingering the turquoise beads. "I wish I could make the whole thing better. I wish your parents could stay together. But it looks like that's not going to happen. You'll be all right, Alley Cat.

Your mommy will take care of you and she loves you so much. And I love you. I'll always be there for you.''

"But I want—I want—'' Alicia's voice dissolved into weeping.

"I know.'' She ran her fingers through Alicia's hair again, touching the beads and wishing the kid could take more home from this week than just those bright turquoise baubles, and a shirt and some nail polish that changed color. She wished Alicia could take home the peaceful wind, the spicy fragrance of the flowers, the magical silence of the fish they'd viewed through their snorkeling masks. She wished Alicia could take home the warmth and the leisurely rhythm of life on the island, the satisfaction of being able to build bridges with just a bit of sand and sea water.

But the one thing Alicia wanted more than anything, Gina couldn't give her. So she only hugged her, and stroked her, and let her cry.

SHE COULDN'T SLEEP.

She'd managed to get Alicia down for the night, though it hadn't been easy. She'd lain beside her in bed and sung to her, not songs from *The Little Mermaid* but traditional lullabies she hoped would soothe the grieving child—"Tu-ra-lu-ra,'' "Hush, Little Baby,'' "All the Pretty Little Horses'' and an old Grateful Dead lullaby with the haunting refrain, "I will take you home.'' That was the song Alicia had fallen asleep to.

Once Alicia was sleeping deeply, Gina packed their suitcases. Venturing to the kitchen to prepare and wrap sandwiches and the few leftover cookies so they'd have something to snack on during their layover at the airport in Miami, she heard no noises from the master bedroom. Had Ethan and Kim departed? Without saying goodbye?

The few items they'd left lying around the living room during the week—shopping directories and catalogs, a tube of imported French sunscreen, beach towels spread across the backs of the dining area chairs to dry—were gone. Maybe Ethan and Kim were gone, too.

Just as well, Gina told herself. Saying goodbye to Ethan would have been awkward. This way they could avoid the whole thing.

Still, just as Alicia had a gaping hole in her heart, Gina had a hole in hers, small-bore but clean through. She'd wanted to say goodbye to Ethan. Actually, no— of all the things she'd wanted to say to Ethan, goodbye wasn't on the list.

Which was why he'd undoubtedly done them both a favor by clearing out with Kim tonight.

By midnight, everything was crammed into the suitcases except Alicia's pajamas, the oversize T-shirt Gina was using as a nightgown, their still-drying swimsuits, which were draped over the shower curtain rod in the bathroom, and the clothing and toiletry items they'd need in the morning. She crawled into bed, closed her eyes, listened to Alicia's faint snores and felt adrenaline zing through her body. No way was she going to be able to sleep.

Sighing, she swung out of bed, tiptoed to the door and stepped out into the hall.

Some of the best moments of her vacation had been spent on the terrace, letting the gorgeous Caribbean night wrap around her. Why not enjoy at least part of her last night out there? Why lie awake in bed, punching her pillow and kicking at the sheets, when she could be sitting outside, listening to the ocean and letting the breezes dance around her?

She had the slider half-open when she spotted Ethan

in his usual chair, so still she thought he might be asleep. But he wasn't. When she didn't push the door the rest of the way, he turned to her. He looked neither pleased nor surprised to see her. In fact, he looked almost resigned.

She hesitated, unsure whether to join him. She was scarcely dressed—a baggy T-shirt and panties didn't exactly qualify as fully clothed. As her gaze took him in, she realized that he was wearing only a loose-fitting pair of athletic shorts. As much of him had been exposed every time they'd gone swimming together. But his skin was dry now, the contours of his muscles barely visible in the hazy moonlight, and his gaze drilled through her.

She hovered in the doorway. He remained silent. "I couldn't sleep," she finally said.

"Neither could I."

That seemed reason enough to take her place beside him. She dropped onto the chair next to his, kicked her feet up on the railing, then quickly lowered them when the hem of her shirt shimmied up to her hips.

"How's Alicia?" he asked. "Did you tell her about her father?"

Tears pricked her eyes. It wasn't enough that he was glorious to look at, with his long, strong swimmer's legs, his broad shoulders and those damn dimples. He also had to be compassionate about the feelings of a seven-year-old kid.

"She pretty much cried herself to sleep," Gina told him.

He winced. "She's lucky she's got you."

"Even if her parents had the best marriage in the world, she'd be lucky to have me," Gina boasted, trying to lighten the mood. She didn't want to fall apart on her last night here, especially in front of Ethan.

"She would," Ethan said without a hint of a smile.

His words moved her. Despite her attempt to remain composed, fresh moisture gathered in her eyes, filling them, overflowing. "It broke my heart, having to tell her. I can't stand causing her pain."

"You didn't cause her pain. Her parents did."

"I was the one who had to tell her." Her voice faltered and she swatted her cheeks with her hands. "It broke my heart, Ethan." She couldn't wipe away the tears fast enough. They streamed through her eyelashes and spilled down her face.

He gazed at her for a moment, then reached for her hand and pulled her out of her chair, into his lap. She was too startled to resist—and then not startled at all. Settling on his bony knees, she sank against him, rested her head on his shoulder, let his chest cushion her body, and wept. He wrapped one arm around her and toyed with the ends of her hair. His other hand held hers, strong and comforting. His skin grew damp as her tears got trapped between her cheek and the hollow above his collarbone. Did he realize how generous he was, letting her sob against him like this? Did he know that, for this one moment, he was everything she needed?

Eventually she wound down. She issued a quick sniffle and a faint hiccup, then subsided, taking long, steady breaths until she was certain she'd run out of tears.

"Are you all right?" he asked. His chest vibrated against her when he spoke.

"Relatively speaking. I'm sorry, Ethan, I shouldn't have—"

"What? You shouldn't have been sad? It's a sad thing Alicia's going through. Why shouldn't you be sad?"

"Well, okay, I should be sad. But I shouldn't have fallen apart." She was glad she couldn't see his face.

Talking about her melodramic little display was embarrassing enough when she was addressing the underside of his jaw.

"Why shouldn't you fall apart?" he persisted. "You're allowed."

"Thanks."

"I mean it, Gina. You've been so strong for Alicia through this whole vacation. Who says you can't be weak now?"

She eased back from him. He was right; she was allowed to be weak for a few minutes. She needed someone to lean on right now, and Ethan was letting her lean on him. He was actually welcoming her weight, inviting it. She was more grateful than she could say.

He stared at her for a long, loaded minute, and her gratitude faded, replaced by other, more troubling, more restless emotions. Oh, she was definitely weak. And maybe he was, too—or maybe he was so strong she had no choice but to surrender as he slid his hands up to her cheeks, pulled her face down and kissed her. Softly at first, just a brush of lips to lips. Then again, a little less gently, a little more resolutely.

With the third kiss, she was ready to wave a white flag.

Her entire body flooded with heat. Her fingers clenched his shoulders, clung to them, and her spine seemed to melt, making her feel limp. His tongue surged against hers, slid over her teeth, traced her lips and surged again. The air around her sang with murmurs and sighs and whispered pleas—whether coming from him or her she didn't know. His hands roamed across the smooth cotton of her shirt, then under the bottom edge and up across her belly, her midriff, her breasts. Her thighs tensed and she felt his arousal through his shorts.

"Ethan." Her voice emerged faint and wavering.

"Shh." He seemed to be trying to calm himself as much as her. One of his hands cupped the underside of her breast, his fingertips moving in teasing circles against her skin. His other hand rested at her waist, holding her so she wouldn't slide off his lap. He rested his forehead against hers, his breathing ragged.

"We can't do this," she said.

He closed his eyes for a long moment, then opened them and kissed the sensitive skin alongside her earlobe. "We can do anything we want," he said.

"What are you, crazy? This is totally insane. We're outdoors—"

"No one else is here. We're all alone."

"Kim is right inside—"

"Kim and I broke up."

"You've been sleeping together every night."

"Sharing a room, that's all."

She leaned back. A part of her wanted to believe him. Another part—the part that was Ramona's loyal sister and Jack Bari's cynical sister-in-law—considered his words a crock. "Sharing a room? Is that what it's called?"

"That's all it is." He kissed that tingly spot by her ear again, and she wanted to slap him—or slap herself for feeling that single seductive kiss throughout her entire her body. "Gina." Another devastating kiss, and his thumb sketched a line toward her nipple, which was hard and burning. His light stroke was so wildly arousing, she moaned. "Just let me kiss you," he said, his low voice rubbing her nerves the way his thumb rubbed her breast.

"You're doing more than kissing me," she pointed out, although she couldn't find it in her to ask him to stop.

He grazed the hinge of her jaw, then kissed under her chin. Apparently, he wasn't going to waste any more time justifying himself to her. He was just going to...*kiss* her.

Her thighs clenched again as his lips found the pulse point in her neck, as he nipped with his teeth. His other hand, the one not on her breast, skimmed up under her shirt and across her back, warm and comforting. She wondered if she should be touching him, too—not just hanging on to his shoulders for dear life but caressing him, tracing his sleek muscles, tasting the skin of his jaw and his brow and his naked chest. That skin would taste like her tears, she thought—and it would taste like Ethan.

She was right—it was crazy, totally insane. But she had to have just one taste.

When her mouth touched his shoulder he let out a muffled groan. That tight, helpless sound made her want to kiss him more, kiss every square inch of his body, including those parts that were currently clothed—yet it also reminded her of who she and Ethan were, where they were and where they'd be tomorrow. Bad enough that she'd never see him again. Far worse that, no matter how he explained it, he'd come to St. Thomas with a woman who was his maybe-almost-potential fiancée, who was presently asleep in the bedroom he was sharing with her. And Gina wasn't going to be someone's Other Woman. She simply wasn't.

Drawing back from him caused a pain in her chest, so sharp she wondered whether she was suffering a heart attack. The fact that she was twenty-six years old, in excellent health, and she could actually feel the strong, steady beat of her heart was enough to convince her the pain lacked a physical source. It was disappointment, regret, frustration and a hefty measure of anger directed at herself.

"I can't do this," she said.

He opened his eyes and sighed. She observed the rise and fall of his chest as he breathed, the gradual clearing of his eyes as they focused on her. His hair was mussed—had she done that?—and his erection still dug into the soft flesh of her bottom—*that* she'd take credit for—but like her, he was regaining control, coming down to earth, back to reality. "Okay," he said hoarsely. "Okay. You're right."

She wanted to thank him for supporting her decision, but this was one of those situations where the less said, the better. "I'll go now," she murmured.

His arms tightened around her for a moment, as if he couldn't bear to let her go. Then he relented, lowering his hands and shifting his knees so she could stand more easily. Her legs wobbled under her for a moment, her thighs and hips aching. He must have noticed her shakiness, because he sprang to his feet and held her again, his hands at her waist—outside her T-shirt, thank God—and his face close enough for his breath to touch her cheeks. "Are you all right?" he asked, just as he had when she'd first joined him on the terrace.

"I'm just fine," she said, not caring if he believed her—or if she believed herself.

He sighed, leaned forward and kissed her forehead. Then he straightened, stared at her with wistful eyes, and whispered, "Good night, Gina."

"Goodbye, Ethan," she said, because she needed to hear the finality of it. Slipping free of his embrace, she crossed to the door and stepped inside, into the air-conditioned darkness of the apartment. *Goodbye, Ethan,*

she repeated silently as she moved away from him, down
the hall to her room. She entered it, shut the door and
pressed the button lock in the knob, not to keep him out
but to keep her longing in.

CHAPTER ELEVEN

"HELLO?"

Bingo. Ethan recognized the voice. He'd heard it once before, about two months ago, when he'd answered the telephone in St. Thomas one morning. The voice sounded similar enough to Gina Morante's to cause pleasure to flash through him—unwarranted pleasure, because it *wasn't* Gina's voice. It was a bit higher, the New York accent a shade more muted.

No matter. He'd dialed the right number and gotten through. Finally.

He'd already tried every possible spelling of Morante he could imagine—Meranti, Maranty and a dozen other varieties. His Internet phone directory had produced a surprisingly paltry number of Morantes of any spelling residing in Manhattan, and none of them had a first initial of *G* or *J*. Why hadn't he thought to ask Gina how she spelled her name? Why couldn't her name have been Mary Jones? He supposed Jones could be spelled "Joans" or "Jowens," though.

In any case, none of the assorted Morante numbers had belonged to Gina.

So he'd decided to track down Alicia, instead. He remembered that she lived in White Plains and that her last name was Barry. Or at least he'd thought it was Barry. He'd just learned, thanks to hearing Gina's sister's voice through his telephone's receiver, that the name was actually Bari; he'd tried that spelling after striking out with all the Barrys in White Plains.

"Hello?" she repeated, jarring him from his victorious thoughts.

He acknowledged that he was a long way from victory. All he'd done was track down Gina's sister. Whether the woman would grant him access to Gina was an entirely new challenge.

She might not, but Alicia would. He and Alicia had—well, *bonded* might be too strong a word, but they'd certainly gotten to be pals during their week in St. Thomas. They'd snorkeled together. They'd discussed iguanas. They'd built the Brooklyn Bridge out of sand. Alicia had told him about her father's girlfriend.

And the wronged wife was waiting on the other end of the line for him to speak. "Yes, hi," he said quickly, reining in his vagrant thoughts. "My name is Ethan Parnell. I'm wondering, is Alicia there?"

"Alicia? You want to talk to Alicia?" Her tone seethed, on the verge of boiling. "Who the hell are you?"

He was a grown man, a total stranger, phoning and asking to speak to a seven-year-old girl. Of course her mother was suspicious. "I'm—"

"Mommy, is it for me?" Alicia chirped in the background.

"Hush, honey. Go review the page in your spelling workbook."

"Is it for me?" Alicia asked again, her voice full of sunshine. She might have cried herself to sleep her last night at Palm Point, but she sounded happy enough now. Had her father seen the light, sent his girlfriend packing and returned to his family? If he hadn't, had her mother and Gina done a phenomenal job of reassuring her that she was still loved and her home was still a safe place?

And when exactly had Ethan become so fascinated by the domestic travails of a spunky little girl?

"I met Alicia in St. Thomas," he said before Gina's sister could lambaste him. "She and Gina wound up accidentally booked into a time-share condo the same week I was there."

"You shared a time-share," the woman said, her suspicion now layered with skepticism.

"Didn't Gina tell you?" He thought of reminding her that he'd answered her call that one morning, but decided to let her search her memory without his assistance.

A long silence ensued. He lifted his gaze from the phone on his desk; sending invisible *trust me* vibes through the wire wasn't going to work. His office was small but tasteful, the furniture blond oak, the area rug a hand-tied Persian, one wall consumed by bookshelves, another by a window that overlooked a small park and a third wall decorated with framed posters and photographs of sites the Gage Foundation had helped to preserve. The door in the fourth wall was firmly closed. He didn't want his secretary eavesdropping on this particular call.

"Who is it?" Alicia shouted in the distance. "Can I talk to them?"

Gina's sister relented. "Okay, so she mentioned something about that," she said, her inflection uncannily similar to Gina's.

What was the sister's name? Mona, perhaps, or Rona… Her sister's name was quite possibly the only thing about Gina that Ethan didn't remember. Everything else about her was etched into his memory, from her coal-black hair to her elegant toes, from her sarcastic wit to her rousing laugh, from her tears to her kisses. Since returning home from St. Thomas, he hadn't lived a day without thinking about her, wondering about her, remembering those few crazed minutes on the terrace their last night, when he'd believed he would have done anything, *anything* to have her.

Maybe they'd both succumbed to vacation madness that night, some sort of tropical fever. Maybe he'd been suffering a bizarre reaction to his breakup with Kim. Or maybe, as the song went, it was just one of those things. He'd never know—unless he saw Gina again.

"I'm trying to reach Gina," he said. "I couldn't find her phone number anywhere—"

"Don't you think she'd have given it to you if she wanted to hear from you?"

"I…" He faltered. Why hadn't he asked for her number before she'd disappeared from his life? "I don't think it occurred to either of us," he said, then considered that answer and decided it was reasonably true. "Things were hectic at the end." More than reasonably true. Those deep, hungry kisses, that desperate groping, the tears, the touches… *Hectic* summed it up. "I don't intend to bother her," he assured the sister. "We were all thrown together for a week, and a friendship developed. I just want to say hi, that's all."

Another pause. The sister took her time mulling things over. Finally she sighed. "You said your name was Ethan?"

"Ethan!" Alicia shrieked, her voice blasting through the phone line. "Is it Ethan, Mommy? I wanna talk to him!"

Bless you, Alicia, he mouthed. He recalled her solemnly informing him, that day at Trunk Bay Beach, that

Gina didn't have a boyfriend, and a smile tugged at his mouth. She'd been in his corner right from the start. "Can I say a quick hello to Alicia?" he asked in his gentlest, least threatening voice.

"Mommy, Mommy, Mommy! Can I talk to Ethan?" Alicia bellowed from her end.

Two against one; Alicia's mother didn't stand a chance. "All right," she said reluctantly. "Just for a minute."

Alicia let out a whoop, and then he heard the rattle of the phone changing hands. "Ethan? It's me!"

"Hey, Alley Cat," he greeted her, loving her even more because she was so damn enthusiastic. "How are you?"

"I'm great. I'm in second grade now," Alicia bragged. "My teacher let me tell the class about snorkeling. I drew a picture of a snorkel on the blackboard, and I talked about the fish and the coral and those water flowers—an-enemies?"

"Anemones," he corrected her.

"Uh-huh. And my best friend, Caitlin, is in my class."

"That's nice."

"And I see my daddy twice a week. He buys me ice cream. My mom thinks that's not healthy, but Aunt Gina let me eat ice cream in St. Thomas. With butterscotch sauce."

He inhaled slowly, hoping to drain any unruly emotion out of his voice before asking, "How's Aunt Gina?"

"She's great! She's got shoes in Fashion Week!"

Ethan had no idea what that meant, but Alicia made it sound like the best possible news. "Wow! That's terrific!"

"Now she's working on something new. She said the new shoes she's making are going to look like fish. I bet they're weird."

"No kidding." She'd hide those beautiful feet of hers in shoes that looked like *fish?*

"Finish up now, Alicia," her mother said. Monica, perhaps? Ethan remembered her name having three syllables. "It's time to say goodbye."

"Will you call me again?" Alicia asked into the phone.

"If your mother lets me."

"Can I see you?"

"I'd like that. I'd like to see your aunt, too. Do you think she'd like to see me?" He cringed as the words rushed out. Did he sound too eager? Would Alicia think he was only using her to get to Gina?

"I don't know. She's very busy with Fashion Week."

"I'm sure she is. And you're busy with school, and I'm busy with work. But it would still be fun for us all to see each other, don't you think?"

"Say goodbye, Alicia," Gina's sister commanded.

"I gotta go. I've got *spelling*," she groaned, as if it were some sort of disease.

"Great talking to you, Ali. Please put your mother back on, okay?"

"Okay. Goodbye!"

He heard more rattling as the phone changed hands again, and then Alicia's mother's voice: "So. You're happy now?"

"No, I'm not happy. I mean, yes, I'm happy, but I'd be happier if you gave me Gina's phone number."

"Forget it. I'm not giving it to you."

"How about her work number?" She worked for a public company, didn't she? A place where Fashion

Week people could get shoes that looked like fish. If only he knew the name of her shoe company, he'd have phoned her there and not wasted hours telephoning all the Barrys and Baris in White Plains.

Yet another long silence ensued while the sister weighed her options. "All right, look," she finally said. "If I hear anything about you pestering her, or stalking her—"

"I'm not going to—"

"Or anything that makes me regret giving you her number at work, I'm going to have the cops on you so fast you'll get whiplash just from their locking you into handcuffs. I can do that, you know. My brother is a cop."

"I know."

"I mean it. I don't want you bothering her."

"I know you mean it, and I won't bother her." Was she this shrewish all the time? Not that he condoned her husband's infidelity, but there were two sides to every story. Maybe the guy had had his reasons for seeking another woman.

"Because if you do bother her—"

"Right. Your brother."

She fell silent again. Had she heard the impatience in his tone? Was she going to punish him for it? He waited anxiously. "Okay," she said. "Here's her work number."

He jotted the digits down and disavowed the nasty thoughts he'd had about her. She wasn't a shrew. She was a saint. He adored Mona-Rona-Monica, whatever her name was. He worshiped her.

He thanked her three times, then decided he was coming across as too obsequious and ended the call. Staring at the phone number he'd scrawled onto his memo pad, he smiled. Alicia's mother might have been right when she'd said that if Gina had wanted to hear from him, she would have given him her number herself. Possessing her work number offered no guarantees that she'd talk to him, let alone agree to see him.

But it was a start.

FORTUNATELY, chaos didn't faze Gina. The main design room of Bruno Castiglio Shoes—a cavernous, brightly lit space in a Seventh Avenue postwar, cluttered with drafting tables, rolls of paper, mock-ups and prototypes of shoes, cartons of samples and boxes of swatches—existed in a permanent state of chaos. Bruno stood near his worktable at the far end of the room, yammering into his telephone. When he was under pressure, his voice rose and became more staccato. As preparations for New York City's Fashion Week raced toward their final stages, he'd come to sound as shrill and rapid as a jackhammer chewing up concrete at a construction site.

In the past, Gina wouldn't have minded. After her trip to St. Thomas, however, she'd lost some of her tolerance for noise. Her week there had given her a taste for tranquillity. Sometimes, when she was walking to work, the din of traffic—blaring horns, wheezing buses, pedestrians babbling into cell phones and the ubiquitous clamor of jackhammers at some construction site or other—actually annoyed her. It never had before.

Not that she'd be able to survive on a full diet of island life. One week hadn't been long enough for her to grow weary of the balmy winds, the soothing surge and ebb of the sea, the brilliance of the stars in a night sky devoid of smog and light pollution. Two weeks in paradise, though, and she would have been tearing at her hair. She *was* an island girl, as long as the island was Manhattan.

But she missed St. Thomas. She missed the salty ocean fragrance, the lush heat, the freedom to do nothing but play in the sand and the high-quality time she'd had with Alicia. St. Thomas haunted her. Over the past few weeks, she'd been working on designs for shoes constructed of iridescent fabrics, some silver, some bluish, some white, like the fish she'd seen while snorkeling.

She was probably fixated on the place because it had been a vacation—a long overdue one, arriving at a time when she'd needed a break from the daily hustle-bustle of her life. Her dreams were filled with St. Thomas because Alicia had been such a sweetie and the beach had been so clean and soft and warm. There was nothing more to it than that.

The abrupt ring of the phone occupying the corner of her drafting table jolted her. The company had three phone lines, and in the days leading up to Fashion Week, Bruno usually tied up all three single-handedly. Right now, apparently, he'd left one line open. She lifted the receiver. "Yes?"

Meg, the administrative assistant who worked in the relative peace of a tiny office adjacent to the design room, said, "Gina? It's for you. Personal, I think, but he wouldn't give his name."

"Wonderful," she groaned. A legitimate personal call would have reached her via her cell phone. This must be some weirdo who'd tracked her down through her job. Whom had she met recently? She hadn't been doing much partying or club hopping in the past few weeks. She'd been too tired, what with all the demands of Fashion Week. At least, that was the best excuse she'd come up with for why she'd been lately spending most of her evenings by herself, quietly.

She did have a plan for tonight, at least. She was taking Carole out for a belated thank-you dinner. She'd wanted to do something special to repay her friend for the use of the time-share at Palm Point, but Carole's recent schedule had been as crazy as her own.

Or maybe that was just another excuse. Gina suspected she'd been putting off the thank-you dinner because she was still assimilating the week she'd spent at Palm Point, still trying to decide how grateful she was for Carole's having crossed wires with some bozo named Paul, forcing Gina and Alicia to share the condo with—

"Hello?" a man's voice broke through her cluttered thoughts.

Not just a man's voice. Ethan's voice.

She pulled the receiver away from her head and stared at it. Why was she hearing Ethan's voice through this piece of molded plastic?

"Gina? Are you there?"

She pressed the receiver back to her ear, clamped her free hand over her other ear to shut out Bruno's abrasive chatter about why some top-name designer wanted to have his runway models shod in Manolo Blahnik instead of Bruno Castiglio, and said, "Ethan?"

"I found you! I can't believe it. I've been trying to track you down for weeks."

"You have?"

"I got this number from your sister."

When had he spoken to Ramona? Did they know each other? Why hadn't Ramona told Gina that Ethan had contacted her? Why did Gina suddenly feel as if she were swimming underwater, lost in that alien universe, sensing no gravity and unsure which way was up?

"I had to twist her arm to give me your work number. She wouldn't give me your home number, and you're not listed in the directory."

"I don't have a land line," she told him. "It's a cell phone. It's not in the directory." Why were they talking about her phone number? She had spent the past two months trying not to think about whatever the hell had flared between them their final night on St. Thomas—whatever the hell had flared between them the entire week they'd been together. She'd berated herself for wasting her mental energy on him. He was a privileged, polished Connecticut fellow, sort-of not-quite engaged to a woman—or at the very least sleeping with her, whatever the hell *that* was all about. Gina and Ethan had become friends the way soldiers sharing a foxhole might; odd circumstances had thrown them together, and there had been a certain amount of chemistry, and that last night those kisses had been a complete and utter mistake. Gina had been sad about leaving St. Thomas, far sadder about her sister's wrecked marriage and its impact on Alicia, and she'd let her emotions carry her away. She was usually not that stupid.

So why was Ethan on the phone? Why had he tracked her down at work? How had he managed to call her at a rare moment when Bruno wasn't tying up all three lines?

"I'd like to see you," he said.

She still felt as if she were underwater, blowing bubbles and kicking against the current. But now, at least she could make out some signposts—a bit of coral reef, the rippled sand below, the sun broken into glints of light across the surface of the water above. *He'd like to see you,* she thought.

Would she like to see him?

She sucked in a deep breath—and coughed, as if some water had come through the snorkel tube along with the air.

"We could meet somewhere, or I could come downtown, if you'll give me the address of your office."

She should have said no—because he was a privileged, polished Connecticut fellow, maybe engaged, and all that. Instead, she said, "When?"

"How about today?"

Today? Was he in New York now? Why did she still feel as though she were caught in a riptide? "What about Kim?" she asked.

"Kim and I ended our relationship in St. Thomas, Gina. Remember? You were there."

"Well…maybe you were just telling me you weren't going to marry her because you wanted to mess around with me."

"I didn't want to 'mess around' with you," he said, pronouncing the phrase as if it disgusted him. "There was something going on between you and me. You know that as well as I do. It wasn't 'messing around.' It was something else."

"What was it?"

"Damned if I know. But I'd like to find out. Can we get together?"

She sighed. Closing her eyes, she tuned out Bruno's hysterical blathering on the other two phone lines, the UPS guy in natty brown shorts who was dumping a carton of samples on the floor near the door, the off-key humming Geoffrey, the company's chief engineer, indulged in when he was concentrating, the blinding fluorescent lights and the scents of leather and solvent and rubber that wafted around her desk. Damned if she knew what was going on between her and Ethan, either—assuming something *was* going on between them. Perhaps they'd only been acting out a tropical fantasy during that week on St. Thomas. If she hadn't been with Alicia and he hadn't been with Kim, maybe they would have continued their act until the final curtain.

He wanted to see her. Today.

"I can't," she said, both disappointed and relieved. "I've got plans."

He took a minute to digest this answer. "How about tomorrow?"

"Why are you so eager to see me, all of a sudden?"

"It's not all of a sudden," he told her. "I've wanted to see you since the moment you left Palm Point. But I had to get things properly squared away with Kim. And then it took me a while to track your sister down, after I tried unsuccessfully to track *you* down." He paused, then asked, "Do you really not want to see me, Gina? Just say so, if that's how you feel. Don't make me come to New York only to make a fool of myself. I want to see you, but if you have no interest at all, no curiosity in seeing where this could take us—"

"No," she blurted out. "I mean, yes. I mean, no, I don't have no interest or curiosity." Great. She was blathering worse than Bruno. She wondered if she sounded like a jackhammer. More important, she wondered if Ethan had any idea what she meant. She wondered if *she* had any idea.

He obviously chose to interpret her mangled words in a way that suited him. "Then we'll get together tomorrow. Where do you live?"

She wasn't about to tell him. She was a savvy New Yorker, and even though she knew Ethan, even though she'd kissed him—a hell of a lot more than that, actually—she knew better than to give him her home address, at least not until she'd seen him again and assured herself that he was safe.

He hadn't been safe in St. Thomas. Oh, he'd been safe when it came to snorkeling…but even an innocent activity like sitting across the table from him at a fancy restaurant in Charlotte Amalie had proven risky. And talking to him, confiding in him, feeling so connected to him—

Not safe. "There's a coffee shop on Ninth Avenue," she informed him, not adding that it was a five-minute walk from her apartment. She often went there for brunch on Saturday mornings. She'd be there tomorrow, if he wanted to meet her. One look at the place, with its pleasantly gloomy ambiance and its multicultural clientele, might scare the Connecticut fellow away.

She provided the address and told him he'd find her there at 10:00 a.m. If he took one peek through the door and ran away—or if he decided between now and tomorrow morning that he really didn't want to see her, after all—she would eat her omelette and get on with her life.

"YOU COULD HAVE seen him tonight," Carole said as she spread her napkin across her lap. She and Gina sat at a corner table at Gina's favorite neighborhood Thai restaurant. Gina had ordered Pad Thai, Carole something with prawns and lemon grass and three little flames printed beside the menu listing, warning that the dish was extremely spicy. The waiter had already brought them bottles of Singha beer. Gina figured Carole would need a few bottles to put out the fire her dinner ignited on her tongue.

"I wanted to see you," Gina said. "If I canceled tonight, it would be months before we could get together.

You've got all those sick kids interfering with your social life.''

Carole laughed. She loved her pediatrics work at St. Vincent's Hospital. She'd been in her final year of residency when Gina had met her; they and three other women had shared a two-bedroom apartment when Gina had first moved to Manhattan. The other three women, one of whom had slept on a sofa bed in the living room, had been monumental slobs, leaving dirty clothing on the floor, food-caked dishes in the sink and open, oozing tubes of toothpaste on the bathroom counter. Carole and Gina had united in their horror, and from that a friendship had blossomed.

Amazing how friendships could flourish when strangers found themselves sharing living quarters.

She and Carole had already discussed Fashion Week, the stretch of days in September when all the major designers came to New York and held runway shows in a huge, glamorous tent in Bryant Park to display the following spring's collections for the fashion columnists and buyers. It wasn't as big a deal for shoe designers as for clothing designers, but Bruno always pushed to get his shoes onto the runway models' feet. The city filled with European royals, American socialites, film stars and cover girls. Parties abounded. Gossip ran rampant. It was like Mardi Gras for the fashion world—exciting but exhausting, requiring an abundant intake of headache remedies.

Gina would much rather have talked about Carole's patients, but Carole wanted to talk about Gina. Specifically, she wanted to talk about the phone call Gina had gotten at work earlier that day. "I'm really sorry about the screwup with the time-share," Carole said. "I still don't know why Paul told those people they could stay in the unit after he told me he wasn't going to use it.''

''You've apologized a zillion times,'' Gina assured her. ''It was obviously just a big misunderstanding.''

''It was more than that, if Paul's friend wants to see you.''

''Why do you keep talking about Paul as if you know him?'' Gina asked.

Carole's usually pale cheeks turned pink. ''Well, I do know him.''

''You do?''

''After you phoned me from St. Thomas, I called him up and tore him a new one. Called him seven different kinds of idiot. I was a little rough, I guess.''

''A little?'' Gina recalled how Carole, a sweet, soft-spoken native of Ann Arbor, Michigan, used to light into their piggish roommates in that East Village walk-up four years ago. She could be pretty fierce herself, but she'd always been glad to be on Carole's side in those fights. Carole was not a woman you'd want to have angry with you.

''The next day, he showed up at the hospital, looking for me. He works down on Wall Street as a fund manager downtown. He said he wanted to set the record straight....'' She faltered, her cheeks growing rosier.

''So?'' Gina goaded her. ''Did he?''

''Well, once we stopped screaming at each other, we…we kind of felt an attraction. We've been seeing each other.''

''You're kidding!''

''I didn't want to tell you over the phone, Gina. I thought you might be angry. His mistake practically ruined your vacation, after all.''

"No, it didn't." It had altered her vacation, but ruined it? Not even close.

So now Carole was seeing Ethan's friend Paul. "Do you like him?"

"We fight a lot. It's fun." She grinned. "He's a little too suburban, but I'm hoping that'll change."

"Do you think it *can* change?" Ethan was too suburban, too. Gina's last boyfriend, Kyle, had been too suburban, even though he'd lived in Queens. She'd hoped he would change, but he didn't. He couldn't.

Why had she agreed to meet Ethan tomorrow? Why did she allow herself a glimmer of excitement at the prospect of seeing him? He was way too suburban. Look at the woman he'd almost married—blond, gorgeous, a walking, breathing embodiment of suburban.

"I changed," Carole said, spreading her hands in display. "I grew up in the Midwest, which is like one huge suburb. And here I am in New York."

"Yeah, but you're a woman. And brilliant. Ethan…"

"Is he brilliant?"

Gina ran a polished nail along the edge of the label on her beer bottle. "He's smart. When it comes to environmental stuff, yeah, he's probably brilliant. But he's definitely not a woman."

"That could be a plus," Carole said, grinning mischievously. "Give him a chance, Gina. He might surprise you."

"He already did, just by calling me up."

"So go for it. What's the worst that'll happen? You'll spoil your Saturday brunch?"

Gina sighed. A lot of things worse than that could happen. Ethan could turn out to be nothing like the man he'd been in St. Thomas, quiet and gentle but steel spined, tough yet sympathetic when sympathy had been exactly what she'd needed. Or he could turn out to be exactly like the man he'd been in St. Thomas, and then she'd fall hard for him, and he'd hop on the train back to suburbia.

The waiter arrived carrying platters of aromatic shrimp soup. Gina managed a smile. Okay, so tomorrow's brunch might be spoiled by the invasion of Ethan Parnell into her life. At least she could enjoy tonight, in the company of a friend who was resolutely not suburban.

ONE THING Ethan liked about Manhattan was that the streets were numbered, making it difficult for a visitor to get lost. He might have taken a cab downtown from Grand Central Station, but his train had gotten into the city a half hour before he was supposed to meet Gina, and the air was crisp, some midway point between summer and autumn, so he decided to walk.

The city was easier to take on a Saturday morning. Traffic was marginally lighter, the sidewalks fractionally less jammed with pedestrians. All right, then—that made two things he liked about Manhattan. Numbered streets and thinner crowds at the start of the weekend.

Still, he wondered how anyone could live in a city so big and overpopulated. A daily diet of New York would leave him too frazzled to think. Gina hadn't seemed particularly frazzled, but she'd been under the influence of the lulling Caribbean atmosphere when he'd gotten to know her last July. Here on her home turf, he might find her as hard and headstrong as most of the New Yorkers he knew. After all, she was in the middle of Fashion Week, whatever that was.

He must have been crazy to force this meeting. He should have contented himself with his sweet memories of Gina: Her intensely dark eyes. The undulations of her body as she'd snorkeled in the clear, warm Caribbean Sea—in one or another of her gloriously revealing swim suits. Her soft hair. The erotic pressure of her weight when she'd sat in his lap. He shouldn't have placed those memories at risk by confronting the real, nonvacation Gina in her natural habitat.

Too late. He was on his way to a coffee shop on Ninth Avenue. He'd see the real her, and maybe his curiosity would be satisfied.

The distance between the avenues was longer than he'd realized. Hiking from Park Avenue west to Ninth took him longer than walking the fifteen blocks from Forty-Second Street to Twenty-Seventh. Somewhere in the vicinity of the Port Authority Building he shed his jacket; ten blocks farther south, he rolled up the sleeves of his tailored shirt. Had he dressed too formally? He'd skipped a tie, but his khakis were pleated and his loafers buffed. What if Gina met him wearing black leather?

He'd probably be very turned on, that was what.

At last he found the coffee shop. No one would mistake it for Starbucks. The sign above the door was faded to illegibility, and the glass windows were grimy, smudged with a thin layer of soot. From the exterior, the place could pass for one of those triple-X clubs that featured lap dancing by women whose chests were pumped full of silicone.

Would Gina have sent him to a strip joint as a joke? Were strip joints even open at ten on a Saturday morning?

Inhaling for courage, he slid his jacket back on as if it were protective armor and shoved open the door.

Beyond the door was a café, not a girlie club, thank God. A handful of women were inside, but he saw only one. She sat at a small, scuffed table against one wall, a massive ceramic mug of coffee steaming near her elbow and that day's edition of the *New York Times* spread open in front of her. He saw her thick black hair sliding forward to obscure her left cheek, and a gold stud and a gold hoop adorning her exposed right ear, and her long legs crossed one over the other, her magnificent feet enclosed in bright-red canvas sneakers. Her faded blue jeans and snug white T-shirt were a hell of a lot more innocent looking than black leather.

It didn't matter. Gina Morante turned him on the way no one ever had.

CHAPTER TWELVE

"COME HERE OFTEN?" he said.

Gina jerked her head up. Her vision of the *New York Times,* all those columns of tiny print enumerating the world's countless disasters and dilemmas, was replaced by the magnificent sight of Ethan.

He had on a crisp white shirt, pleated trousers, loafers and a blazer—clothes that just about screamed Connecticut. He looked like someone scheduled for tea at the Plaza, cocktails at the Carlisle, dinner at the Harvard Club—anything other than brunch at a grungy Chelsea coffee shop.

Yet his hair was the same tawny shade she'd found so attractive, and thick with waves. His green eyes were as bright with intelligence and generosity as they'd been in St. Thomas. He still had dimples. He was tall, lean, poised and exactly as attractive as she'd remembered—although her memories of him were dominated by their final night at the resort, when he'd been wearing a lot less clothing.

Heat crept up the back of her neck as she recalled that night. She realized he was waiting for her to speak. She folded her newspaper and gestured toward the empty chair across from her. "Just about every week," she answered his question. "The omelettes are great."

He glanced around him before lowering himself into the chair. The wall beside their table was decorated with a poster advertising a circus performing at Madison Square Garden—four years ago. Someone had carved the words "Domino rules" into the tabletop, the letters sharply angled because curves would have been difficult to cut into the varnished wood surface. A napkin dispenser and a cylindrical jar of sugar were as close as the table came to a centerpiece. No candlelight and fresh flowers here.

A waiter Gina had gotten to know over the course of many Saturday brunches materialized at their table. His hair was pulled back into a ponytail, and a tiny silver hoop pierced one nostril. "You guys ready?" he asked.

"I'll have a mushroom omelette," Gina ordered. "And a refill on the coffee, please."

Ethan studied the menu, which was posted on a wall above the cash register. "I don't suppose you've got anything healthy here," he muttered.

"We've got whole-wheat toast," the waiter said helpfully. "I can tell 'em not to smear any butter on it."

"Live it up," Gina urged Ethan. "Omelettes are good for you. High in calcium."

He relented with a smile. "Okay. I'll have a mushroom omelette, too. And a cup of coffee."

Apparently satisfied, the waiter abandoned their table. Gina grinned at Ethan. "Six mornings a week a person can eat a healthy breakfast. You've got to have an omelette every now and then."

"I've got to, huh?" His smile seemed to melt her organs. She felt a luscious warmth, sweet and liquid, seeping through her. This wasn't good. She didn't want his smile to make her so happy. "So," he asked, "what exactly is Fashion Week?"

She told him. While the waiter delivered coffee to Ethan and topped off Gina's mug, while the tables around them filled and emptied and filled again, while the waiter returned once more with their omelettes, bright yellow and glistening with butter, and garnished with whole-wheat toast also drenched in butter, Gina told him about the runway shows, the parties, the frenetic planning and preparation, the competition among designers for the press's attention, the taunting and schmoozing, deal making and scene making. She told him about the celebrities who attended the shows, and the rich old men who squired teenage supermodels around town in their limos.

She described this season's Bruno Castiglio line, which featured brightly colored patches of leather—purple vamps with lime-green bows and bright red heels, turquoise T-straps with orange toes. "They're wild," she said. "Everyone on the design team loves them."

"But you're not wearing shoes like that," Ethan noted, peeking under the table.

"They aren't in stores yet," she said. "And once they are, well, they'll be *big,* you know? Not big in size, but big in their ability to attract attention. A woman would wear them only if she wanted the world to notice her feet."

"If you want the world to notice your feet, you should go barefoot," Ethan suggested.

She laughed, even as she felt more of that syrupy warmth spreading through her, caused not just by his flattery—she was used to people complimenting her feet—but by the ease she felt talking to him. Whenever she reminisced about the week she'd spent getting to know him in St. Thomas, she thought mostly about the way he'd looked that last night, or in a swimsuit with his torso wet and sleek and his hair slicked back. She hadn't remembered how much she'd enjoyed those nights they'd shared out on the terrace, just talking. But talking with Ethan had definitely been one of her favorite activities that week. How had she forgotten that?

"Tell me how Alicia's doing," he prompted her before breaking off a chunk of omelette and forking it into his mouth.

She was touched that he wanted to know. "She's doing well. So's Ramona—my sister."

He nodded.

"Once Jack moved out of the house, the tension level dropped way down. It made life much more pleasant for everyone. Mo was no longer cooking and cleaning up and doing the housewife thing for a guy she was totally pissed at, and she stopped being so resentful. And Jack's been really good about seeing Ali and sending money. Don't get me wrong—he's still a schmuck. But he's turned out to be a responsible schmuck. So things are going okay. I try to get up to White Plains at least once a week for dinner with Ali and Mo—although with all the Fashion Week hysteria, that's been impossible lately." She sipped some coffee, then continued. "Ali wants to take scuba lessons for her birthday. I looked into it, and the scuba schools said she's too young. But in a few years, we'll see. And Ramona plans to go back to work, which is something she probably should have done when Ali started kindergarten, instead of sitting around the house feeling useless and maybe taking it out on Jack a little. So yeah, they're all right."

"I'm glad." He nodded again. "Alicia's a terrific kid."

"Terrific is an understatement. She's a goddess." Perhaps she didn't seem so to others, but to Gina, her spunky little niece was as close to perfect as a seven-year-old could get. "Now—" she took another sip of coffee, hot and deliciously bitter "—it's your turn to tell me about you, Ethan. Tell me what's going on in your life."

He launched into a description of his current work. The Gage Foundation would be hosting an important fund-raising dinner in November, which was a major undertaking. He was also preparing position papers on logging in old-growth forests for a couple of senators to use in hearings in Washington. Gina listened, fascinated. But his work wasn't the part of his life she'd most wanted to hear about.

"How is Kim?" she asked.

He lowered his fork and reached for his mug. His expression implied that the question didn't surprise him. "I haven't seen her since this summer," he said. "I assume she's fine. I think I would have heard if she wasn't."

"She's the most beautiful woman I've ever met," Gina blurted out. She didn't want to talk Kim up to him—she certainly didn't *have* to. He wasn't blind; he knew how beautiful Kim was. But the words seemed to erupt from her without any forethought, perhaps to test him, to make sure his relationship with Kim was truly dead and buried before Gina allowed herself to give in to that deep, thick attraction she felt for him. "I know lots of models, Ethan, but they're all so, I don't know, *thin.* And striking. They don't look real. Kim looked real."

"She was real. And beautiful." He offered a crooked smile. "Why are we talking about her as if she were dead?"

"Well…she isn't in my life anymore," Gina rationalized.

"Nor in mine."

"Don't you miss her? When I broke up with my boyfriend last year, I missed him for a long time."

"Maybe you really loved him."

"You didn't really love Kim?"

He drank some more coffee, then lowered his mug and let out a long breath. "I assumed I did—but I never really thought about it the way I should have. Mostly I thought about how beautiful she was. That's not love."

"So you don't miss her at all?"

He shrugged. "I wish her well."

"Jeez, you sound so civilized." Gina wasn't sure she believed him. In her world, when people broke up, they most certainly didn't wish each other well, at least not for the first twelve months after the breakup. As peaceful as life had grown at Ramona's house, Gina was sure that before her sister crawled beneath the covers and turned off the light at the end of each day, she prayed for God to rain curses down upon her estranged husband's head.

And if Gina were Kim, she'd probably pray for Ethan to be drowned in a cloudburst of curses, too.

Well, she wasn't Kim. She wasn't a fancy-schmancy debutante suburbanite. She'd never be almost-engaged to someone like Ethan. No point even contemplating such an eventuality.

The waiter returned to their table with the coffeepot, but Ethan waved him away from his mug. "Do you want any more?" he asked Gina.

She'd already had three cups. "No, thanks."

"Just the check, please," Ethan requested. The waiter dug it out of a pocket in his apron and handed it to Ethan, who barely glanced at it before pulling out his wallet and handing over a twenty-dollar bill. "Let's go," he said.

Go where? Gina wanted to ask. She hadn't planned

any activities for the day. She hadn't known how this brunch would go, or even if Ethan would show up.

He'd shown up, and it had gone wonderfully. He was still smiling, his eyes still radiant. Maybe he'd made plans for them. Eyeing his preppy outfit, she wondered whether those plans included spiriting her off to Connecticut.

As she wove among the tables, he placed his hand on her shoulder. His palm was warm, lightly possessive, and it reminded her of the way he'd touched her that last night in St. Thomas. And suddenly a plan took shape in her mind, a plan she didn't want to want, a plan that was probably the worst idea she'd ever had.

A plan that was undoubtedly nothing like whatever he had in mind. He'd touched her shoulder only as a courtesy, one of those chivalrous things men like him did when they escorted women out of restaurants.

Exiting into the bright sunshine, they blinked and squinted until their eyes adjusted. He tightened his grip slightly, and turned her to face him.

"Well," Gina said.

"Gina," Ethan said simultaneously. His hand lingered on her shoulder, his fingers gentle but firm, and he searched her face with his gaze.

She inclined her head, inviting him to continue talking, since she couldn't come up with any profound comments.

"Gina," he said again, then sighed. "There's no simple way to say this."

Oh, great. Hadn't Kyle uttered words like that the night he'd told her he didn't think things were working between them? That she'd agreed with his assessment hadn't taken the sting out of his statement. Of course, there was nothing between her and Ethan to be working or not working, no way he could break up a relationship that didn't exist.

Except that his eyes were telling her he thought a relationship *did* exist, and that maybe his plans bore a dangerous resemblance to what she'd been thinking as they left the restaurant. "It's still there," he said. "That's why I had to see you, why I've been trying to track you down for the past month. It was there in St. Thomas. We both felt it. We both knew it. But you were dealing with Alicia and I was dealing with Kim, and..." He paused, as if aware he was rambling. "I had to see you again once our lives were resolved and we were back on familiar territory, just to find out if it was still there. Now I've seen you and found out."

He didn't have to spell out what "it" was. She knew. It was there, just as it had been there during their shared vacation. They were in a different place now, at a different time, and she couldn't deny what Ethan was saying. The pull between them, the heat, the connection, the fact that he didn't have to define "it" for her to know exactly what he meant...

It was still there.

His hand remained on her shoulder, his other hand rose to her other shoulder, and she couldn't keep from leaning toward him. His mouth brushed hers and he made a sound halfway between a gasp and a groan. Then his mouth came down on hers hard. This kiss felt as much like a homecoming as landing in LaGuardia Airport had, and riding in a cab through the familiar streets of New York, and wiggling her key into the lock of her apartment door, and stepping inside. Kissing Ethan was like crossing a threshold.

She reached under his jacket to grip his waist and he made that sound again. She made a sound, too, half gratitude and half begging for more. This was probably a stupid move—she and Ethan knew each other hardly any better than they had in St. Thomas—but she lacked the willpower to fight her longing for him.

She wasn't going to fall in love with him, at least. She'd keep her heart out of it, and accept whatever Ethan had to offer the way a tourist might, visiting this exciting place, experiencing it, temporarily immersing herself in it, but never forgetting that she belonged somewhere else. For now, she would just enjoy the trip.

Two teenage boys on skateboards whizzed past them down Ninth Avenue, shouting obscenities. Ethan eased back from her, glared at the boys as they skated off the edge of the curb and away, and then turned back to Gina. His smile was hesitant.

"I live around the corner," she said before she could stop herself.

He took her hand and let her lead the way to her apartment.

She briefly contemplated what he'd think of the building, with its drab brownstone facade and its dingy glass front door. The vestibule was cramped and stark, two rows of mailboxes and an intercom panel occupying one wall. No doorman in her building, no polished marble floor, no potted plants—not even plastic ones. She wasn't going to apologize for her modest residence, though. Given the exorbitant rent she paid, the landlord ought to be apologizing to her.

They rode up the elevator in silence, Ethan's fingers twined through hers. Fortunately, they had the elevator to themselves. She wouldn't have been able to make small talk with any of her neighbors, not with him standing beside her, not with her heart thundering against her ribs and her mouth still tingling from his kiss.

They arrived at her floor, and she ushered him down the hall to her apartment. She hoped he didn't notice the slight tremor in her hand as she manipulated the key into the door's three locks. She wasn't used to being this nervous, even when sex was imminent. She didn't have sex that often—in fact, she hadn't slept with anybody since the breakup with Kyle—but she usually faced the prospect of it with poise and confidence.

She felt confident now—sort of. But poised? Not even close. Not with Ethan hovering behind her. Not with her awareness of how seductive his kisses and caresses could be, her memory of his arousal that night, her comprehension that he'd spent the past two months thinking about her, searching for her and traveling all the way from Connecticut to see her. Was it only for this? Would sex be enough?

Sex and conversation, she reminded herself. Sex and connection. Sex and "it." There was a lot going on, and it would indeed be enough.

She jammed her hip against the door to shove it open. Ethan followed her into the entry and closed the door behind them. She tossed her keys into the lumpy, lop-sided ceramic dish Alicia had made for her in art class last year, and stepped aside so he could view the entire apartment.

He circled the main room with his gaze, taking in the single window, the flea-market furniture, the palm-tree-shaped floor lamp, the footlocker that doubled as a coffee table, the bed that doubled as a couch, the rectangular carpet remnant covering most of the hardwood floor, the coat tree draped with scarves, purses and belts. He scrutinized the paintings hanging on the wall—a couple of abstract acrylics from her college days, and a lot of smaller, simpler watercolors of street scenes, the arch in

Washington Square Park, the view from the fire escape outside her window, a chic lady sipping a cosmopolitan at a sidewalk café table and a study of Gina's own feet as observed from the opposite end of her body. He peered into the kitchenette, which wasn't much bigger than a bus-stop shelter but was clean and cockroach-free, then returned his attention to the paintings. "Wow," he said.

"I know. I've got too many scarves," she admitted as he wandered around the room.

"No, the paintings. They're amazing." He studied the one of her feet for a long moment, then the one next to it, of a cluster of pigeons pecking at bread crumbs beside a park bench. "You painted all of them?"

Gina nodded. She didn't pretend humility; she knew she was talented. That Ethan recognized her talent gratified her.

He turned toward her, apparently awed. "I know this is a huge thing to ask, but would you make a painting for me someday?"

His question implied that they weren't just dealing with "it" anymore. "Someday" had been added to the equation. Did Ethan think that whatever existed between them would last all the way to "someday"? Did Gina believe that? She shouldn't let herself—a woman needed to protect her emotions—but she wanted to. When Ethan turned back to her, his eyes captivating her, his hands reaching for her, she wanted to believe it more than anything she'd ever wanted before.

"Yes," she said, although whether she was speaking about creating a painting for him or something else she couldn't say. And then it didn't matter. He pulled her into his arms, bowed to kiss her and nothing mattered, nothing at all.

She skimmed her hands to his shoulders and shoved off his jacket. It hit the floor with a soft thump. He lifted his hands to her cheeks, threaded his fingers into her hair and kissed her deeply, his tongue filling her mouth. She played her tongue against his and caught her breath when he stroked the skin behind her earlobes. Shimmers of heat spread through her, ripples of a desire so powerful it might have alarmed her if she'd been thinking clearly.

Clear thinking didn't seem terribly necessary right now. What did seem necessary was stripping off his shirt. She brought her hands forward and tugged at the buttons. He released her to join in the effort, and within seconds his shirt was off. And then hers. He yanked it free of her jeans, lifted it over her head and let it fall. She had on one of her less inspired bras—under a white T-shirt, she hadn't wanted to wear anything colorful— but he clearly didn't care. He opened the hook with a flick of his fingers, and the bra joined the growing pile of clothes on the rug.

"Oh, Gina," he whispered, bending his knees so he could nuzzle the skin between her breasts. She combed her fingers through his hair, holding him to her, loving the damp friction of his tongue on her skin, loving everything he was doing to her, everything sensation he was awakening inside her. "Gina…" He straightened up and pulled her to the sofa bed. She shoved off the pillows and cushions to give them more room, and he urged her back until she was lying across the bedspread, exposed from the waist up and feeling utterly vulnerable as he gazed down at her.

The late-morning sun seeped through the pleated shade covering her window, filling the room with a dreamy light. She watched as Ethan lowered himself beside her on the mattress, as he slid his hand over one breast, the other and then her belly, his fingers splayed to cover all the skin above her belt. His touch was like her mood, confident yet not entirely poised, his hands caressing but not quite claiming. He lifted his face and she saw the question in his eyes.

"Take off my pants," she said, hearing a faint tremor in her voice.

He undid the buckle, then the zipper. She watched him ease the denim over her hips, dragging down her panties, as well, and stopping only when everything got jammed up at her ankles, blocked by her sneakers. He unlaced them, wrenched them from her feet, and flung them across the room. She kicked her legs free of her jeans.

He touched her bare feet, traced the bones of her insteps, gave each toe a gentle pinch. He ran his thumb over the silver ring circling the second toe of her left foot, then sketched a ticklish line down the arch of each foot. Bowing, he kissed her ankle. When he straightened, he looked abashed. "I've never been a foot person before," he confessed.

"Didn't you say something about being a breast man in St. Thomas?" she asked, once again hearing a quaver in her voice. What he'd done to her feet had aroused her far too much.

He directed his attention to her chest. "I'm a breast man, too." His gaze skimmed down her body and she saw him swallow. "I think I'm a Gina man," he conceded as he tackled his own belt.

Gina remained sprawled out on the bed, watching as he shed the last of his clothes. She felt like a voyeur, except that he knew she was there, staring at his body as he stripped naked. She'd seen plenty of men in her life—all those life drawing classes she'd attended at art school had given her a comprehensive education in the subject of male anatomy. She briefly entertained the desire to draw Ethan, his long, lean legs, his streamlined torso, the dusting of hair on his stomach, the thicker hair at his groin. He was gorgeous, every feature wonderfully proportioned.

He was also fully erect. They'd barely begun, she thought, and he was as aroused as she was. They could skip the foreplay and just get down to it.

For a moment, she suspected that he had the same idea. Sitting on the bed, he reached into the pocket of his slacks and pulled out a condom. But instead of putting it on, he tossed the foil square onto the foot locker and then stretched out next to her, sliding one arm under her and tracing her cheek with his other hand.

"You came here expecting sex," she said, gesturing toward the footlocker. She wasn't sure how she felt about his having brought birth control with him.

"I came here with no expectations at all," he murmured, touching his lips lightly to her forehead. "But I came prepared for anything. Maybe you wouldn't be at the coffee shop. Or maybe you'd be there and you'd tell me to go away. Or maybe—" he brushed her mouth with his "—maybe you would be happy to see me."

"I guess that third option comes closest," she admitted, running her hands over his chest. His skin was hot and silky, shaped by hard male muscle and bone.

He ran his hand over her body, too, riding the curves, teasing her nipples, exploring her belly button, scaling the rise of her hip. *Happy* wasn't the right word, she realized as his touches became more adventurous, more demanding, as he probed the curve of her bottom and wedged his leg between her thighs. *Happy* seemed so safe, so placid. When he flexed against her, she felt anything but safe and placid. Quite the contrary, she felt as if she were racing toward the edge of a cliff, unable to slow down, eager to jump.

He rolled onto his back, lifting her on top of him and freeing both his hands. They roamed her back and sides, kneaded her breasts, spread her legs around him. He pulled her down so he could kiss her, and arched against her. When he grazed the hollow of her throat with his teeth, she managed only a helpless sigh.

He must have heard the plea in that sound, because he groped for the condom and tore off the wrapper. Her fingers collided with his as she helped him roll on the sheath. Then she sank onto him, guiding him where she needed him to be.

He clamped his hands over her hips, refusing to let her move. She reared back and gazed down at him, and she saw the sublime strain in his face, his need as desperate as hers. "Gina."

"Let me," she said, fighting his hands as she rocked her hips.

"If you do that…" He swore when she moved her hips again. "Don't, Gina. I'm not going to last."

"Ethan…" He didn't have to last. She was so close to gone all she wanted was him, hard and fast, now. She writhed against him and he reluctantly yielded, loosening his hold on her, letting her take him, surging deep into her. He cupped one hand behind her head and moved the other to where their bodies were joined. One touch was all it took to set her off. Her body convulsed and she collapsed on top of him, savoring his last, fierce thrust as he came.

She closed her eyes and rested her head against his shoulder. His chest rose and fell beneath her as he struggled for breath, and she felt the wild pounding of his heart against her breasts. His hands wandered down her legs to her feet; with her knees bent at his hips, he was able to reach as far as her heels. He rubbed them tenderly.

"I'm usually a little better at this," he finally said.

"You hear me complaining?"

He chuckled, and she smiled at the sensation of his rib cage vibrating beneath her. "I just hope you'll let me do it properly next time."

"Properly?" She propped herself up and peered down at him. A laugh slipped out. "What—is there a fancy Connecticut way to do it that I don't know about?"

He joined her laughter. "I don't know what ways you know or don't know. I'm hoping I'll have a chance to find out. And I'm hoping—" he eased her off him and onto her back "—you'll give me a chance to make love to you slowly." He kissed her throat. "With a little more control." He touched his tongue to one breast. "Like a grown man instead of a horny teenager." He licked her other breast.

Her thighs tensed. Her belly clenched. He sucked her nipple into his mouth, cupped his hand between her legs and stroked her until she came again, moaning, lost in a pulsing rush of ecstasy and love.

"Like that," he whispered.

If she could have spoken, she would have promised to give him all the chances he wanted. But speech seemed impossible, so she only gathered him to herself and hugged him, and hoped he would know.

CHAPTER THIRTEEN

HOW CAN SHE live in this place?

Ethan tried not to be judgmental. And indeed, her apartment had some things going for it—specifically, her paintings, which were phenomenal. The large acrylics on canvas were vibrant with color, bursting with energy. They captured her personality—unpredictable and exciting. The watercolors were more subdued but exquisitely precise, revealing an elegance that fascinated him. He'd never guessed, when he'd watched her constructing sand castles with Alicia on the beach at Palm Point, that she had such talent.

He sat on her bed in his boxers. She had ducked into her minuscule kitchenette to answer her cell phone, grabbing a robe from among the scarves on the coat tree along the way. The robe was a kimono style, scarlet with yellow and blue parrots on it, and it fell only to mid-thigh, revealing her glorious legs. Since she'd opted for discretion, he figured he ought to put on his shorts. He contemplated putting on the rest of his clothing, too. A trip outside—to a drugstore—might be necessary, unless she had some condoms in the apartment. He'd been speaking the truth when he'd told her he'd come to New York with no expectations. He'd brought one condom, just in case, but he hadn't dared to hope he would use it, let alone need more than one.

Just as he hadn't expected to use that condom, he

hadn't expected Gina to be living in such cramped quarters. Anyone who tried to pace in an apartment as small as hers would risk stubbing his toes. Claustrophobics would need years of therapy to overcome the trauma of spending time in a place like this. And if a person wanted fresh air, he'd have to ride down an elevator just to get outside—into air so dense with auto exhausts and soot that it hardly qualified as fresh.

He *was* being judgmental. But viewing Gina's home with a critical eye was essential if he was going to evaluate whether whatever existed between them was worth pursuing. He'd tracked Gina down not only because he wanted to see her but because he had to know who she really was. And here was his answer: she was someone who had chosen to live in an apartment not much grander than a prison cell—no bars on the window, and the toilet was hidden behind a door, but other than that...

Sitting on her bed, hearing her spicy laughter as she chatted with her sister, he was forced to acknowledge that her choice to live in this cramped little room in a part of New York that was only halfway to gentrification was a significant indication of who she was.

He stood, crossed to the window—all of three steps away—and drew up the shade. Craning his neck, he could see a tiny scrap of sky. The only greenery visible through the glass was a lawn chair perched on the third-floor fire escape of a building across the street. The seat of the chair consisted of woven green strips of plastic.

He lowered the shade and turned back toward the couch. ''No kidding, really?'' she was saying into the phone. ''Mo, that's so cool!''

He gazed at the rumpled sofa bed and felt his mouth curve in a smile. All right, so she lived in a too small dwelling and ate overly greasy omelettes at a neighborhood dive. Remembering what had just occurred on her bed helped him to overlook the worrisome details of her life. The bed was one place where they were in sync. He recalled her warmth, her weight on top of him, the satiny smoothness of her skin, her responsiveness and honesty. The way she'd felt coming. The way he'd felt.

Damn. They were definitely going to have to buy more condoms.

He glanced toward the kitchenette and saw her leaning against the counter beside the sink. She grinned at him, then said into the phone, "I'd love to, Ramona, but I can't. Not tonight. I've got plans."

Plans to spend the evening with him? Or plans with someone else? When he'd called her yesterday and begged for the chance to see her, he hadn't demanded that she free up her entire day for him.

"You know," she explained, averting her eyes. "All the Fashion Week stuff. Parties out the wazoo. Why don't you use that teenager who lives down the street from you? Yeah, I know, Alicia likes me better. I like her better, too. But I can't do it tonight."

He returned to the bed, trying not to worry about whether her plans for that evening included him. She'd made love with him, hadn't she? She'd lain on these very cushions with him, her skin still golden from the week she'd spent soaking up the sun in St. Thomas, her eyes so wide and dark, her feet so pretty. She'd given him everything, held nothing back. If she could love him like that just minutes ago, knowing all the while that she was going to be spending the evening with another man…well, he'd be surprised. And gravely disappointed. And pretty damn mad.

"Hi, sweetie!" she chirped into the phone. "No, I

can't baby-sit you tonight. I'd love to, but I can't....
Right—Fashion Week.''

Was Fashion Week her justification for everything?
Would she use it as an excuse to send him on his way?

''She did? Well, maybe you could sleep over at Caitlin's house tonight. Then Mommy won't have to get a
baby-sitter.... Yeah, you should check with Caitlin and
see. Of course it's a good idea. Don't I always get good
ideas?''

Her voice mesmerized him. He loved its gritty texture,
its brash accent. He wanted her to get off the phone and
talk to him. And kiss him. And untie the sash of that
sexy little robe of hers, and let it fall open, and...

''Sorry about that.'' Her voice was normal, aimed at
him. She strolled across the room to the bed and tossed
her cell phone onto the footlocker. ''Ramona's got a
date. Her first one since Jack moved out. This is big
news.''

He nodded, pretending he gave a hoot about Ramona's romantic adventures. His fingers itched to tug at
the sash. His hands ached to roam her body. When she
flopped down onto the sofa bed beside him, it took all
his willpower not to haul her onto his lap and kiss her
senseless.

''It's a guy who works for my father. Nick Balducci.
He's known Ramona for years. I think he's loved her
for years. Now that Jack's out of the picture, he's making his move.''

''Good for him,'' Ethan said. He wanted to make his
own move. How could he ask her about the condoms
without sounding as if he had a one-track mind?

''She wanted me to baby-sit Alicia tonight.''

''But you've already got plans,'' he said, searching

her face for an indication of what those plans might entail.

Her smile reassured him. "There are always tons of parties around Fashion Week. They're crazy but fun. I was figuring on hitting at least one of them. Will you come with me?"

"To a fashion party?" He could think of a lot of things he'd rather do, but as long as she wasn't sending him away, he'd count his blessings.

"It's not a 'fashion' party. Just a bash with folks involved in Fashion Week. I've actually got three different invitations for tonight, but I'd just as soon go to Jean-Claude LeMonde's blowout in SoHo. He always has the most interesting people, and he doesn't blast the music so loud you can't talk."

"That sounds fine," Ethan said. And it did, really. Just as he'd needed to see Gina's home, he needed to learn about her social circle. He needed to know whether the compatibility they shared when they talked—and when they got naked—existed in the world beyond just the two of them. He stared at her cell phone until she leaned toward him and kissed his shoulder.

One little kiss, and he was as hard as steel. But his gaze remained on the phone. "Gina."

"What?" She traced a meandering line across his chest with her index finger. Her nails were polished a creamy shade, like pearls. He watched her hand move on him and felt himself grow impossibly harder.

"A few things, actually," he said, amazed that he could keep his voice calm and steady while her aimless touches were driving him crazy. "One—you haven't given me your phone number."

She recited the ten digits, then grinned. "I'll write it down for you later."

"Okay." Better than okay. When a woman gave a man her phone number, it meant she wanted him to stay in touch. Gina had already opened herself to him, her apartment, her body, her mind. But giving him her phone number meant opening her future to him.

"Also..." He sighed as she teased one of his nipples into a little point. "Your name."

"What about it?"

"How is it spelled?"

She burst into laughter.

"I mean it. With a *J* or a *G?* And Morante—"

"G," she told him. "G-I-N-A. M-O-R-A-N-T-E. You want my social security number, too?"

"No." Her caresses were too distracting. He covered her hand with his and peeled it off his chest. "This is important, Gina. I don't have any more condoms with me."

She drew back and stared at him. "You only brought one?"

"And I was afraid it might be one too many."

Slowly her smile returned. "Today's your lucky day, Ethan." She rose, strolled to the bathroom and vanished inside. When she returned, she was carrying a cellophane-wrapped box of prophylactics. She dropped it into his lap and resumed her seat beside him. "I was wondering when I was going to get around to using them."

He grinned. "You can stop wondering now," he said, attacking the knot of her sash.

THEY FELL ASLEEP at some point during the afternoon— between the second and third time they made love. A good thing, too. Ethan would never have had the energy to face a night at a crazy but fun fashion party with Gina if he hadn't gotten some rest. He was relieved he could even walk after all that sex.

Not that he was complaining. Every moment of it had been spectacular. Gina was as passionate underneath him as she was above him. She was as tender, as adventurous, as attuned to him no matter what they tried, what position they found themselves in. She wasn't afraid to laugh, or to guide him, or to let out a cry when she climaxed. As a lover, she was fearless.

She was fearless as a woman, too, he was beginning to recognize. The rumble-tumble of the city didn't faze her. She had no hesitancy about marching into the middle of Ninth Avenue, dodging cars, trucks and bicycles as she flagged down a cab, or about fending off the man who'd appeared out of nowhere and tried to climb into the cab Gina succeeded in summoning for Ethan and her.

Ethan did his part by paying the driver, who deposited them in SoHo, a part of the city he'd never visited before. Large industrial-looking buildings stood interspersed with more residential-looking buildings, and galleries and boutiques lined the sidewalks of roads that didn't follow the familiar numbered grid of the midtown streets. Ethan held Gina's hand; if he lost her, he'd never find his way out of this neighborhood.

He also held her hand because he wanted to. She looked ravishing, in a snug-fitting black top, even snugger black jeans and a pair of flamboyant shoes constructed of patches of bright turquoise and orange leather. "They're a prototype," she told him, modeling the vivid shoes. "Bruno—my boss—would kill me if I didn't wear them to the parties."

"Are they comfortable?"

"Well, the heels are a little high, but other than that, yeah."

The heels weren't *that* high; he still stood a couple of inches taller than her. But they made her legs look even longer, and those tight black jeans made her legs look longer yet. Holding her hand made him realize he'd rather be back in the privacy of her microscopic apartment than out on the town with her.

He forced himself to act as enthusiastic as she seemed to be. She swept him into a sushi bar on a corner, saying, "We probably should eat something, but not anything heavy. Jean-Claude usually has excellent catering at his parties, and all the models are anorexic, so we don't have to worry about all the food being gone before we get there."

Ethan would have been content with a sandwich, or even another greasy omelette. Raw fish had never appealed to him. But tonight belonged to Gina. She was showing him her world, and he couldn't act like a close-minded tourist, contemptuous of the local customs.

He managed to get down some raw tuna and a few shrimp thingies that were cooked and actually tasted pretty good. Gina dipped everything she ate into a puddle of soy sauce mixed with wasabi before popping it into her mouth. She wore little makeup, and she didn't need much. Her lashes were so thick and black, mascara would have been redundant. Her lips were full and alluringly rosy. Those lips had done some amazing things to him that afternoon. Merely remembering the way they'd felt on him, nibbling his belly, tasting his shoulder, luring his tongue into her mouth renewed his appetite, not just for the sushi but for this entire evening. He was with Gina, in her world and at her command. Wherever she led him in her garish turquoise-and-orange shoes, he'd gladly follow.

They'd finished snacking on cold fish and seaweed by

ten, which Gina pronounced a good time to show up at Jean-Claude's. She hooked her arm through the bend in his elbow and promenaded with him down a narrow block to a warehouselike building with several limousines double-parked in front of it. A uniformed guard at the door stopped them. Gina provided her name and told him Ethan was her guest. He scanned a list of invited guests, checked her off and held the door open for them.

They entered a dark, vaulted room swarming with people—mostly tall, thin people, mostly clad in black. In his white shirt and khakis, Ethan felt like a beacon, glowing through the gloom. The crowd was dense enough for him to tighten his hold on Gina's hand as she pulled him along. She'd told him the music wouldn't be blasting at this party, but the mechanical beat of European techno-punk was loud enough to resonate painfully in his molars. The din of voices was almost as loud as the din of music.

Gina moved with a purposeful stride through the crowd. Occasionally, she shouted a greeting to someone or paused to kiss an offered cheek. But she appeared to be on a mission, and Ethan, clutching her hand, dutifully followed. To his left, he spotted a fellow whose hair settled around his face in a cloud of tight pink curls; to his right, two skinny women in sheer blouses that hid nothing danced erotically with each other. Enough people held classic martini glasses with pale liquids in them to make him suspect that getting a beer at this bash would be something of a challenge.

At last Gina reached her destination—a quiet pocket of space around a corner, where the light was marginally better and a bartender was busy filling orders. Ethan released a pent-up breath. The bartender had a row of beer bottles lined up on his table like icy brown soldiers. Things were looking up.

When Gina asked for a beer for herself, things looked even more up. She might belong at a chichi downtown party like this, but in her heart she was a down-to-earth beer drinker like him.

"Do you know a lot of the people here?" he asked, gazing around the bend in the wall at the crowd, enough of whom were moving in some sort of rhythm to make him realize they'd trekked across a dance floor to reach this oasis.

"What's a lot?" She shrugged, accepted an open bottle from the bartender, then waited while the bartender snapped open another bottle for Ethan. A wisp of vapor rose from the mouth of the bottle before he lifted it and took a bracing sip. "I recognize plenty of faces. Some of the players, yeah, I know them. And here's a person I know very well," she added, waving to someone behind Ethan. He turned in time to see a compact man with leonine brown hair and strong features. He was about Gina's height—or about what her height would be if she weren't wearing her multicolored shoes.

The man's gaze zeroed in on them and he smiled. "Sweetheart! How do they feel?"

"You know me—I hate heels," she said before air-kissing his cheeks, one and then the other. "Other than that, they're fine."

"Is the leather soft enough?"

"Like a second skin."

"And don't complain about the heels. Those are, what, inch and a half?"

"I'm spoiled. I'm used to flats."

"We ought to drag you in front of the cameras, wrestle your tootsies into some three-inch stilettos."

"You'd have to kill me first." She gave Ethan's arm a squeeze. "Ethan, this is my boss, Bruno Castiglio. Not everyone cares as much about shoes as he does."

"They should care," Bruno said indignantly. "Your job and mine depend on them caring. You gonna go out there and circulate? Anyone comment on them yet?"

"I just got here," Gina told him. "And it's kind of dark and crowded in there. I don't know if anyone's going to notice them."

"You should dance. People'll see your feet if you dance."

"Don't be a pain in the butt, Bruno. In fact, if you'd shut up a minute, I could introduce you to my friend Ethan Parnell."

"Ethan. A pleasure," Bruno said, pumping his hand. "You in the business?"

Ethan swallowed a laugh. Surely it was obvious, from his staid apparel and boring hairstyle, that he was not a card-carrying member of the Fashion Week Brigade. "No. I direct a foundation for environmental protection."

"Uh-oh. An environmentalist? You're not gonna give us a hard time over the use of leather in the shoes, are you?" Bruno touched the lapel of his leather jacket as he spoke.

"No," Ethan assured him. "My shoes are leather, too."

"So's his belt," Gina said, shooting him a sly grin. Evidently, his belt was a point of particular interest to her.

Bruno's gaze shifted toward the dance floor for a moment, and then he smiled at Gina. "Isn't that Delores de la Mancini?" he whispered, as if a woman standing in the current of that loud music could hear them talking by the bar.

"The little princess?" Gina squinted, then nodded. "Yeah, that's her."

"I want her to see those shoes. Go make nice."

"I'm not kissing her hand," Gina warned, then patted Ethan's shoulder. "I'll be back," she promised before abandoning him to cozy up to the petite woman in the silver lamé minidress hovering near the edge of the dance floor.

"The little princess?" Ethan echoed.

"She's some kind of minor royalty," Bruno told him. "A duchess, a countess, I can't keep all those titles straight. But she's a shoe fanatic. She's the doyenne of European shoe fanatics. She's gonna love our new line. And thank God Gina's the one wearing the shoes. She can make any pair of shoes look special."

That was only one of her assets, Ethan thought, watching from the safety of the bar as Gina embraced the smaller woman, began chattering, then kicked up a leg so the woman could view her shoes without bending over.

"So, you're a friend of hers?" Bruno asked, drawing Ethan's attention away from the sales job Gina was performing on the European shoe doyenne.

Gina had warned him that Fashion Week thrived on gossip. He didn't believe anyone would care about his identity, but he was willing to protect Gina's reputation if he could. "Yes, we're friends," he said noncommittally.

"She's in love with you," Bruno guessed.

Ethan felt his eyebrows rise. "I don't think—"

"Last guy she fell in love with was a straight arrow,

too,'' Bruno said. "Neat, quiet, wouldn't know cashmere from mohair. He was a cop."

"Her brother's a cop, isn't he?" Ethan said, eager to steer the discussion away from love.

"That's the thing about her. She's a city girl, funky, brilliantly talented—but on those rare occasions when she falls in love, it's usually with a clean-cut guy in an oxford shirt."

Ethan opened his mouth and then shut it. What could he say in his defense? He was a clean-cut guy in an oxford shirt. "I don't think she's in love with me," he assured Bruno. "We just...we met in St. Thomas last summer and became friends."

"Be that as it may..." Bruno smoothed the collar of his jacket and edged over to the bar. "A Campari on ice," he requested, then turned back to Ethan. "Just do me a favor and don't break her heart, okay? Last time she fell in love, with that cop, he broke her heart. I swear, I would have gone after him with both fists if he hadn't been a law enforcement professional. You can't avenge a friend's heartbreak when the heartbreaker carries a service revolver, you know what I mean?"

"I can imagine." Ethan decided he liked Bruno. Anyone who'd want to avenge Gina's heartbreak was all right in his book. "I have no intention of breaking her heart," he promised, hoping that was a promise he could keep.

"Because I'll tell you—" Bruno leaned toward him "—if I were hetero, I swear, I'd marry her in an instant. She's one hell of a woman."

"She is," Ethan agreed. Admitting that he considered her one hell of a woman was practically the same as admitting that they were more than friends. And after the day he'd spent with her, he'd be lying to call what they had going for them mere friendship. Friends didn't dive into passion like snorkelers, holding their breaths and submerging, letting the tide carry them into deep waters. Friends didn't give themselves to each other the way he and Gina had.

He had come to New York to find out what existed between them. He knew now that it was something real, something scary, something he couldn't label. Something that would likely cause problems for him and her both—because there he was, the clean-cut straight-arrow out-of-towner in her high-style world. He didn't feel comfortable here. He wasn't sure he belonged.

But they were more than friends. And damned if he was going to break her heart.

With a nod to Bruno, he ventured away from the safety of the bar to the edge of the dance floor, where Gina had attracted a cluster of people who were gushing over her shoes. He touched her shoulder, and she turned and gave him a dazzling smile. "Let's dance," he said, taking her free hand and leading her deep into the too-too fashionable crowd.

CHAPTER FOURTEEN

"SO, IT'S GOING WELL with this Ethan guy?" Ramona asked.

Gina leaned back in her chair and stretched her legs under the kitchen table in Ramona's cheery country-style kitchen. Her definition of luxury was being able to take a weekday off to travel up to White Plains to see Ramona. Her reward for having worked eighty-hour weeks leading up to Fashion Week—and having generated great interest among buyers in their colorful line of shoes—was to be allowed to work only thirty-hour weeks once Fashion Week was nothing but a memory with a mild hangover.

Gina sipped her Diet Coke and smiled. "It's going okay," she said—an understatement, but she didn't dare to say more. Claiming that a relationship was flying high would jinx it. Gina was superstitious enough not to take chances.

Ethan had been coming to New York City to see her every weekend in the month since Fashion Week ended. He and Gina spent those weekends talking, eating, roaming the streets, visiting museums and making love. And partying. In his crisp pleated trousers, crew-neck sweaters and tailored shirts, Ethan always looked grossly out of place at the parties and clubs she took him to, but he was a good sport, dancing with her and shooting the breeze with her pierced, tattooed friends and never showing a hint of revulsion or impatience when someone like her sculptor pal Willie, who insisted on wearing spiked collars even though they were so yesterday, launched into a diatribe about how it was more important for the government to fund the arts than to support old-growth forests, because a lack of art destroyed society more effectively than a lack of sequoias in Northern California did.

After each party, their heads still ringing with music and conversation, they'd return to her apartment and make love again. She wasn't the most experienced woman in the world—those sisters at Our Lady of Mercy had done a decent job of brainwashing her before they'd kicked her out of their school—but she understood that what happened between her and Ethan in bed was a rare thing. The honesty, the sharing, the trust—she'd never known anything like it before. She'd never known a man willing to talk during lovemaking, to suggest things, to accept her suggestions, and afterward to hold her, and stroke her, and make her feel precious to him. Neither she nor Ethan dared to use the *L*-word—talk about jinxing a relationship!—but with him, Gina felt deeply loved.

So yeah, it was going okay.

A major test loomed, however, and anxiety nibbled at the edges of her contentment whenever she thought about it. "I've got my doubts regarding this fund-raising party he wants to take me to," she said, then took another sip of soda to keep from blurting out that she was scared to death about venturing onto Ethan's upper-crust Connecticut turf. She prided herself on being scared of nothing. But this had her in a chronic state of low-grade anxiety.

"Once we get you the perfect dress, you'll feel better

about it," Ramona assured her. "I'm sure we'll find just the thing today at the mall."

Gina tried not to shudder. She couldn't remember the last time she'd shopped at a mall. Malls were so suburban.

But Ramona had insisted she couldn't attend Ethan's swanky fund-raising gala in Connecticut wearing an outfit she'd picked up at one of her funky consignment shops, or an ensemble thrown together by some up-and-coming designer she'd met at a party. "I live in the suburbs, Gina," Ramona had reminded her over the phone yesterday, "and I'm telling you, when you get out of New York City you've got to dress appropriately. The suburbs are very into appropriateness."

"You mean I'm going to have to *act* appropriately at this shindig, too?"

"Look it, act it, live it. Ethan's taking you with him because he wants to show you off. You don't want to embarrass him, do you?"

Gina had never considered herself embarrassing. Anyone who might be embarrassed by her was not a person she'd want to spend time with. She wasn't embarrassed by Ethan when he wore khakis while club hopping with her. He was who he was—a clean-cut kind of guy. And she was who she was—not the sort of woman who shopped at malls.

It was more than just going to the fund-raiser that had her spooked. The benefit, scheduled for two weeks from that Saturday, would be her first time visiting Ethan in Connecticut. Her first time viewing his house, her first time cruising through his town, her first time seeing him in his own element. She and not Ethan would be the outsider.

What if Connecticut proved to be too far away—not

in miles, but in manner? What if traveling there proved to her that the distance between her and Ethan was just too great to be overcome? Ramona could dress her in the most bland, conservative, *appropriate* outfit in the entire mall, and Gina might still feel as if she didn't belong. No wonder she was scared.

Her panic must have shown on her face. Ramona carried her own soda to the table and patted Gina's hand. "You don't have to dress like a senator's wife, Gina. We'll find something appropriate *and* cool."

"Really?" She forced a laugh. "Is it possible for a dress to be both?"

Ramona joined her laughter, but the sudden chime of the doorbell interrupted their giggles. Ramona reflexively glanced at the clock built into her wall oven and frowned—11:00 a.m. "I'm not expecting anyone," she said as she left the kitchen to answer the door.

A mixture of curiosity and concern propelled Gina out of her chair and down the hall behind her sister. Maybe someone had sent Ramona flowers—someone named Nick Balducci. They'd gone out a few times. Why not? Flowers, or a guy in a gorilla suit who would sing a love song, or a parcel service delivering some sort of romantic gift, or—

"Jack? What are you doing here?"

Gina's apprehension about her shopping mission and the party that necessitated it vanished, replaced by defensiveness and anger. She hadn't seen Ramona's estranged husband since July, just before she and Alicia had departed for St. Thomas. Once he'd moved out of Ramona's house, he'd moved out of Gina's life, as far as she was concerned.

But now he filled the doorway of Ramona's tidy, tree-shaded split-level. He was as tall and devastatingly hand-

some as Gina remembered, his hair as black, his eyes as
chilly a blue. He still had broad shoulders, a dimpled
chin and a cocky smile that women—at least the woman
who happened to be Gina's sister—had once found ir-
resistible.

Ramona was apparently able to resist him now. She
bristled with impatience as she stared at him looming on
her front porch. She'd been dealing with him on a regular basis since his departure last summer; he came twice
a week to visit Alicia, and Gina supposed they also
spoke frequently on the phone, working out the logistics
of their separation. They weren't fighting anymore; they
were simply relating to each other as dispassionately as
possible. Or so Ramona had told Gina.

Dispassionate or not, she felt all her protective-sister
urges boil to the surface. If Jack gave Ramona a hard
time—even if he gave her a soft time—he'd have Gina
to answer to.

"Ali isn't here," Ramona told him. "She's at
school."

"I know that." Jack's voice was muted. He wore a
traditional gray suit, his tie hanging loose at his throat.
He must have come directly from the bank where he
worked as a branch manager. "You're the one I came
to see." His gaze strayed past Ramona and he glowered.
Clearly, he hadn't come to see Gina. But his frown
ebbed and he offered her a polite nod. "Gina. How're
you doing?"

She could be polite, too. "I'm fine, Jack. And you?"

"Not complaining."

Okay. They'd gotten through that exchange without
bloodshed. If she could handle that, she could probably
handle an evening of small talk with the fat cats and

tycoons she'd have to socialize with at the Gage Foundation benefit dinner.

"If it's business you want to discuss," Ramona said, folding her arms across her chest, "maybe we should have the lawyers—"

"It's not business." Jack shoved his hand through his hair and sighed. "Can I come in?"

Cool late-October air spilled into the entry hall. After a long minute, Ramona sighed, waved him in and closed the door behind him. "Gina and I are on our way out," she warned, as if she had to justify her lack of cordiality.

"I won't take long," Jack promised, passing Gina as he followed Ramona through the hall to the kitchen.

Gina decided to make herself scarce. She trailed them as far as the kitchen doorway, then spotted her half-full glass of soda on the table. "Let me just get my glass, and I'll give you two some privacy."

"We don't need any privacy," Ramona declared, pointing to the chair Gina had been occupying. "Sit. Finish your Coke."

Jack eyed Gina with mild resentment. She didn't want to be there any more than he wanted her to be there. But if Ramona wanted her there, she wouldn't leave. Shooting him a defiant look, she dropped into her seat and raised her drink to her lips.

He scrubbed his hand through his hair again and flexed his mouth as though rehearsing what he was going to say. "Look," he began, then cleared his throat and shifted to face Ramona—a physical attempt to cut Gina out of the conversation. "It's just—well, I ran into your brother the other day."

"You ran into Bobby? You were in an accident?" Ramona asked, deliberately misunderstanding him.

Jack scowled. "He came into the bank, all right? He

was ordering new checks. I don't know why he didn't do it at his local branch instead of coming to mine. No, I *do* know why. He came because he wanted to tell me you were seeing someone.'' Jack glanced toward Gina, apparently measuring her reaction.

She hoped her face gave nothing away. Jack had a hell of a nerve questioning Ramona about her love life after he himself had left her for another woman. On the other hand, Gina understood why he hadn't wanted her to sit in on this conversation. It was between his wife and him. Gina didn't belong in the room.

Ramona glanced toward her, too, her look saying she was grateful Gina was close by. She didn't seem to need any backup, though. She leaned casually against the counter, her arms still crossed, her chin tilted at a pugnacious angle, her poise unshaken, and returned her husband's steady stare.

When she didn't speak, Jack did. ''Your brother said it was a guy who works at your father's store. Nick something.''

''Nick Balducci,'' Ramona informed him.

Pain flickered across his face. ''Yeah, that was it.'' Once again, the two of them stared each other down in silence. Was Ramona supposed to apologize for dating Nick? Why should she?

''He's a clerk in a hardware store,'' Jack finally said.

''My father's a clerk in a hardware store.''

''Your father owns the store.''

''And Nick's been there a long time. It wouldn't surprise me if my father makes him a partner in the place someday.''

''Yeah, especially if he's seeing your father's daughter.''

Anger flared in Ramona's eyes. "You think he's seeing me to get close to Dad?"

"The possibility crossed my mind, yeah."

Gina *really* didn't want to be here for this. Even shopping for a dress at the mall would be more fun than witnessing a blowup between Ramona and Jack. She started to push out of her chair, but when Ramona erupted, she decided the wisest course would be to stay put. "How dare you come in here and make snide remarks about who I'm dating? You're the bastard who left me for another woman, remember? You're the one who told me you wanted to move in with her. You're the one who broke up our marriage, because you were so much in love with What's-her-face. Correct me if I'm wrong, but I think you lost the right to criticize my social life when you walked out that door."

"Mo. Come on. Just because we're separated doesn't mean I don't worry about you."

"Oh, so you've got my best interests at heart? Can you believe this, Gina? He's worried about me. He's afraid Nick's taking advantage of me. What a guy!"

Gina held her hands up in surrender. She had no intention of contributing to the debate.

"I just don't want you getting used," Jack insisted. Despite Ramona's rage, he kept his voice low. "I don't want you getting hurt."

"You're a little late on that score, Jack. Nobody, including Nick Balducci, could hurt me as badly as you did." Gina could tell that Ramona regretted the words as soon as they were out by the way she averted her eyes and took a long sip of her drink. Jack looked chastened and rueful, and Ramona stared at her soda as if it were tea and she hoped to divine the future from leaves swirling at the bottom of the glass.

Actually, Gina thought Ramona's outburst was a good thing. Why not let Jack know he'd hurt her? Why not be human, and honest?

That was one of the best aspects of her relationship with Ethan. They were honest. When they made the rounds of the galleries and he didn't like a painting, he'd say so, even if it was a piece she considered brilliant. If he didn't like the cuisine at a restaurant she chose, he'd speak up. And when he'd told her he really wanted her to accompany him to the fund-raising dinner, she'd honestly told him she didn't think she would fit in. And he'd honestly told her he wanted her there anyway.

And she was honestly petrified about how the evening would go. But at least she was honest.

"So what's this really about?" Ramona asked, more calmly. "Things aren't going so well between you and your sweetie?"

"I don't know," Jack mumbled.

"What do you mean, you don't know?" Ramona asked. Gina pushed determinedly to her feet, but Ramona glared at her. "Sit down," she commanded. Like an obedient child, Gina sat.

"Things are going fine with Vickie," Jack insisted. "But I miss being home. I miss Ali. I miss…home." He obviously wasn't going to admit that he missed Ramona, but the unspoken sentiment hung in the air.

"You left home."

"And I miss it. I'm not saying things are bad with Vickie. I'm just saying I miss what I gave up."

"Well, here's a news flash, Jack. You made a choice. Nobody forced you. It was your decision, and you made it. If you're having second thoughts—"

"Damn it, I *am* having second thoughts. What do you want me to say, Ramona? I made a mistake? Okay. Here

I am, admitting it. I made a mistake. And I'm not asking you to forgive me or take me back. I don't know if that would be the best thing for us right now. All I'm saying is, I'm allowed to care about what happens to you. If this guy, this Nick dude, sees you as a way to kiss up to your father, I'm allowed to care that you might get hurt in the process." He let out a tired breath and pivoted toward the hall. "All right. That's it. I've got to get back to work." Before Ramona could show him to the door, he was gone.

Silence descended upon the kitchen, similar to the silence left in the wake of an ambulance after it's raced away and its siren is no longer audible. At first the atmosphere was tense, and then, gradually, Gina eyed Ramona and realized that, ambulance or no ambulance, disaster or no disaster, they'd both survived.

Ramona gave Gina a faint smile. "That was interesting," she said.

"More interesting than going to the mall."

"Don't even think about it." Ramona set her glass in the sink, then crossed the table and seized Gina's glass. "We need the mall now more than ever. I can hear my Visa card crying for release." She placed Gina's glass beside hers in the sink, then grabbed her keys and purse from the counter. "Get your jacket and let's go. There's an appropriate dress with your name on it in one of those stores."

CONNECTICUT WAS…pretty.

She'd found a window seat on the train and, ignoring the paperback novel she'd tossed into her purse to keep her occupied during the trip, she gazed out at the scenery on the other side of the glass. The towers and tenements of New York City had receded behind her forty-five minutes ago, replaced first by row houses and the occasional factory or warehouse, and then by brittle, straw-dry grass and trees, evergreens dense with dark green needles and deciduous trees clinging to a few final, brown leaves. The sky was a crisp blue, dotted with a few fluffy white clouds. It wasn't exactly rural, but it was pretty—in an unsettling way.

Gina shifted her folding bag on the empty seat beside her. Actually, it wasn't her bag. She'd borrowed it from Carole because her dress would have gotten wrinkled beyond repair in her duffel. Carole had also taken her shopping for earrings. "You can't wear double hoops to a thing like this," Carole had said, and since she was from the Midwest, Gina assumed her to be an expert in appropriateness. "What you need is little gold posts in the upper holes and something elegant and dangly in the lower holes. Diamond posts would be even better than gold. Do you have any?"

"Me? Diamonds?" Gina had laughed.

"Then buy some."

She'd bought new gold posts, instead. The diamond posts she'd checked out, even the tiny ones that didn't sparkle much, had sported outrageously high prices. If only she'd known, when she'd been in St. Thomas, that in a few months' time she'd be expected to dress appropriately for a snooty fund-raising party, she could have bought some diamond earrings there. Kim Hamilton would have helped her pick out the right stones. She'd owned that book on the buying diamonds. No doubt she was an expert in appropriateness, too.

Ethan could have invited Kim to be his date for this gala. Perhaps he had, back when they were still almost-engaged. But now he was stuck with Gina, the inappropriate New Yorker. His choice, she reminded herself. He wouldn't have asked her if he hadn't wanted her to accompany him. She'd wear her appropriate dress and her appropriate earrings—both posts and elegant, dangly ones—and she'd be as courteous while Ethan's colleagues discussed spotted owls and snail darters as he was while her colleagues discussed open toes and arch support.

He was waiting for her on the platform when the train chugged to a stop at the Arlington station. In the brisk breeze, his hair was windblown, and he'd turned up the collar on his jacket—which, she noted with some satisfaction, was leather. Brown leather, but still. And he was wearing blue jeans. They weren't terribly broken in, but at least they didn't have creases pressed into them. She'd never seen him in jeans before, and the sight reassured her.

Spotting her as she stepped onto the platform, he raced over. His hug reassured her even more. He seemed genuinely thrilled that she was there. In Connecticut. In his home territory.

"How was your trip?" he asked, lifting the suitcase out of her hand and leading her down the platform steps to the parking lot.

The air smelled different here. It smelled…empty. The other passengers who'd disembarked in Arlington were climbing into cars and starting their engines, but there was a hollowness to the sounds, a lack of reverberation. And the colors—grays and browns and lingering greens, fallen leaves swirling along the edges of the parking lot, the peaked roof of the station… Ethan had told her Arlington was a city. Not in her book, it wasn't. Cities weren't this quiet.

"The trip was fine," she remembered to answer.

He led her to a Volvo sedan and tossed her bag into

the trunk. Then he opened her door for her. She sank onto the leather seat and recalled the last time she'd been a passenger in a car he was driving. That time, she'd shared her seat belt with Alicia and Ethan had driven on the wrong side of the road.

She'd loved the tranquillity of St. Thomas. Why didn't she love the tranquillity of Connecticut?

Maybe because St. Thomas was a vacation. It wasn't *real*. It wasn't Ethan's home.

"You seem nervous," Ethan remarked as he steered out of the parking lot.

Much as she loved the honesty in their relationship, she wished he'd been a little less honest about how obvious her tension was. She sighed. "I guess I am."

"Why?"

"Well, this party, this fund-raiser— Ethan, that's just not my scene. I keep thinking I'm going to say the wrong thing, or use the wrong fork."

"No one cares which fork you use, as long as you don't use it to stab anyone. And I can't imagine what wrong thing you'd say."

"Oh, you know—something like, 'Hey, I grew up in the Bronx. How about you?'"

"No one cares where you grew up, either. They're going to think you're the epitome of glamour, Gina."

"Glamour?" She snorted. "My dress isn't glamorous. It's…appropriate."

"You're glamorous because you work in the fashion industry. Most of the guests are businesspeople and professionals. They're boring. Compared with them, you're going to glow."

"You think so?"

He glanced toward her, then turned back to the road. "As far as I'm concerned, you're always glowing."

She hoped that comment was more of his honesty. She wanted to glow for him.

He drove them to a comfortable colonial-style house in a serene neighborhood. As he pulled into the attached garage, she conceded that she would like having a garage—and a car. How convenient it would be on a rainy day if she were loaded with bags of groceries. Or purchases from the mall, she thought with a private smile.

Inside, his house was what she'd expected. Just like him, it was tasteful, unobtrusive, the walls white and the den's carpet a tan color awfully close to khaki. The artwork on his walls consisted mostly of framed photographs of nature scenes. The furniture was large and solid-looking—big overstuffed chairs and sofas, and occasional tables you could kick your feet up on without causing damage. His kitchen had less clutter in it than her much smaller kitchen. On the counter, a wooden bowl filled with apples imparted a tart fragrance to the air.

He led her from room to room, saying little more than, "This is the kitchen," and "This is the den." Apparently, he wanted her to convey her impressions of his home, and she did: "That dishwasher is really nice, Ethan," and "Wow, what a huge TV. What size screen is that?" The TV in his den, angled between a wall of books and a brick fireplace, was as wide as her bathtub. Her TV was a tiny box perched on a shelf. Fortunately, she didn't watch much, so the size had never bothered her.

He laughed, although he didn't sound happy. "You're still nervous."

"I'm not glowing?" She turned to him and smiled, all too aware that her smile couldn't hide her apprehension. It sat inside her like a living thing, a stir-crazy monster, larger than his damn TV. "I want to love Connecticut," she confessed. "I really do."

He clearly heard what she wasn't saying: *I want to, but I don't.* As her smile waned, his widened. He eased her coat off her shoulders and down her arms and tossed it onto one of those massive chairs. "Come here," he murmured, drawing her into an hug. "You don't have to love Connecticut. You just have to relax a little."

Fifteen minutes later, lying naked with him on that nondescript tan carpet, feeling rug burn on her bare butt and struggling to catch her breath, she felt a bit more relaxed and significantly fonder of Connecticut. The groan Ethan had emitted when he came had sounded better than the cacophony of New York's streets, and the heat of his hand still moving lazily over her belly felt better than New York's giddy, raucous embrace. She thought vaguely about unpacking her appropriate dress so any wrinkles caused by the suitcase would shake out, but that didn't seem as important as nestling against Ethan's hard, hot body, sandwiching one of his legs between hers and reminding herself of what really mattered: *this*. Not Connecticut, but *them*.

"Maybe we could skip the fund-raiser tonight," she suggested hopefully as she twirled her fingers through his hair.

He chuckled. "We're going to the fund-raiser, Gina. I've got to make a speech."

"Tonight? You have to make a speech?"

He lifted his head to peer at her. His eyes were slightly glazed, his smile weary. She noticed a faint red mark on his neck—a love bite. She hoped it would fade before the party, or his shirt's collar would conceal it. If he had to make a speech in front of all those wealthy benefactors and they all saw a hickey on his throat...

"Gina," he said, his tone solemn in spite of his smile. "I have to be there. I'm the head honcho. They've donated money to my organization. It's part of my job."

"I know, Ethan—"

He brushed his fingers over her lips to silence her. "I *want* to be there. I love my job. Fund-raising isn't my favorite part of it, but I'm grateful to these people who make it possible for the Gage Foundation to protect the environment. I want to thank them, and celebrate our accomplishments with them."

Of course he did. Of course she recognized the importance of this night to him. Gazing up into his eyes, however, she understood what he was really trying to tell her: this was his world. This was what mattered to him. If she cared about him, she had to accept the truth about him. Connecticut, fund-raising parties and Ethan giving speeches, with or without a hickey on his neck— this was who he was.

"We'll have fun tonight," she vowed, trying to convince herself. "Not as much fun as we had just now—" she raised her head off the floor to kiss his cheek "—but it'll be cool."

"Oh, yeah," he said, allowing himself a genuine laugh. "Real cool. Trust me, Gina—" he kissed her back, on the mouth, a much longer, deeper kiss "—you'll be the coolest thing about it."

CHAPTER FIFTEEN

GINA WAS DEFINITELY the coolest person in the room.

Her dress was more conservative than he would have expected—a simple thing in midnight blue, with long, slender sleeves, a seductively scooped neckline and a lace-trimmed hem that fell midway between her knees and her ankles. Her hair was pinned back from her face, held in a velvet clip the same dark blue as her dress. The hairdo exposed her long graceful throat and her ears, from which dangled remarkably sexy gold earrings. Her makeup was light, her muted-red lipstick matching her muted-red nail polish.

And then there were her shoes. An elaborate puzzle of straps set atop a thick heel, they shimmered, an iridescent combination of silver and turquoise. Her fish shoes, he realized, recalling Alicia's description of them. They had to be some version of those shoes Gina had been designing, inspired by the fish she'd seen while snorkeling in St. Thomas.

He wished he could be snorkeling with her right now. As spectacular as she looked, she'd looked ten times better in a swimsuit, her body sleek and wet and her eyes wide with awe at the sight of all that magnificent underwater scenery. But instead of snorkeling, he had to spend the evening fishing—for money, for contacts, for praise.

Actually, he didn't mind these fund-raising galas. He

was grateful for the generosity of the Gage Foundation's supporters. And he had to admit that making small talk with insurance company presidents and nationally renowned cardiologists was more stimulating than debating the merits of extreme snowboarding with three multi-braided, multipierced slackers at some unlit basement club Gina dragged him to in the East Village, where the music was so heavily amplified it swallowed half the conversation. The music at this party, located in the banquet room of the Arlington Inn, a charming hotel nearly two hundred years old and lovingly restored, was provided by a trio—harp, flute and cello. No one had to shout.

The room's appointments were luxurious. Heavy cream-colored linens draped the tables, and crystal and silver winked in the light shed by several colonial-style brass chandeliers. Waiters meandered among the milling guests, carrying trays of champagne and hors d'oeuvres. Gina stood within arm's reach of Ethan, although she was involved in a conversation with two silver-haired women while Ethan entertained the husband of one them. Melvin Reinhardt was the president of a supermarket chain and a longtime supporter of the Gage Foundation. Ethan owed him his full attention, but he could give at most ninety percent. The other ten percent belonged to Gina.

What was she discussing with Agnes Reinhardt and her friend? Organic carrots? Hiking the Appalachian Trail? The Reinhardts had backpacked their way from one end of the trail to the other—over a thousand miles of wilderness—more than once, and Ethan realized Agnes was doing all the talking. Gina listened and occasionally nodded. When a waiter skirted near them, she grabbed a glass of champagne.

He had to stop worrying about her. She could cope with a discussion about the Appalachian Trail if she had to. She was a grown-up.

After a few minutes, Melvin released Ethan. "I'm sure you've got lots of other guests to greet," he said, gesturing toward the double doors. Every time Ethan checked them, he saw more people entering. The foundation had sold a record number of tickets to this dinner, and it looked as if everyone who'd bought a ticket was using it.

Ethan shook Melvin's hand and inched over to Gina. He waited until Melvin escorted Agnes and the other silver-haired woman away before whispering, "How are you doing?"

"This place is so *fifties*," she whispered back.

He frowned. "What does that mean?"

"Like the 1950s. When people behaved and everyone knew their place." The way she'd said *behaved* implied that she considered the word distasteful. "All these people have New England accents."

"There are some New Yorkers here," he assured her.

"I bet even they have New England accents."

"You're gorgeous," he murmured, in part because he suspected that her critical stance was a ploy to hide her insecurities, but mostly because it was true.

A surprised smile crossed her lips. Then her insecurities slipped back into place. "How many glasses of champagne will it take to get me drunk?" she asked.

"Let's not find out." A couple approached them, the man, like Ethan, dressed in a classic tuxedo and the woman in an elaborate beaded dress that did not strike Ethan as *fifties*. Gina's eyebrows rose slightly, then settled back into place as Ethan introduced her to the Eldridges, both professors at Yale.

For all her attitude, Gina performed as smoothly here as he did at her wingdings in New York. He'd never actually doubted that she'd be able to handle this party, but *she'd* doubted it, and her doubt had seeped into him, making him wonder just how difficult it would be for her to mix and mingle with the elite who attended benefit dinners like this. Maybe it was difficult for her, but she was pulling off the act with panache. She seemed particularly excited by the Eldridges, pumping Madelyn Eldridge for information on where she'd gotten her dress and who had designed it. When Madelyn confessed she'd purchased it at a consignment shop, Gina looked blissful. "I'm in the fashion business," she confided, "and I shop consignment all the time. Not this thing," she added, waving dismissively at the beautiful blue dress she had on. "My sister made me buy this at the mall in Westchester County. She's got more class than me. She wouldn't even let me buy something on sale for this dinner."

"I always say, the more money a person can save by buying a bargain dress, the more she's got to donate to worthy causes," said Madelyn.

Ethan relaxed. Gina had a friend at the party now. Everything would be fine.

They bantered, Ethan laughed and Gina smiled at a joke Rick Eldridge told poorly, they talked soberly about some research going on at Yale that the Gage Foundation was funding, and then the Eldridges moved on. It was like a square dance, couples drifting around the room in a smooth choreography. Gina seemed to pick up the steps easily enough. "Is it possible to get another kind of drink?" she asked as she set her empty glass down on a passing waiter's tray. "Do they have beer or mixed drinks?"

"Champagne before dinner, and wine with," he told her. "If you had as much class as your sister, you'd know that."

She shot him an angry look, then softened when she realized he was teasing her. "My sister's got so much class you should have asked her to be your date tonight, instead of me. She's available."

"I thought you told me her husband is trying to get back into her good graces." Gina had mentioned something about that the last time he'd been in New York City.

"He's trying," Gina muttered. Then added, "He's *very* trying."

"How's Alicia dealing with it?"

"She's not real clear on what's going on," Gina said. "She loves her daddy. She loves her mommy. She loves you, too. She talks about you constantly. I told her we'd figure a time when she could see you. I hope you don't mind."

Ethan didn't mind, although getting together with Alicia implied something he wasn't sure he was ready for. Granted, seeing Alicia wouldn't be the same thing as, for example, meeting Gina's parents. After all, he already knew Alicia; he'd shared living quarters with her for a week. Meeting parents was a much more significant step, one he wasn't about to rush into with Gina. He'd learned his lesson with Kim, whom he'd convinced himself he loved when it had simply been a matter of convenience and great sex.

That wasn't what was going on with Gina, he assured himself. The sex was great, but no one could call their long-distance arrangement convenient. And the fact that he was even thinking about meeting her parents indicated something. He wasn't going to define what that something was, though, not tonight. Tonight was for backslapping and glad-handing, doing his job as the head of the foundation.

"I've got to find the ladies' room," Gina murmured, patting his arm and wandering off. Ten minutes ago, he might have helped her to locate it, but at this point he had faith in her ability to navigate through the party and the hotel lobby without his assistance. She could hold her own in this crowd, just as he'd expected.

He continued working the room in her absence, thanking benefactors, meeting their spouses, plunging into an intense discussion with a local congressman about the prospects of an environmental bill currently in committee, plunging into an equally arcane dialogue about whale migrations with a researcher from the Woods Hole Oceanographic Institution on Cape Cod. Whenever he had a spare moment he scanned the room, searching for Gina, but as more and more people filtered in, he couldn't find her. Not that he was worried, but…well, it would be nice if she could see him shooting the breeze with such esteemed individuals. He didn't have to knock himself out to impress her, but…it would be nice.

The woman from Woods Hole finished her oration on endangered whale populations and Ethan moved on. Once again he searched the room—and spotted an astonishingly beautiful blond woman entering the room on the arm of a tall, thin, nondescript young man.

What the hell was Kim Hamilton doing here?

He vaguely remembered that back in July, just before they'd left for St. Thomas, she had arranged for her company to buy an entire table for the dinner. The table seated ten. Surely she hadn't had to be among the ten.

Yet here she was.

The good news was, she'd brought a date. At least,

Ethan hoped the man whose elbow she'd hooked her hand around was an actual date and not a colleague from the company, doing his part to fill the table they'd sponsored. He hoped the man was passionately in love with Kim, and Kim—well, he couldn't imagine her passionately in love with anybody, but she could be deeply in *like* with him. Maybe she was engaged to him. He hoped she was wearing a big, fat diamond ring on her left hand, and her life had developed exactly the way she'd wanted it to. He hoped she was happy.

He also hoped he could find Gina before Kim did, just to alert her. Gina could handle Kim—she'd handled her better than Ethan himself had when they were all together in St. Thomas. But still…a little warning wouldn't hurt.

OKAY, GINA THOUGHT. Two glasses aren't enough. Three could be too many, but since she'd already had that many, she figured she might as well go on to four.

In the bathroom, she'd come upon two extremely prissy women applying powder to their noses with precise dabs while they gossiped about someone's au pair, who came from the Hebrides and swore she was speaking English although no one could understand a word she said. "Aren't people from the Hebrides Scottish or something?" one of the women asked as she fussed with her blindingly bejeweled earrings.

"Well, you know Scottish accents. They're even thicker than New York accents."

Gina had considered opening her mouth at that point, and really amping her Bronx accent, but she'd opted for discretion and dried her hands without speaking a word. Poor, benighted souls, she thought as she sauntered out of the rest room. If they couldn't handle New York accents, they were obviously too provincial.

Ethan was barely visible when she returned to the banquet room. She glimpsed him surrounded by a knot of people, all of them blathering at him, and she grabbed a glass of champagne from a passing waiter and observed him from afar. He was so debonair in his tuxedo. A lot of guys looked goofy in formal attire, but the tux suited him. She wasn't sure if that was a good thing, but given the situation, she saw no reason not to ogle him.

At one point, the cluster of people around him loosened slightly, and he glanced her way. Even from all the way across the room, she detected a glimmer of concern in his eyes.

She smiled and raised her champagne flute in a toast, then sipped. She didn't want to interfere. Let him make nice with his guests. Playing the proper host was his job, his purpose for being here. She could take care of herself and pretend she knew what the hell she was doing.

Her gaze broke from his and she drank a little more champagne. The multiple conversations around her blurred into a pleasant, indecipherable hum, underlined by the wistful strains of the musicians plucking and tooting on their instruments in their corner of the room. People promenaded elegantly back and forth, looking patrician and confident. She wondered whether they were all pretending, too, or whether they actually had a better idea than she did of how to behave correctly at a party like this.

Anyone having any doubts about proper behavior ought to drink some champagne, she thought. The tart bubbles refreshed her palate, and the alcohol acted like a muffler, softening the world's edges. She spotted that Yale professor in the beaded dress, Something Eldridge, who was chattering with a man in a pretentious green brocade dinner jacket, and the woman who'd hiked the Appalachian Trail, who was pondering the canapé pinched between her fingers. Gina ought to grab something to eat, but the waiters who ventured near her were all serving only drinks, no food.

She spotted a vivid splash of blond hair contrasting with all the dark outfits in another small knot of people. That blond was a great color; Gina tried to guess if it was natural. This probably wasn't the sort of gathering where she could ask the woman what hair products she used—although Professor Eldridge hadn't seemed to mind Gina's comments about her dress, all of which Gina had intended as compliments. Maybe the blond woman standing with all those folks in classic black would be flattered if Gina complimented her hair color.

She moved around a table, approaching the blond woman, who abruptly turned around. Gina nearly dropped her glass.

"Kim?" she asked the beautiful woman in the black silk.

"Gina?" Kim asked back.

They stood several feet apart, staring at each other. Gina supposed she shouldn't have been shocked, and maybe if she'd stopped at three champagnes she would have been able to process more efficiently the information that Kim Hamilton, Ethan's former lover, was at this party. Kim lived in Connecticut; apparently, she supported the work of the Gage Foundation; ergo, she'd chosen to attend the fund-raiser.

Or else she'd attended because she'd known Ethan would be there, and she'd wanted to see him again. Not that Gina felt jealous or in any way threatened by Kim's presence. If Ethan had wanted to have Kim with him at this dinner party, he wouldn't have invited Gina to take the train up to Connecticut. He wouldn't have made love to her on the floor of his den, and he wouldn't have brought her here tonight.

Still, the situation was kind of strange.

Kim pursed her perfect little lips. "What a surprise," she finally said.

"How've you been?" Gina inquired, relying on good manners to see her through.

"How have I been?" Kim clutched a sequined silver minaudière before her. "I've been absolutely fine. And you? Are you a benefactor?"

Good manners didn't require lying. "No," she said. "I'm here as a guest."

"I didn't know you had friends traveling in this circle," Kim remarked, her impeccable eyebrows flexing energetically in contrast to her deliberately cool voice.

"Well, I do." Professor Eldridge might count as a friend. That would allow Gina to claim friends, plural.

"What a small world."

"New York…Connecticut—not a huge distance," Gina noted.

Kim studied her for a long moment. "Your shoes look like fish."

"That was the idea. What do you think?" She extended one leg, lifting her foot off the carpet so Kim could get a better look.

"What odd shoes!" a man standing near Kim remarked. "They change color, don't they?"

"Not really." Gina tried not to boast, but she couldn't help swelling with pride as more people gathered around to scrutinize her feet. "They seem to because of the way the light hits them. It's a material we're still experimenting with. Luminescent, we call it. Silver is the most obvious color, but we're going to see what we can do with some other shades.''

"They're certainly…unique," a woman in the crowd murmured.

"I designed them," Gina said. "I'm a shoe designer."

"You designed those?"

She explained that she worked with Bruno Castiglio. Evidently, several of the women had heard of him. "He's famous for very peculiar shoes," one of them commented, and it dawned on Gina that maybe these people weren't complimenting her. They were calling her shoes *peculiar,* which really couldn't pass for a compliment. She tried to explain the way snorkeling among tropical fish in the Virgin Islands had inspired her, but the people around her simply smiled and murmured and drifted away, Kim along with the rest of them.

She felt a strong hand on her elbow, and Ethan's hushed whisper. "It's time for dinner."

"I'd like another glass of champagne," she whispered back, uneasiness overtaking her.

Ethan led her among the tables to one near a lectern at the side of the room across from the musicians. "I think we're done with champagne for now."

"What do you mean, *we're* done?" That was the way Ramona chided Alicia when she wanted more cookies: *I think we've had enough cookies. Go brush your teeth.*

Gina was not going to brush her teeth. Nor was she going to let Ethan tell her what to drink. She was at his damn party, wasn't she? She was socializing, wasn't she? She'd talked about her shoes, and if the snobs and fat cats Ethan counted among his friends didn't like it, tough.

"The champagne disappears after eight," he explained. "They'll be serving wine for a while."

"Oh." So he wasn't chastising her. Just explaining the liquor schedule for the evening. She hadn't realized champagne after 8:00 p.m. was a no-no.

Mere seconds after she'd taken her seat next to Ethan, a waiter asked her if she preferred red or white wine. The champagne had been white, so she stuck with that. Ethan introduced her to some of the other people at their table—a bank president and his wife, the head of cardiology at Arlington Memorial Hospital and her husband, a haze of names and fancy titles she was unable to memorize. She wished Ethan had thought to offer those stick-um labels that said, "Hello, my name is…" that people could have filled out and glued to their chests. At the parties she'd taken him to, downtown, names weren't important. But here, when her tablemates addressed her, they called her Gina, and she felt guilty that she couldn't reciprocate by using their names.

Remembering her name was easy for them, she realized. She was the only unfamiliar face at this party. The rest knew one another. They were a circle, as Kim had mentioned, all attending the same events, contributing to the same causes. They were the suburban elite. She was the outsider—just one new name to learn.

At least they included her in their conversation. They asked her how she and Ethan had become acquainted, and she regaled them with the story. "We both wound up in the same time-share at the same time," she explained. "Ethan wasn't supposed to be there, but—"

"That's a matter of opinion," Ethan gently teased.

"Well, his friend messed up, but—"

"I believe it was your friend who messed up."

She sent him a gritted-teeth smile. "*Someone* messed up."

"I recall your talking about that trip last spring," the

lady from the hospital said. "At the Leukemia Society dinner, remember? Weren't you going with a group of people?"

"Not a group of people," Gina clarified with a smile. "His almost-fiancée."

"Gina," Ethan said quietly, then smiled at the rest of the table. "I went with a friend, Gina went with her niece and we all wound up sharing a condo for the week."

"Did you know Kim is here?" Gina asked him.

"Yes." His jaw was tense, his eyes telegraphing some sort of message she couldn't quite decipher.

"Did you get to say hello to her?"

"Not yet."

Dinner was served, course after course. The clam chowder was so thick with starch she almost needed a fork and knife to eat it. The salad was pedestrian, mostly iceberg lettuce and out-of-season tomatoes that tasted mealy. The prime rib wasn't bad, if you liked prime rib. Gina wasn't crazy about it. She sipped her wine and picked at the food, wondering how much people had paid for their meals. A hundred dollars a plate? Five hundred? They ought to have gotten better food for their money. This food was...suburban. Appropriate. Safe for people who had no taste in shoes.

As soon as his plate was cleared, Ethan touched her shoulder, then stood. "I'm on," he said to the rest of the diners at their table, then turned and strode to the lectern. He tapped on the microphone to make sure it was working and said, "Welcome, everyone. I hope you've enjoyed your dinner. Dessert is on its way, but I know you're all dying to have me bore you to tears with my speech, so try not to scrape your plates too loudly while I'm up here."

Friendly laughter greeted him.

Gina rotated her chair so she could see him without straining her neck. He launched into a speech about the work the Gage Foundation had funded in the past year, the projects it was hoping to support in the upcoming year, the importance of its work in protecting the nation's resources and the necessity for people like all these benefactors to keep the fund financially healthy so it could continue its worthy work. He used no notes, not even scribbles on index cards, but simply spoke, in complete command of the room. She observed his posture, his easy smile, the way he moved his hands, the way glow of the fake candles in the chandeliers brought out the fiery highlights in his hair. She observed the way his strong shoulders filled the jacket of his tux, the way the narrow black bow made his chin look even more chiseled, the way the trousers emphasized the length of his legs.

He was at home here. This was his milieu, and these were his people. All the champagne and wine in the world couldn't muddle her brain enough to lose track of that obvious truth. She was playing "let's pretend" in her fancy dress and her gold-stud earrings, and Ethan was being Ethan.

She shouldn't have come. She didn't belong. Somewhere in the room, Kim Hamilton was sitting beside some other person instead of next to Ethan. Kim was at home here, too. She'd grown up in this rarefied world, a world of clean air and silence and houses surrounded by grassy yards. Her shoes were demure. She would know what to say about a nanny from the Hebrides. She would also know how much champagne was too much.

Gina's head hurt. She should have stopped after that third glass—after the second. She'd made a fool of herself at the table, talking indiscreetly about how she and Ethan had met. Surely she'd embarrassed him. She couldn't help it. He was so poised up at the lectern, so articulate, so impassioned about the work the Gage Foundation did.

She loved him. How could she not, when he was so smart, so self-assured, so considerate? Even when they made love, when he wasn't surrounded by his social caste, when he wasn't buttoned up inside a tuxedo, he was smart and self-assured and considerate, letting her lead as much as follow, letting her take chances with him. Loving him was the biggest chance she'd ever taken—and tonight she felt like a fraud. She'd managed to fake her way through this evening, but in her heart she knew she didn't belong here.

He finished his speech to thunderous applause. Gina clapped along with everyone else, but she felt tears gathering along her eyelids. She struggled to blink them away before he noticed.

He took his seat next to her, glanced at the melting ice-cream cake that had been left for him while he'd been speaking—and her untouched puddle of vanilla and crumbled cake beside it, and then studied her face. "That was wonderful," she said, meaning it.

"Are you okay?"

"I'm fine," she lied.

He didn't seem convinced. "I wish we could leave now, but we can't."

"I know." Maybe there was some way she could leave without him, so she wouldn't embarrass him further. "Ethan—"

She couldn't finish her thought, not when so many guests were swooping down on him, praising his speech, promising more donations, commenting on some of the projects he'd mentioned. Rising to his feet, he accepted their congratulations and thanked them for their generosity. "The Gage family gave us a great start," he said, "but the growth of the fund has really enabled us to take our work to the next level."

More handshakes, more congratulations. At one point, Ethan managed to grab her hand and give it a squeeze—a sweet acknowledgment of her, although his attention had to remain with the dinner guests. Then his fingers slipped from hers as someone edged between them, insistent on hyping some new research he was pursuing on prairie dogs.

In the crowd swarming around Ethan, Gina spotted that magnificent blond hair again, and the equally magnificent face framed by it. God, Kim looked glorious. As confident as Ethan, as appropriate. As right.

No wonder he'd considered marrying her. She and her simple black pumps belonged in his world in a way Gina never would. When she rose on tiptoe to kiss Ethan's cheek, Gina felt the truth rush at her like a tidal wave, strong enough to knock her over. It wasn't jealousy. It wasn't resentment.

It was the understanding that she was all wrong for Ethan.

CHAPTER SIXTEEN

PEOPLE WERE STILL milling around the hotel's lobby, schmoozing, networking and lingering over farewells, when Ethan tried to track Gina down. He'd been so busy networking and schmoozing and lingering himself that he couldn't be sure exactly when she'd disappeared. After his speech, she'd been right next to him, and then he'd gotten mobbed, and the next time he tried to check for her, she'd vanished.

He was furious.

Anxious, too, of course. Worried about her safety. But for God's sake, it was midnight, he was exhausted and he wanted to go home. With her. This was not a good time to pull a diva act—if that, indeed, was what she'd done.

He tugged his bow tie loose as he wandered through the lobby, his footsteps silent on the plush carpeting. The Neilsons called to him from the coat-check counter, and he detoured to thank them for coming. Playing the courteous host with them wasn't easy when all he wanted to do was survey every chair and couch in the lobby, every table in the cocktail lounge, every possible nook or niche where Gina might be hiding.

A few polite words with the Neilsons, and he was able to break away and resume his search. She wasn't in the cocktail lounge. Nor was she in the restaurant, although he would hardly have expected her to duck in there for a snack after having been served a four-course dinner in the banquet room. He inched the ladies' room door open and received an appalled glare from a woman edging past him to use the facilities. "I'm sorry," he said, backing away. "I'm looking for someone. I thought she might be in there."

Mollified, the woman entered the ladies' room and then returned to the door to report that no one was inside. Ethan thanked her and continued his search.

Not down the hallway. Not hovering outside beneath the front door's awning with the smokers who'd had to leave the building to light up.

Where the hell was she? Why had she pulled this stunt?

Swallowing his humiliation, he approached the night clerk behind the polished mahogany check-in desk. "Have you seen a tall woman in a dark blue evening dress, with black hair and—"

"Silvery shoes?" the clerk asked. "I couldn't help noticing them—they were so weird. She went outside a while ago."

"Outside?" He started toward the front door again.

"No—the other door," said the clerk, gesturing toward a glass door on the opposite side of the lobby. "To the pool patio. The pool is closed, but the patio's still open."

"Thanks." Ethan sprinted across the lobby to the glass door and shoved it open.

He spotted Gina perched on a carved marble bench, hugging her arms around herself in the chilly November night and staring at the large rectangular black tarp that covered the pool. She was all alone on the patio, a solitary figure surrounded by wrought-iron tables and chairs and folded sun umbrellas, a few leafless trees, dead patches of grass and a tall white security fence. He was overcome with a rush of relief—followed by a fresh surge of anger.

"Gina. What are you doing out here?"

She turned to him. Her smile was the saddest thing he'd ever seen. "I was just…cooling off," she said.

"Cooling off? It's freezing!" Even in his jacket he felt the air's chilly nip.

Her smile grew, if anything, more enigmatic. "Ethan…" As he approached, she sighed and turned back to the pool. "I just needed to clear my head a little."

"Why? Did you have too much champagne?"

Her smile vanished, and she shot him a fierce look. "No, I did *not* have too much champagne," she retorted, sounding grossly insulted.

He wasn't sure what she'd do if he sat beside her. He didn't really want to; the marble bench would be icy and uncomfortably hard. More important, he just wanted to go home, and settling himself in for a heart-to-heart with Gina by an abandoned hotel pool wasn't the most efficient way to accomplish that goal. If they had to have a heart-to-heart, they could do it just as easily in the comfort of his den—if he could keep himself from staring at the carpet and remembering what they'd done the last time they'd been in the den.

God, he hated heart-to-hearts with women. They made him as uncomfortable as the word *relationship*. He was crazy about Gina; they had something amazing going, something spectacular—but he didn't want to talk about it. And he had the feeling that if he sat on that bench next to her, talking about it was what they'd wind up doing.

Unsure what to say, he let his gaze drift to her shoes.

The night clerk was right; they were weird. Funny. Striking. Like Gina herself.

"I don't belong here," she said abruptly.

He took a deep breath and weighed his response. "Neither of us belongs here," he finally said. "The pool is closed and the party's over. Let's go."

"No, I meant—" She pursed her lips, then sighed again and rose from the bench. "All right. Let's go."

She'd meant something else, obviously. But he wasn't going to ask her to clarify herself out here, in the cold. In the warmth of his car, he could demand an explanation.

She stood patiently in the lobby while he finalized some paperwork with the hotel's banquet manager, and then they headed out the front door to the parking lot. He helped her into his car, took the wheel, blasted the heat and steered away from the hotel, all the while waiting for her to explain her cryptic comment. But she said nothing, just tapped her fingertips together in her lap and let her head loll back against the headrest.

The silence ate at him. "Did something happen to you?" he finally asked. "At the dinner—did someone say something to you?"

"Lots of people said lots of things," she answered vaguely.

"Don't play games, Gina. Something's bugging you, and I can't do a damn thing about it if you don't tell me what it is."

"You can't do a damn thing about it anyway," she said, straightening up. At a red light, he allowed himself a glimpse of her. Her mouth was set, her eyes luminous in the car's shadows. "I didn't belong at that party tonight, Ethan."

He sat up straighter, too, concern running the length

of his spine like a buzz of electricity. This wasn't a minor snit. Gina had a real grievance. Whether or not it was justified, he had to take it seriously.

"What makes you say that?" he asked.

"It was obvious. I was like an exchange student there. Everyone was talking a different language. Except that professor from Yale—Madelyn? She understood about buying clothes on sale. But then I asked her about her research, and I had no idea what she was talking about. I had no idea what most of those people were talking about. They might as well been speaking Greek."

"You're not in Greece, Gina. You're in Connecticut. It's not a foreign country."

"It is to me."

"Come on! It's not even another part of America. Connecticut and New York are contiguous."

"*Contiguous?*" She snorted a laugh. "*Contiguous!* Now, there's a great word."

Oh, boy. This was worse than discussing their relationship—although Ethan had a creeping suspicion that that was exactly what they were doing. "Okay," he said in the calmest voice he could muster. "What's wrong with *contiguous?*"

"Normal people don't use the word *contiguous*. At least, not normal people where I come from."

"And that would be where? New York City? I bet there are people even in the Bronx who use the word *contiguous*."

"Then you should have brought those people to your fancy party, instead." She let out a long breath. When she spoke again, her tone held no sarcasm, no derision. She sounded wistful, as sad as her smile by the pool had been. "Ethan, I didn't belong at that party tonight. I went, and I tried my best. But I fit in about as well as a whoopee cushion at the ballet. They hated my shoes.''

"Nobody hated your shoes,'' he assured her. The clerk had called them weird, but that wasn't the same as hating them.

"They did. They were polite, but they made sure I understood that my shoes weren't appropriate. My shoes were the most *me* thing at that party, and they didn't fit in. And neither did I.''

"Gina—''

"I saw you there with your friends, Ethan. Your associates, your colleagues…I saw you with Kim. She belonged there. I didn't.''

Damn. Was that what this was about? Jealousy over Kim? "There's nothing between me and Kim. I told you—''

"And I believe you. Of course I do. What I'm saying…'' She paused, clearly struggling with her thoughts. "All I'm saying is, you belonged there. A woman like Kim belonged there. I saw the two of you together and thought, What is he doing with me? I don't belong in this world.''

"I wanted you in that world,'' he argued. "I wanted you with me. I wouldn't have asked you to be there with me if I hadn't wanted you.''

"I know that, Ethan. Just like I want you with me when I go club hopping downtown. How do you feel when we do that? Do you feel like you belong?''

God, no. But he couldn't admit as much. If he did, Gina would use his admission as proof that he was an exchange student in her world, or her friends hated his loafers, or some such thing.

"I mean, it's so sweet of you, going to parties with me and trying so hard to make small talk with people you have nothing in common with. I can imagine how hard it must be for you. I love it that you do that for me. But it's hard. You know I'm right about that.''

"Gina—"

"I'm being honest here. And the honest truth is, you don't feel any more comfortable with me in my world than I do with you in your world.''

All right. The honest truth: he didn't feel comfortable in her world. But he could tolerate a few hours of small talk with punks with pierced noses and green hair if it meant spending the rest of the night in Gina's bed. Given how spectacular life in her bed could be, he was willing to tolerate a hell of a lot to get there.

The honesty she was demanding of him forced him to follow that thought to its end. If he was tolerating the head-banging music, the cheap beer and the vapid conversations about which neighborhood sushi bar had the best aki-aki and which cover girl was overdoing it with Ecstasy, just so he could have sex with Gina, what did that say about him? Other than the fact that he really, really enjoyed sex with Gina.

She was talking about life beyond her bed and his, life beyond the magical sphere they entered when it was just the two of them. Even this awkward, painful conversation in his car, late at night, was part of the magic. He'd never before been involved with a woman who compelled such honesty from him, who wanted it. Kim would have happily married him without ever knowing how he felt about most things—let alone such personal issues as how comfortable he felt in societies that weren't like his own. Kim would never have pressed him to consider such questions. She hadn't cared.

Gina did. And she was right. When they were alone, they were great. But when they ventured out into each other's worlds, they needed a passport and a Berlitz book.

"Your friend Carole and my friend Paul get along okay," he pointed out.

"Carole is a doctor. Paul is a businessman. And they both work so hard neither has the time nor energy to go to the other's parties, anyway."

"That's true." He turned onto his street and slowed as he neared his driveway. "Maybe they should schedule a week together in Palm Point so they can get to know each other."

"Or two weeks," Gina said. "His and hers. Of course, if they spend that time together, they might find out they don't like each other. It's been known to happen."

It had happened with him and Kim, he acknowledged silently. But he hadn't minded losing Kim. Gina... God, he didn't want to lose her.

He yanked the parking brake and turned off the engine. "Let's not talk about this anymore tonight," he said, holding out the promise that they could resume the discussion tomorrow if she insisted. They could compare their worlds and bare their souls and figure out a way to build a bridge between downtown funk and suburban posh, something more substantial than the sand bridges Alicia had created on the beach outside their time-share condo. Right now it was late and they were both tired, and a guy could handle only so much honesty when all he wanted was to take his woman in his arms and make love to her, and then drift off to sleep with her body warm and soft next to his.

Within minutes they were in his bedroom, naked, and she was as warm and soft as he could have dreamed.

But when he kissed her he tasted tears on her cheeks, and he understood that even in bed, a person couldn't hide from the truth.

"YOU BROKE UP with him?" Ramona shrieked into Gina's ear. "What are you—crazy?"

Gina was sitting across from Carole at a tiny table in a tapas bar, and she should have turned off her cell phone once the waiter had brought their wine and tapas. But she hadn't, and when it had beeped, Carole had conveniently announced that she had to go to the bathroom, so Gina had taken the call. Now she was stuck listening to her sister scream at her.

"I get home, there's this message on my machine saying, 'This weekend didn't work out, so I guess I won't be seeing Ethan anymore,'" Ramona wailed. "How could the weekend not work out? You had the perfect dress!"

"The dress was perfect for the weekend," Gina explained, sending an apologetic look to Carole as she returned from the ladies' room. "It just wasn't perfect for me."

"You promised Ali she could see this guy. She's half in love with him herself. And now you've gone and broken up with him? How is she going to see him?"

"Look, Mo, I can't talk right now, okay? Carole is eating all the tapas and I'm not getting any." Hearing her words, Carole snagged a salty sliver of fried anchovy from the platter between them.

"You looked gorgeous in that dress," Ramona insisted. "I can't believe he'd let you walk out on him. What happened? Did that bastard break your heart?"

"We'll talk about it later, okay? I've got to go." She hit the disconnect button before Ramona could say anything more.

Carole nudged the platter closer to Gina. She picked up a piece of smoked chorizo and listlessly bit into it. She honestly didn't care if Carole ate all the tapas. Ever since she'd left Ethan's house that overcast Sunday morning, she hadn't really cared about much.

"So you broke up with him, huh?" Carole said.

"Not really," Gina said, then sighed. "Yeah." She took a sip of her Rioja to still the quaver in her voice. "It just wasn't going to work, Carole. That's the bottom line."

"It worked for a few months."

"Not even. Mid-September to early November. That's less than two months."

Carole pulled a face. "It started working while you and he were in my St. Thomas condo. So don't give me that." She took another anchovy, which was just as well since Gina wasn't crazy about the anchovies. They were too salty. Then again, all tapas were salty—the bars that served them went heavy on the salt in order to make customers thirsty. Then the customers would buy more drinks. Gina and Carole were on their first glasses of wine, but it might take a few rounds to get Gina through the story of her breakup with Ethan.

"I was like a fish out of water in Connecticut," she said. "When we were in St. Thomas, we did a lot of snorkeling. Have you ever gone snorkeling down there?"

Carole swallowed and nodded. "Sure. The snorkeling is wonderful."

"You know how, when you snorkel, the fish just sort of accept you? You know you don't belong there, and the fish know it, but everyone pretends it's okay that you're there among them."

Carole nodded again.

"When I went to that party with Ethan," Gina explained, "it was like snorkeling. The fish would pump their little mouths at me and then swim away. I was trying to be part of their world, but I knew I wasn't. They pretended it was okay that I was there, but I wasn't one of them."

"Do you have to be?" Carole asked sympathetically.

"No, except that Ethan is one of them." She sipped a little more wine. "When we talked on Sunday, he said I only felt weird at the party because I'd drunk too much champagne. I mean, puh-leez."

"Do you think he was trying to make light of your discomfort?"

One reason Gina loved Carole was that she approached every conversation like the doctor she was. She dissected each idea and then diagnosed it. "Exactly," Gina agreed. "He didn't want to believe I really felt out of place. But the thing is, his old girlfriend was at the dinner."

"Uh-oh."

"No, really, I was fine with that." Gina held her hands up, as if to prove she had nothing to hide. "Kim and I got along okay in St. Thomas. There's nothing particularly *wrong* with her. Ethan seems to think she wasn't the woman for him, and he might be right about that. But I saw her at the dinner—I saw her with him— and I realized she belonged there as much as he did. They were like two beautiful, graceful fish, and I was the big, clumsy human being."

"You are *not* clumsy."

"You know what I'm saying." Gina picked up another slice of chorizo and forced herself to nibble at it. She considered mentioning what had happened with her shoes, but decided not to go into it. Carole would dissect that, too. She'd want to know why Gina had worn inappropriate shoes, whether she'd done so deliberately, to test Ethan's social circle. And maybe Gina had. Maybe, despite her perfect dress, she'd wanted to make sure everyone knew who she truly was. Those shoes were who she was.

She didn't need Carole to analyze that.

"So," she said, lifting her glass and then putting it back down so she wouldn't empty it too quickly, "I asked him how he felt at my parties. He started out all righteous, insisting he thought my parties were great, thought visiting Lower Manhattan was a big adventure, he thought loud music and microbrewery beer were just swell and it was such a kick talking to people with spiky hair and visible nipples about whether graffiti is the people's art."

"You didn't believe him," Carole guessed.

"He didn't believe himself," Gina said. "I pressed him, and he finally admitted that he'd rather listen to a classical music trio—that's what they had at the benefit dinner—than Jimmy Eats World. And he'd rather talk about the peregrine falcon population than whether squatters ought to be evicted when they've made improvements to the properties they've been squatting on."

"Peregrine falcons are important," Carole pointed out.

"So are squatters." Gina sighed. She didn't want to argue with Carole. "There we were in his big, bright, eat-in kitchen, drinking coffee, and I looked across at him and thought, *I love this man. I love him.*"

"And you broke up with him?"

Gina nodded again. "How can I drag him to my downtown parties? He doesn't like them. He's only going to them for me. He's as much a fish out of water in

Manhattan as I am in Connecticut. And if I love him, how can I keep him out of his water? He doesn't belong here. He isn't comfortable here. He comes to the city for my sake, but it doesn't make him happy.''

"He said all this? Or are you projecting?"

"No, he said it. I mean, he didn't say he wasn't happy. But he did say he came to the city only because it made *me* happy, and he hung out with my friends because he thought I wanted him to. He didn't have to say more than that.'' She finally swallowed the last tidbit of chorizo, then washed it down with another sip of red wine. "If I didn't love him, I wouldn't care about his happiness, you know? I'd drag him to parties and not care if he felt comfortable. But I *do* love him, and I can't stand the idea that he's forcing himself to do this stuff for me.''

"But if he's willing to do it—"

"What's the point? He's not going to be happy. I want him happy.''

Carole shook her head. "Maybe if you saw each other less. I mean, Paul and I haven't had a chance to figure out if we're making each other happy. If we can catch a dinner together once a week, we're satisfied.''

"You should be with him tonight, instead of me.''

"He wasn't free,'' Carole told her. "He had some sort of investors' dinner at the New York Racquet Club. Maybe we're perfect for each other,'' she said with a crooked smile. "It's so rare we can see each other. That's the way to make a relationship work.''

Gina considered that possibility. She thought about how much fonder her sister had become of Jack once he'd moved out of her house. She wasn't letting him move back in. She said that was because he was still sort of involved with his girlfriend, but Gina suspected he was clinging to the girlfriend on the chance that Ramona refused a reconciliation. Gina also suspected that her sister wouldn't let him move home because they got along so much better this way, when they didn't see each other all the time.

She didn't think that would work with Ethan, though. For one thing, she wanted to be with him all the time. She loved talking to him, laughing with him, falling asleep and waking up with him. For another, she wasn't about to model her relationship on her sister's screwed-up marriage.

Gina had tried to explain all that to Ethan, too. But every time she'd uttered the word *relationship,* he'd winced.

"So what are you going to do now?" Carole asked. "Mope?"

"Mope and eat tapas," Gina said, spearing a wedge of pickle with a toothpick and popping it into her mouth. Tapas wouldn't lighten her heart. But they would help the wine go down more easily.

CHAPTER SEVENTEEN

THE ADDRESS was about a mile from the expressway exit. Ethan had downloaded the directions from Map-Quest, and he'd meticulously followed them—.23 of a mile, turn left, .41 of a mile turn right—through a non-descript middle-class housing development that must have sprung up not long after World War II. He pulled to the curb in front of the Bari house and turned off the engine.

The house was a modest split-level with brick-and-vinyl siding. Its lawn was trimmed but basically dead, frozen into a late-November state of crunchy brown. Evergreen shrubs flanked the front porch, and the leafless trees edging the property looked skeletal.

Ethan wondered whether Ramona would be willing to talk to him. He'd knocked himself out trying to reach Gina, but after a few frustrating phone conversations, during which she'd told him it would hurt less if they just cut things off, she'd relegated him to her phone mail and never returned his messages. He'd even traveled down to New York City last Saturday, figuring she'd be forced to deal with him if he presented himself in person, but she hadn't been home. Nor had she been at her favorite brunch place around the corner from her apartment. He'd walked over to the building that housed Bruno Castiglio Shoes, but it was locked.

So he'd decided to try Ramona. He'd considered

phoning her, but he'd learned from past experience that she could be scathing on the telephone. Maybe if she saw him—and if Alicia vouched for him—she'd be more willing to help him connect with Gina.

Two and a half weeks had passed since the benefit dinner. Two and a half weeks during which he'd logically and calmly analyzed everything Gina had said, all her concerns about and criticisms of their situation. All right, so their backgrounds weren't that similar. So they operated in different spheres. So she had a Bronx accent, and designed bizarre shoes, and spent her weekend nights at noisy parties with tattooed people.

None of it mattered to him. All that mattered was that ever since she'd stepped onto the New York City train and out of his life, he'd been miserable, empty and angry and given to fits of temper. He had always prided himself on being even-keeled. Maybe it was easier for a man to be even-keeled when he wasn't suffering—and it was easier to escape suffering when he wasn't in a *relationship*.

In the past, he'd avoided the *R*-word because he'd avoided the institution. Breaking up with Kim, just like every other time he'd broken up with a woman, hadn't been painful because those relationships hadn't been *relationships*.

What he had with Gina was a genuine *relationship*. And even though she was eluding him, refusing to return his calls, daring to be out—or at least not answering her door buzzer—when he'd journeyed all the way into the city to see her…if it wasn't a *relationship*, he wouldn't be hurting so much.

He stared at her sister's front door in White Plains and tried to gather his courage. He'd departed from his office at around one, telling his secretary he had an appointment, and now it was a few minutes past two. Would Ramona be home? If she was, would she let him into her house?

He'd have to be charming. Ingratiating. Totally unthreatening.

He reached for the door handle, then paused at the growl of a motor behind him. Glancing into his rearview mirror, he saw a yellow school bus rumbling around the corner and down the street. It cruised past him and slowed as it neared the corner up ahead. Its lights flashed red and its door swung open.

A handful of children tumbled out. A few sloppy, noisy boys, an older girl, a younger one...and Alicia. He recognized her instantly, even though she hardly resembled the cute little squirt he'd gotten to know in St. Thomas last July.

What was he thinking? Of course she resembled the girl she'd been then. But she seemed a little taller now, a little more mature. She had on denim bell-bottoms, a cherry-red fleece jacket and sneakers with patches of brightly colored leather on them. Her hair was longer than it had been last summer, and the two decorative braids with the turquoise beads adorning them were gone. The watery November sunlight glinted off her tiny hoop earrings. Slung over her shoulders was a bulging blue backpack.

He hadn't known she would be arriving home from school this early, but her appearance was a good omen. As she sauntered along the sidewalk to her front walk, he eased open his door and stood.

She couldn't miss him, since he was parked right in front of her house. Her eyes grew round, and she broke into a run. "Ethan!"

"Hey, Alley Cat!" He circled the car to the sidewalk

in time to catch her in a hug as she barreled into him. She was cold and smelled of autumn, and her giggle cheered him as nothing else had in the past two and a half weeks.

"I knew you'd come see me!" Alicia's arms were too short to reach far around him, but he savored her hug. "I knew it! Mommy said I should forget about you, but I didn't. Guess what happened in school today?"

"What?" he asked, surprised to find himself genuinely curious.

"Mr. Sonnenberg, that's the principal? He dressed up in a turkey costume and marched around the school making gobbly-gobbly noises. It was a Thanksgiving surprise. He looked so funny!"

"I bet he did."

"Everybody was laughing so hard my teacher got mad and said if we didn't calm down we'd miss recess. She's such a grouch. I wish Mr. Sonnenberg could be our teacher. He's so nice. Did I tell you my best friend, Caitlin, is in my class this year?"

That rang a bell. "I believe you did."

"Well, let's go in. Mommy'll give us a snack. She always gives me a snack when I get home from school." Alicia slipped her small, icy hand into his and led him up the walk to the door. She unzipped her jacket a couple of inches and pulled out a key, which hung around her neck on a navy-blue cord with Nike Swooshes imprinted on it. "Mommy said I was old enough for my own key this year," she bragged as she unlocked the door and shoved it open. "Mommy?" she hollered into the house as she bounded inside. "Mommy, I'm home, and guess what?"

Ethan wished he'd get as enthusiastic a greeting from Ramona as he'd gotten from Alicia, but he knew that wish wouldn't come true. Indeed, when a woman who bore a strong resemblance to Gina—a bit shorter, a bit plumper, but with the same large, angled eyes, sharp nose and sculpted cheeks—entered the front hallway from the kitchen, her gaze narrowed suspiciously. "Who are you?"

"This is Ethan, Mommy," Alicia chirped, tossing her backpack onto the floor and unzipping her jacket all the way. "He came to see us."

Ramona definitely didn't look thrilled. She opened her mouth, then glanced at her daughter and pressed her lips together. Ethan imagined she'd been on the verge of saying something nasty to him, but thanks to Alicia's presence, he was being spared.

He didn't know why she should feel negative about him. He wasn't the one who'd broken up with Gina. He'd never inflicted pain on her. Quite the contrary—he was the inflictee.

But just like Ramona, he exercised discretion in front of Alicia. He extended his right hand to her and attempted a smile. "It's about time we met," he said. "I'm Ethan Parnell."

She grudgingly shook his hand, then turned to Alicia. "Hang your coat up, honey. I'm making cocoa. It's cold out there."

"Cocoa! Make some for Ethan, too," Alicia reminded her as she carried her jacket to the closet near the front door.

A few minutes later, they were all tucked into Ramona's cozy kitchen. Frilly blue curtains framed the window, a ceramic cookie jar shaped like a snowman stood on a counter and the refrigerator door had been transformed into a magnetic bulletin board of reminders, shopping lists and schedules orbiting around a school photo of Alicia.

Alicia couldn't sit still, and she couldn't shut up. "What do you think of my sneakers?" she asked Ethan. "Aunt Gina made them for me. They're kind of like the shoes her company makes. Only, they don't make shoes for children, so she sort of made these on her own for me. Have you seen her fish shoes? I want a pair like that, but she said no. I bet that means she's going to give them to me for Christmas, and I'll have to act surprised...."

Ethan remembered Gina's fish shoes too well. Maybe if she hadn't worn those fish shoes the night of the fundraising dinner, she wouldn't have concluded that she could never fit in with Ethan's crowd. Frankly, he didn't give a damn if she never fit in with his crowd. He'd really liked those shoes.

He let Alicia dominate the conversation while he sipped his cocoa. Ramona grilled her about school and homework. Alicia regaled her mother with the story of her school's principal in a turkey costume, and described a fracas between two boys who were real jerks in the playground during recess, and mentioned a field trip her class would be taking to the Museum of Natural History. "That's in New York City, where Aunt Gina lives," she informed Ethan.

"I know."

"They've got dinosaur bones there. Have you seen Aunt Gina?"

"Not as much as I'd like to," he said carefully, letting his gaze slide to Ramona.

She leaned against the counter, arms folded, lips pursed. But her eyes seemed to soften. He might be imagining it, but she seemed measurably less hostile than when he'd first entered her home.

"Have *you* seen Gina?" he asked her.

"I see Gina all the time," Ramona answered.

"Not as much as we'd like to," Alicia added.

"Ali, maybe you should do your homework," Ramona said as Alicia set down her empty mug. "Mr. Parnell and I have to talk about grown-up things."

Alicia rolled her eyes, as if her mother had suggested something barely tolerable. "Come see me when you're done with Mommy," she requested as she climbed down from her chair. "I'll show you my bedroom. I still have some of the nail polish we bought in St. Thomas, the stuff that changes colors." She plodded out of the kitchen, then turned at the doorway and sent Ethan an adoring look before she disappeared up the stairs with her backpack.

Ramona let out a long breath and joined Ethan at the table. "So what are you, an idiot?" she asked.

He flinched. "I beg your pardon?"

"Why did you stop seeing my sister?"

"I'm dying to see your sister!" He lowered his voice, not wanting Alicia to hear him. "Your sister walked out on me, and I'm going crazy. She doesn't return my calls. She doesn't want to see me. She says we're wrong for each other. *She's* the idiot."

Ramona bristled. "You're calling my sister an idiot?"

This wasn't going well. "I love your sister, okay? I want a relationship with your sister. I think I'm already in a relationship with her." He loved Gina so much he was freely using the *R*-word. "I don't know why she won't talk to me."

"She thinks you're wrong for each other," Ramona reminded him.

"If she thinks that, she's an idiot." He sighed. "I want to be with her. I was hoping you'd help me."

"You just called my sister an idiot, and I'm supposed to help you?

"We're not wrong for each other," he insisted. "We belong together. I don't give a damn if she never attends another benefit dinner with me. I don't care if she wants to drag me to head-banger parties in strange lofts with inadequate lighting. All I know is, we belong together. In a *relationship*. And I'm hoping…" He'd run out of breath, and he paused to drag air into his lungs. "I'm hoping you'll help me get that message to her."

Ramona seemed visibly touched by his desperation. "So what am I supposed to do?" she asked gently.

"Tell her I'm not a bad guy," he suggested. "Tell her I'll take good care of her, and I'll love her, and I'll go to her damn parties if she wants me to. Tell her I miss her pretty feet." He clamped his mouth shut, concerned that he might be coming across as a lunatic.

Ramona smiled, and he realized the lunatic approach had been effective. "She does have the prettiest feet in the family," she said. "I always envied her feet."

"I'm sure your feet are nice, too."

"Nothing like hers." Ramona shook her head. "She told me you and she came from two different worlds, and all I could think was, my husband, Jack, and I came from the same world, and our marriage is a mess. We grew up in the same neighborhood, went to the same high school—I mean, does it matter whether two people come from the same world? If you love her, you should be with her."

He dared to hope. "So you'll help me?"

Ramona thought for a minute. "I myself can't always

reach her. She's down in the city, doing her thing, you know? And she turns off her cell phone half the time.''

''I've noticed,'' Ethan muttered.

''My parents are hosting Thanksgiving,'' she said. ''So at least I know where she'll be on Thursday—at my parents' house in the Bronx. She'll probably arrive there around noon. You could catch her then.''

''At your parents' Thanksgiving?'' The idea didn't please him. He'd only just met Gina's sister; he wasn't sure he could handle meeting her parents, too. Thanksgiving was a day for people to spend with their own families. He and his father were supposed to meet at his aunt Marcie's house in Darien for the holiday.

Seeing Gina was more important. Aunt Marcie and his father would understand. Maybe he could confront Gina at her parents' house at noon, get their *relationship* back on track and then cruise up I-95 to Darien. Aunt Marcie didn't usually start serving cocktails until around four, anyway.

And if he missed not just the cocktails but Aunt Marcie's turkey, cranberry sauce and pumpkin pie, so be it. He would gladly starve for the chance to see Gina and beg her to let him back into her life so he could start smiling again, and laughing, and making love to her, and waking up joyful and energized and ready to take on the universe.

''Sure,'' he said. ''Can you give me directions to your parents' home?''

THE MORANTE HOUSE was one step down the socioeconomic ladder from Ramona's. A tidy brick row house in a proud working-class neighborhood, it shared its side walls with the adjacent row houses, and its front yard was consumed mostly by a concrete driveway sloping down to a basement-level garage. The windows were filled with bright light. It looked like a warm house, a happy place.

He wondered if Gina would be happy to see him.

Or if her parents would, for that matter. Ramona had assured him that she'd make sure her parents knew he was dropping by, but he still had misgivings. Wiggling his car into a tight parking space, he flashed back on the last time he'd met a woman's parents. He and Kim had been in the airport in Atlanta, at the gate where their connecting flight would take them to St. Thomas. Her parents had arrived at the gate from their flight out of Reagan Airport in Washington, all buffed and glossy and exuding privilege.

The minute Ethan had seen them, he'd known the trip would not be the idyllic little getaway he'd dreamed of. Forcing himself to talk to Ross about golf, listening to Ross criticize his left-side-of-the-road driving, hearing Delia go on and on—and on—about the shopping in Charlotte Amalie... He would have rather undergone a root canal.

What if Gina's parents were obnoxious? What if they fell into the root-canal category?

Well, they'd created Gina, hadn't they? He'd forgive them a lot, just because of that.

He climbed out of his car, turned up the collar of his leather jacket against the blustery breeze and scaled the steps to the front door, clutching the flowers he'd brought for Gina's mother. He wasn't planning to stay for dinner—Aunt Marcie was expecting him—but he figured the bouquet would gain him a few points. After all, he was barging in on Mrs. Morante when she was undoubtedly up to her elbows fixing turkey and stuffing and pie. He had no idea how welcome he might be; he'd never even spoken to Mrs. Morante or her husband. Ramona had told him they wouldn't mind his stopping by, but Ramona had her own agenda.

Fortunately, it seemed to coincide with his.

He rang the bell, heard it chime through the door and waited for someone to answer. After a minute, the door swung open and he wound up face-to-face—well, actually, his face was a good two feet higher than hers—with Alicia. "He's here!" she shrieked, making him fall back a step and clutch the Autumn Abundance Arrangement, as the florist had called the bouquet he'd chosen, more tightly. No one was supposed to be excited by his arrival. He was just dropping in, just here to see Gina. He shouldn't be treated as the guest of honor.

But before he could figure out how to lower Alicia's expectations, a tall, beefy man with steel-gray hair and a warm smile clamped a hand over Ethan's shoulder and dragged him inside. "Come on in, shut the door—it's cold out there!" he said, continuing to drag him through the entry as Alicia had slammed the door shut. Through an arched doorway, Ethan glimpsed a lanky, casually dressed young man draped across an overstuffed sofa, watching a football game on TV. He glanced toward the doorway, smiled and waved at Ethan—and his smile was a reflection of Gina's smile. Her brother, he deduced. The cop.

He didn't have a chance to say hello, however, because Gina's father continued to pull him down the hall, which ended in a small, crowded kitchen. The room was warm from the oven and aromatic with mouthwatering smells. Ramona stood at the table, fussing with a cranberry mold. Behind her, stirring something on the stove, stood an older version of Ramona, dark haired and curvy, wearing an apron over a pair of wool slacks and a turtleneck.

"He's here," Gina's father announced. "The boyfriend."

"I'm not—" Ethan began, then shut up. He might not be Gina's boyfriend at this particular moment, but by the time he was finished talking to her, he hoped that would change.

"She's not here yet," Ramona told him, while her mother set down her stirring spoon, wiped her hands on a towel and turned to face him.

Amazing how all the Morantes had the same smile— a smile as warm as the Hamiltons' smiles had been chilly. Smiles like the Morantes' made a man want to shed his jacket and bask in the warmth. They made him feel…accepted.

"I'm Tony Morante," Gina's father said, shaking his hand. "And this is my wife, Rosa."

Rosa clasped both her hands around his free hand, releasing him only when he extended the flowers to her. "These are for you."

"You shouldn't have," she protested, although she eagerly snatched the flowers out of his hand and dipped her nose to sniff them. "Mo, get me a vase, would you? You know which one? The one Grandma Alba gave me. Not the crystal one, the milk glass. You know which one I'm talking about?"

Ethan allowed himself a smile. Gina's mother's Bronx accent was classic.

Ramona abandoned the cranberry mold to attend to the flowers. Gina's mother folded her hands over her apron and gazed up at Ethan, studying him. "I hope you don't mind onions in the stuffing. I always put onions in it. I figure, everybody's eating it, so we all wind up with bad breath together."

"And then we eat mints," Alicia piped up, perching herself on a chair and busying herself with a stack of paper napkins in need of folding.

"I'm sorry, but…I'm not here to eat, Mrs. Morante."

She didn't look alarmed. "Of course you have to eat something. It's Thanksgiving."

"I came only to see Gina." *Because I haven't been able to see her anywhere else. Except in my dreams,* he added silently. *Except every time I close my eyes.*

"So you'll see her and you'll eat something. No big deal." Before he could object, she patted his shoulder, then turned her back to him and resumed stirring whatever was in the pot on the stove.

"It's okay," Ramona mouthed as she arranged the flowers, stem by stem, in the vase.

What was okay? His aunt Marcie was expecting him. His father and cousins would be at the house in Darien, eating off bone china with real silver. No way could he devour two Thanksgiving dinners. As it was, he was nervous enough about confronting Gina to question whether he'd be able to swallow anything at all.

Nothing was okay at all. Gina's family obviously welcomed him, but would she? Were they being nice to him because Ramona told them to, or because they wanted their unwed daughter to settle down? He hadn't come here to propose to Gina, of course. He only wanted to talk to her, to promise her she wouldn't have to attend any more fancy fund-raisers with him. To assure her that what they shared was special and mustn't be tossed away.

The doorbell rang. His breath caught in his throat. Alicia jumped down from the chair, bellowing, "I bet that's Aunt Gina!"

"You can talk to her upstairs," Ramona coached him

in a quick whisper. "You'll have some privacy up there. Down here, everybody's—"

"Mommy, it's Daddy!" Alicia yelled from the entry.

"Oh, God, what's he doing here?" Ramona groaned.

"Go say hello to him," her mother urged. "He's your daughter's father."

Ramona shot her parents a suspicious look, then stormed out of the kitchen. Gina's father gazed after her for a moment before turning to Ethan. "There's a good game on TV. You want to watch?"

Ethan shrugged and, pulling off his jacket, followed Tony Morante through the dining room, around to the living room. In the entry, Ramona and yet another tall, dark-haired man conferred softly. If they were arguing, they were doing so peacefully. Alicia stood between them, an arm wrapped around each one's waist, even though she had to stretch upward to reach.

The football game was between two universities to which Ethan had no emotional attachment. Gina's brother straightened up and greeted him with a nod. "So you're Ethan?"

"Has Gina talked about me?"

"Nah. She doesn't talk about anyone. Ramona does all the talking. I'm Bobby," he added, extending his hand.

Ethan shook it. The guy didn't look like a cop, although that might have been because he was dressed in a sweater and jeans rather than a uniform with a gun hanging from a holster at his hip. "Gina's told me a little about you," he said.

"Don't believe a word of it," Bobby said with a chuckle. Then he leaned across the overstuffed cushions toward Ethan. "Let me tell you something. My sister Gina? She's a little crazy, you know?"

"What do you mean?" Once again, apprehension nibbled at Ethan.

"Well, you know, with the shoes, and her single-chick attitude. But don't let that fool you. She's a family girl, you know? She would take a bullet for any of us. Especially Alicia."

"I'm aware of that." He'd seen how close, how loving and protective she'd been with her niece in St. Thomas. That maternalism was one of the things that had made him fall for her. Just remembering caused a strange image to flash in his mind: a picture of Gina holding a baby in her arms. Gina holding *their* baby, hers and Ethan's.

Oh, God. He *had* come here to propose to her. That was the ultimate relationship—and that was what he wanted with her.

The doorbell rang again. Ramona's husband was still standing by the door, so he spun around and opened it. "Hey!" Gina's voice rolled over the din of the television announcers' voices. "Who invited you, Jack? Hold the door for me, would you? I've got my hands full with the salad here—hey, Ali! Can you carry this bag into the kitchen for me? It's a loaf of that sourdough bread Grandma loves, that I can get at that bakery on Ninth Avenue...." Her voice faded to silence as she peered through the arched doorway and saw Ethan.

Yes. He had come here for her, forever. To be his lover, his wife, the mother of his children. The moment he saw her, he knew.

GINA VERY NEARLY dropped the salad bowl. It wouldn't have broken—it was wood—but the foil would have torn off and her parents would have wound up with shreds of oil-and-vinegar-soaked romaine lettuce scattered all over the carpet.

Why was Ethan here? Who the hell had invited him? And why did he have to look so damn handsome?

Her vision blurred, but she blinked to clear it. He rose to his feet, a strangely confident smile curving his beautiful mouth, and she briefly considered hurling the salad at him and running. By the time he'd picked all the oily bits of lettuce off his cable-knit sweater, she'd be long gone.

It wasn't that she was scared of him. Rather, she was scared of herself, scared of the way just seeing him made her remember how good things were when it was just the two of them, when he wasn't gritting his teeth and trooping along to her assorted social gatherings, when she wasn't trying to blend in with his upper-crust associates but failing because her shoes were weird. She wondered what he thought about her parents' humble house, located in the city's least classy borough.

As a matter of fact, he looked pretty comfortable. Comfortable enough to toss his jacket onto the sofa and cross the room to her. "Ramona, could you take this?" he asked, lifting the salad bowl out of Gina's hands and placing it in her sister's. "Gina and I have to go upstairs."

"Sure." Ramona pointed toward the stairs with her elbow.

"I don't want to go upstairs," Gina objected. She had nothing against the bedroom level of her parents' house, but she didn't like being railroaded. She especially didn't like being railroaded by her sister and Ethan.

"This won't take long," Ethan promised, clasping her arm and steering her up ahead of him.

"Can I at least remove my gloves?" she muttered.

"You can remove as much of your clothing as you'd like." He marched her down the second-floor hall to the first open door and through it. The room was appallingly pink, the walls pink, the narrow twin beds covered with flowery pink spreads, the curtains sewn from the same flowery pink fabric and a carved wood rocking chair in one corner with a pink seat cushion tied to it. "This wouldn't be your brother's bedroom, would it?" Ethan asked as he closed the door behind them.

She laughed, then silenced herself. She didn't want to enjoy Ethan's sense of humor. She didn't want to be happy around him. "Stop being funny. I feel like you kidnapped me."

"In your own parents' house. And now I'm holding you hostage in your own childhood bedroom."

"How did you get here, anyway?"

"I drove," he answered, then had mercy on her. "Ramona invited me."

"That bitch! Why did she do that?"

"Because I love you," he said, his voice so steady and calm she had no choice but to believe him. "And she seems to think maybe you love me, too. She could be wrong about that, but I'm going to pretend she's right. I'm going to assume we both love each other, and you've got it in your head that we shouldn't be together because some people at a party I took you to didn't like your shoes."

"It's not just the shoes, Ethan." She heard despair in her voice—despair because he was right and Ramona was right. She loved him, and it pissed the hell out of her that he was belittling the very real problem between them. "It's me. It's being completely out of place in your world, sticking out like a sore thumb."

"You stuck out like a goddess," he told her, still sounding calm and confident. "And I loved your shoes. I thought they were great. I don't give a damn what anyone else thought of them, and I don't know why you do."

Her vision blurred again, and this time no amount of blinking cleared it. Tears leaked through her lashes and down her cheeks. She pulled off her gloves so she could wipe her face. "If I were going to be with you," she finally said, the words wobbly and damp, "I'd want to be good for you. I'd want to be able to help you in your work. I'd want to stand next to you and say all the right things so people would give your foundation money. You deserve that, Ethan. And I don't think I can give that to you. I don't know how."

"What I deserve is irrelevant," he said, gathering her hands in his. "What I need is important. I need you, Gina. I need your thoughts and your humor and your sexy body. And your silver fish shoes. I can manage my foundation without your help. My life, though—I don't think I can manage that without you."

The tears kept flowing, but with him holding her hands she couldn't brush them away.

"You do love me, don't you?"

"Yes," she murmured.

"Then say you'll marry me."

"What?"

"Say you'll marry me. I'll fly with you to St. Thomas and buy you a big diamond ring. I hear they've got incredible prices on diamond jewelry down there."

In spite of her tears, she laughed. "I don't want a big diamond ring."

He pulled her closer. "Then we'll go to St. Thomas and snorkel."

"That sounds like fun."

He brushed his mouth over hers. Her lips must have tasted salty from her tears, but he didn't seem to mind. "You still haven't said you'll marry me," he reminded her.

"Where will we live?"

"Someplace equidistant from our jobs? That would probably put us not too far from your sister and the Alley Cat." He kissed her again, a little longer, a little deeper. "Say yes already."

"You make it all sound so easy," she said dubiously.

"It *is* easy. It's as easy as we want to make it. If you want to live in Arlington, great. I would prefer not to live in Manhattan. We could keep an apartment there, though, for weekends and visits. We managed to live together in that time-share for a whole week. Compared with that, figuring out where to live now ought to be a cinch." He peered into her eyes. "None of this is hard, Gina, not if we want it."

"Well…"

"Marry me."

"Okay," she said.

He smiled. His lips were so close to hers she could practically taste his smile. "Now, here's the really tricky part," he warned her, his voice low and hypnotically romantic. "Your mother wants us to eat dinner here. My aunt is expecting me at her house at four. Can we cram in two dinners?"

"No way. My stomach would explode."

"Then how about if I call my aunt and say we'll get there in time for dessert?"

"That sounds like a good compromise."

His smile expanded. "See? That wasn't so hard. The rest is going to be even easier."

"You think so, huh?"

"I know so," he whispered before kissing her again.

* * * * *

*Turn the page for another exciting story
from Judith Arnold,*
HEART ON THE LINE.
Coming from Mira Books in August 2003.

One

Leaning out over the platform and staring down the tracks wasn't going to make the train arrive sooner. But Loretta leaned and stared anyway, and prayed for the 7:51 westbound to chug into the station so she could say goodbye to Nicky, climb aboard and go home.

She wished she could tune him out, but she'd learned long ago that her family was un-tune-out-able. "It's not like I care or anything," he droned. "It's your life. You wanna throw it away, that's your choice. It's nothing to me."

"I'm not throwing my life away," she argued. "Come on, Nicky. Today is my birthday. Back off."

"Yeah, it's your birthday. The big twenty-nine, baby. The last year of your youth. After thirty, it's all downhill."

"Maybe in your case," Loretta needled him. "You've sure gone downhill in the past few years."

He ignored the dig. "We're talking about you. Where the hell are you going with your life?"

Where the hell she was going with her life was back to Manhattan, if the damn train ever showed up. She wished Al had driven her to the station instead of Nicky. As the oldest, Nicky seemed to feel a special obligation to lecture his wayward sister. He loved playing the role of the wise elder, although his propensity for dressing like Gilligan, in plaid shorts and inverted sailor hats, disqualified him for any mantle of wisdom, as far as she was concerned.

"All I'm saying," he continued as she gazed desperately down the tracks, "is your first reaction shouldn't always be no."

"I don't want to meet your friend, Nicky. Okay?"

"Why not?"

"He's a dentist."

"Like this is a bad thing. I'm a dentist. Al's a dentist. Dad's a dentist. What's the problem?"

The problem was that Nicky, Al and Dad were dentists. Dentistry was the family trade, and her family's reaction, when she had militantly refused to take even a basic biology class in college, let alone anything that might smack of predentistry, was "That's okay—she'll marry a dentist."

She had no plans to marry a dentist. It wasn't as if she was ever going to lose sleep over where her next plaque scraping was coming from. One of the reasons she'd become engaged to Gary had been that he was in advertising. A worthless occupation, according to her family, but what did she care? It wasn't dentistry.

So now her brother was trying to fix her up with a colleague. He thought Loretta would have a good time sharing drinks and dinner with some guy who got paid to stick his fingers into other people's mouths.

"Kathy vouched for Marty, didn't she?" Nicky reminded her. "She said he was nice."

"She said he was brilliant and he looked like Mel Gibson, only taller. Yeah, right."

"Are you calling my wife a liar?"

"I'm just saying maybe she was trying a little too hard

to sell me on this buddy of yours. Tell me the truth. Does he really look like Mel Gibson?''

''Well…'' Nicky considered. ''He's taller.''

The distant rattle of the train tickled her ears. She perked up with all the excitement of a dog hearing the whine of a can opener.

''Just this once, okay? Let me give him your number. It's nothing to me, but you could do worse. You *have* done worse. Not to mention any names, but *Gary*. Okay? Marty Calabrese is a nice guy.''

''Gary was a nice guy, too,'' Loretta argued, meaning it. Her family would never forgive him for having broken up with her at a late-enough date that they'd had to sacrifice half the deposit they'd put down at the Roslyn Harbor Inn, but Loretta had forgiven him long ago. In fact, once she'd gotten over the shock, she'd realized she was grateful to him for figuring out that if they didn't love each other, getting married might not be the wisest option.

''You know,'' she added, wishing the train would glide up to the platform already, ''I don't need my brothers soliciting dates for me. I can get dates on my own.''

''Yeah? When was the last time you were on a date?''

''Wouldn't you like to know.'' He *would* like to know, she admitted silently. He'd love to know that it had been weeks, months—and going club hopping with Bob from work one evening when he'd been between girlfriends didn't really count as a date, because they were just pals. Nicky would love to know that she was everything her family feared: twenty-nine and single, with no prospects in sight, no wedding bells ringing on the horizon, no suburban tract house and two-point-three kids in her foreseeable future.

She wouldn't object terribly to having a husband

someday, and even a kid or two. She wasn't too keen on the suburban tract house, but she was sure her parents would give her a pass on that if she'd do the marriage-and-children thing. But God, the pressure! They just wouldn't let up—and now that she was twenty-nine, it was only going to get worse. Loretta didn't respond to pressure well. When anyone—especially her blood relatives—applied it, she dug in her heels. As long as they pressured her about marriage, she was going to stay single.

Nicky peered down at her, all six brawny feet of him, and gave her a smile that displayed his extremely white teeth. He'd be handsome if he took off the dorky hat and did something about the paunch budding above his belt. "It's just that you're my sister and I care about you. And it bothers me that you won't keep an open mind about things."

She wouldn't keep an open mind? Nicky and the rest of her family were the ones who were close minded. But the train was squeaking to a halt at the station, and she saw no reason to get into an argument with him about open minds. "Okay, look. I've got to go," she said, sounding much too relieved.

"Yeah, well, think about it, would you? He's a really nice guy. It wouldn't kill you to spend an evening with a nice guy."

"Uh-huh." She rose on tiptoe to kiss Nicky's cheek, then started toward the door, trying not to sprint.

"You got your ticket?" he called after her.

"Yeah, I got it. Bye, Nicky. Thanks again for the book."

"Kathy picked it out," he reminded her.

"Well, thank her again for me." She stepped onto the train and waved, then entered the car and let out a long, weary breath. Though the car wasn't packed, most of the bench seats held at least one passenger. The only unoccupied seat was the backward one just inside the door. She dropped onto the stiff upholstery, stifled a groan and closed her eyes so she wouldn't have to view all the passengers staring at her from the forward-facing seats.

The book Nicky and Kathy had given her for her birthday was called *The Secret to Success in Love*. Her brother Al and his wife had also given her a book, entitled *Two by Two: How To Find Your True Partner in Life*. Her parents had given her a simple gold bracelet with a small heart-shaped charm hanging from a link. She'd understood the message they were conveying with their sweet gift: poor Loretta didn't have a man in her life to give her a romantic bracelet for her birthday, so her parents had to step into the breach.

The gifts had prompted her to request a refill on her wine. It was her birthday party, after all, and if she needed vast quantities of wine to survive the day, so be it. If ever she'd shared her family's yearning for her to have a boyfriend, it had been today; with a boyfriend, she could have begged off the family barbecue her parents had insisted on hosting in her honor. *Sorry, Mr. Wonderful is taking me out for dinner tonight,* she could have said, and they'd have been so ecstatic they wouldn't have minded that she wasn't spending her birthday with them. Or else she could have brought Mr. Wonderful with her to her parents' raised ranch in Plainview, and he could have been her ally. He and she could have exchanged amused glances whenever the discussion veered to tartar treatments or quadrant cleaning, or her mother aimed sly criticisms at her: *So, Loretta, are you ever going to get a haircut?* or *So, are people still threatening to tear each other limb from limb on that show you work for?*

But she'd attended the party alone, because alone was her current social status. After faking delight over her presents, she'd dined with her family on grilled steaks and salad and bruschetta and more red wine, followed by a too-sweet golden cake from Rocco's Bakery, the white frosting decorated with pink roses and the words "Happy Birthday, Dear Loretta," as if her family might need some help with the lyrics when they sang the traditional birthday song. Nicky's and Al's kids had run around the lawn after dinner, squealing and howling, while the adults had remained seated on the deck, where they'd been dive-bombed by mosquitoes that seemed passionately attracted to the pungent smoke from the citronella candles her mother had lit and placed on every available vertical surface. Her father had drunk quite a few toasts filled with unsubtle hints: "Here's to my grandchildren—the beautiful grandchildren I already have and the ones Loretta will give me someday," he'd announce before taking a long chug of his Valpolicella. Or "Here's a toast to my birthday girl, whose beauty is so overwhelming she scares the men away."

Loretta could think of plenty of things more overwhelming—and scary—than her beauty. Her family, for instance...

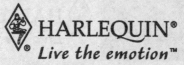

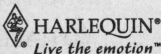

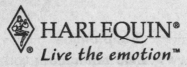

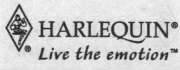

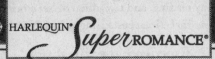

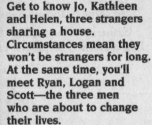
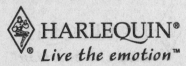